OTHER TONGUES

mixed-race women speak out

OTHER TONGUES

mixed-race women speak out

edited by

Adebe DeRango-Adem and Andrea Thompson

INANNA Publications and Education Inc.
Toronto, Canada

Published in Canada by
Inanna Publications and Education Inc.
210 Founders College, York University
4700 Keele Street, Toronto, Ontario M3J 1P3
Telephone: (416) 736-5356 Fax (416) 736-5765
Email: inanna@yorku.ca Website: www.yorku.ca/inanna

   Canada Council   Conseil des Arts   ONTARIO ARTS COUNCIL
for the Arts   du Canada   CONSEIL DES ARTS DE L'ONTARIO

The publisher gratefully acknowledges the support of the Canada Council for the Arts and the Ontario Arts Council for its publishing program.

The publisher is also grateful for the kind support received from an Anonymous Fund at The Calgary Foundation.

THE CALGARY
FOUNDATION

Printed and Bound in Canada.

Cover Design: Val Fullard
Interior Design: Luciana Ricciutelli

Library and Archives Canada Cataloguing in Publication:

     Other tongues : mixed-race women speak out / edited
by Adebe DeRango-Adem and Andrea Thompson.

Includes bibliographical references.
ISBN 978-1-926708-14-0

     1. Canadian literature (English) – Women authors.
2. Racially mixed women – Race identity – Canada – Literary collections. 3. Racially mixed women –Literary collections.
4. Racially mixed women – Canada--Biography. 5. Women – Canada – Literary collections. 6. Women – Canada – Biography.
7. Canadian literature (English) – 21st century.
I. DeRango-Adem, Adebe, 1986– II. Thompson, Andrea, 1967–

PS8235.W7O85 2010   C810.8'092870971090511   C2010-907030-5

*To all those who encourage, support, and honour
the importance of voice in the creation of unity and the
transformative potential of speaking truth to power.*

CONTENTS

REVELATIONS

Acknowledgements

FIRST AND FOREMOST, THANK you to our families, friends, fellow writers, supporters, and all the incredible women who graciously shared their stories and creative visions with us.

We would also like to acknowledge Carol Camper, Natasha Trethewey, George Elliott Clarke, Karina Vernon, Lise Funderberg, and Charlyn Ellis for offering us their invaluable support and wisdom.

Finally, a special thank you to Luciana Ricciutelli, Editor-in-Chief at Inanna Publications, for her encouragement, dedication, and belief in our vision for this book.

"Open Letter," "Prism Woman," "Blanqueamiento," and "Colour Lesson I" "Concealed Things," and "Colour Lesson II," by Adebe DeRango-Adem, were originally published in *Ex Nihilo,* by Adebe D.A. (Frontenac House, 2010). Reprinted with permission.

"FireBelly," by Andrea Thompson, was originally published in *Eating the Seed* by Andrea Thompson (Ekstasis Editions, 2000). Reprinted with permission.

"I, too, hear the drums," by Peta Gaye-Nash, was also published in *I Too Hear the Drums: Stories,* by Peta Gaye-Nash (In Our Words Inc., 2010). Reprinted with permission.

"Miscegenation," "Blond," and "Southern Gothic" are from *Native Guard: Poems* by Natasha Trethewey. Copyright © 2006 by Natasha Trethewey. Reprinted by permission of Houghton Mifflin Harcourt Publishing Company. All rights reserved.

—*Adebe DeRango-Adem and Andrea Thompson*

Preface

Other Tongues: Mixed-Race Women Speak Out is an important contribution to the body of autobiographical work that is critical to any discussion about racial mixing. Although at a physiological level racial separation barely exists, the convergence of races within the individual continues to be a focal point of pain, confusion, defiance and love. When *Miscegenation Blues: Voices of Mixed-Race Women* was published in 1994 there was very little extant in terms of personal accounts of mixed-race experience. That left the stories of racially mixed women in the hands of the scientists or popular culture. Result? We were either case studies or sad/sexy light-skinned courtesans in a movie or music video. I received criticism from a couple of readers who decried the fact that the book wasn't more "scientific" and therefore authentic. This highlighted the importance and radical-ness of auto-biography for people of colour. We are speaking for ourselves. We don't need to be validated by "science." We are the experts on our own lives. In 1994, this was enough to really vex some people. Although there are some wonderful personal accounts that have been published since then, they are not many in number.

The personal has turned out to be critical. Mixed-race people aren't subjects to be studied, analysed and categorized. We are people of lived experience who can represent ourselves. All persons struggle with issues of identity as they journey through life. The mixed-race person's struggle is often not conducted with privacy and dignity. Our very bodies are subject to dispute, discussion, and suspicion. Our families often have histories of pain—the provenance of which sometimes is our very existence. Family, for us, often is not the place of support, refuge and commonality that we long for.

My own struggle for identity and refuge continues and I am surprised at how much of it still centres on what I look like. Not long after the publication of *Miscegenation Blues*, I met a woman who I thought might be mixed Black and White. Her hair was long and black with natural-looking corkscrew curls. She was wearing large hoop earrings and a matching black leather jacket and pants cut in a very '70s, Foxy Brown (the original, as portrayed by the incredible Pam Grier) kind of way. Her eyes were brown and her skin was coppery. I wondered, "is she mixed?" I was attempting to reach out to mixed-race people and let them know about my book so I decided to ask her about her ethnicity. I began by identifying myself as mixed-race Black. The woman was not Black it turned out, she was Italian and her skin colour was fake, achieved through tanning salons and perhaps the tanning pills that used to turn skin orange. She expressed surprise to hear that I was Black, she hadn't realized that—and so I had a "moment." I was profoundly shocked that she had not been able to see my Blackness. The moment was so impactful for me that I wrote a poem to record it and investigate some of the issues at play:

Wanda B.
Hoping for an agreeable brown she ended up with an unadmitted
Orange
Skin she took for herself not really even approximating
but she tried anyway.
Hair black she hoped and corkscrew ringlets
maybe okay dreadlocks but definitely not the naps definitely not
the hair that doesn't move except
to move her much too far from where
she'd never leave her feminine pride her womanly self
(preferring her forefathers' thoughtful injection of herself wayback
  anticipating her
fashionable emulations) no
definitely not.
She thought
"This is how they do it —
I will wear the big golden earrings the bracelets the
'I will be a hip chick Cleopatra Jones' in the black leathers
(the only kind of black skin I really want — removable)
hugging hips holding to my skin
the closest thing the hippest thing going
down this street your street — hold on — My street and
I will still tell you how to be you
I will still tell you who you are and
I will still own you 'cause
I can go back to the real white world anytime."

I had lived by that time for twenty-five years in one of the most cosmopolitan cities on earth with Black people of all hues. This woman had gone to some lengths to emulate the "mixed, light-skinned look" of the hip-hop video vixen. She had made a study of Blackness—and couldn't tell that I was Black. What I experienced in that moment felt like a reality shift on a seismic scale. I had settled comfortably into my Blackness by that point. I knew many people of Caribbean and American Black descent who looked like me. I had been a board member of a Black community organization and a member of a Black women's political organization. I had attended Black Pride in Washington, DC. Hadn't I earned my Blackness? And here was this woman who couldn't tell! I still haven't quite recovered from that.

So I am still haunted by the spectre of racial ambiguity. I am almost afraid to even broach the subject when Black people are around. I expect them to say "Girl! There's nothing ambiguous about you! You're Black!" I would be so relieved to hear that and yet I'd wonder, "Do they think I'm running from my Blackness?" I realized that I have actually depended on Black people to know that I'm Black and to confirm that for me. A couple of years ago a Black co-worker (unambiguously Black) told me that my name had come up at work in the context of some conversation about Blackness. One of my co-workers apparently had said that I wasn't "really Black." I felt the words stab at my soul. That bitter surprise again. I didn't ask who said it because I didn't want to know if the person was Black or White. It would have been more painful if it had been a Black co-worker. I'd understand (though still be pissed) if it had been a White co-worker—but if it had been a Black co-worker … betrayal, pain.

These days I'm not feeling any resolution about my racial looks. I look at my increasingly grey hair and wonder, "Am I even more racially ambiguous now? Now that I don't even have dark hair anymore?" Should I announce my Blackness? Should I carry cards to announce my Blackness like artist Adrian Piper? Am I no longer authentic? Should I just dye my hair? My hybridity has re-emerged as a contentious thing. When I wrote the introductory essay for *Miscegenation Blues* I was more confident than I am now about my racial location. Time moves on and as I age, I struggle with my changing looks which unexpectedly has included a change in my racial looks, making my identity more ambiguous—or so I fear. It's not comfortable these days.

So I continue my interior monologue about race and racial location. Although, scientifically the existence of race is questionable (persons of "different races" often have more in common with one another genetically than persons within the "same race"), there is no question that historically, politically and socially race does indeed exist. Genotypically we all may be very similar but the phenotypical often arranges itself in a way that leads to conflict. It is what we see that makes the biggest difference. *Other Tongues* features the writings of mixed-race women whose bodies are on the line—who are called upon constantly to declare identity and loyalty.

Identity and loyalty are questions we ask ourselves about. We have different conclusions at different times in our lives. Context is critical. Those of us whose entire families are mixed have at least the relief of resembling one another, despite other divisive conflicts that might exist. We look like the whole family. We aren't the living, breathing, unsimilarly-visaged evidence of shame, alienation or "other"-seeking rebelliousness as is sometimes the case when our parents are married interracially. We do have something in common; maybe even community with other mixed-race people. One of the impacts of *Miscegenation Blues* was that it reached many who experience the struggle of living "in between." So mixed-race women are again speaking the truth of their lives. *Other Tongues* contributes significantly to an important conversation. Who are we? We are defining that and we're letting you know.

—*Carol Camper, 2010*

Mixed Manifesto

An Introduction

Other Tongues: Mixed-Race Women Speak Out was born from a combination of necessity and a desire to see a new and refreshing literature that could be at the forefront of mixed-race discourse and women's studies. The idea behind this anthology of writing by and about mixed-race women in North America was planted in our minds when we each came across a similarly-themed collection of writing and images, *Miscegenation Blues: Voices of Mixed-Race Women* (1994), edited by Carol Camper. While we picked up this groundbreaking book at different times in our lives, the anthology had a lasting impact on both of us, an impact that would set the stage for the collaboration that became *Other Tongues.*

After a few years of following each others' creative trails as poets, we formally met for the first time in 2009. We had strangely felt like we'd known each other for years. Shortly after realizing our kinship creatively and culturally, we began to discuss the need for a new collection of work by mixed-race women in order to reflect upon the changing racial landscape that had occurred over the last decade. We extended an invitation to Carol Camper to write the preface to the collection as a natural way for us to honour the history that framed *Other Tongues,* and were thrilled when she accepted.

This collection represents a truly collaborative process. As co-editors, we both brought to the project our own diverse mix of literary, academic and performing backgrounds. Andrea, being nearly two decades older, brought an understanding of issues women of her generation. With over fifteen years under her belt as a mainstay of the Canadian and International performance poetry scene, and author and creator of two CDs (*One, Two*) a spoken word play (*Mating Rituals of the Urban Cougar*), and a collection of poetry (*Eating the Seed*, 2000), Andrea offered the project her sensibilities garnered as a working artist, as well as a returning MFA student. Adebe, an MA graduate with a background in literary studies and critical race theory, also came to the table as a recently published poet—her debut poetry collection, *Ex Nihilo* (2010), considers the ability of art to respond to the annihilation of particular identities struggling to exist in an impossibly post-racial world.

On this fertile ground we created a clearing for the creative expression and critical analysis of the issues that mixed-race women across North America face today. *Other Tongues* is an exploration of the multiplicity of mixed-race women's experiences, and a documentation of a journey over time, as well as through the stories each woman has to share. The book chronicles the changes in social attitudes towards race, mixed-race, gender, and identity over the last few decades, and the each of the contributors' particular reactions to those attitudes.

In seeking work for this book, we asked our prospective contributors to share their own individual experiences and tell their unique stories in relation to the way(s) in which they identified themselves. This process led to the excavation of perspectives of women from diverse backgrounds, ideologies, racial mixes, ages, social classes, sexual orientations and geographical locations.

While some of the burning questions you will find here have been addressed, many continue to smolder in our social consciousness. In this way, this collection has also become like a snapshot of the North American terrain of questions about race, mixed-race, racial identity, and how mixed-race women in North America identify in the twenty-first century.

We feel that *Other Tongues* has something to offer everyone, from all walks of life and all fields of inquiry. During the process of bringing the project to fruition, we were pleased to find the anthology making a difference: offering a timely opportunity to poets, artists, and academics to become part of the discourse surrounding race and gender as it pertains to mixed-race women in this specific time in herstory, which is, of course, also one that marks the inauguration of the first mixed-race/Black president in North America.

This groundbreaking event will go down as one of the most pivotal points in North American history, yet its ramifications are still being uncovered as we move through the age that many have both seriously and ironically referred to as "post-racial." Did the election of a mixed-race president trumpet in the end of racism? Is our work here done? Or did it just bring brewing tensions to a boil? What is the significance of Obama being referred to as a Black president rather than a mixed-race or bi-racial one? What happened to the fervor of backlash from factions of both the Black and white communities that claimed Obama was not black enough? What do we make of the choice of mixed-race figures to identify as either Black or white in particular instances where they gain popularity, or enter into the public eye?

In any case, *Other Tongues* talks about race and mixed-race explicitly, refusing to throw conversations on race into abstraction. In turn, it is through these honest conversations that we can discuss instances of racial oppression and explore the conundrum of race in all its complexity. Even if race is primarily a social construction—that is, channeled through social mechanisms—the point is that we remain committed to unpacking those mechanisms. Just because racial categories are compartmentalizing doesn't mean being mixed-race is automatically freeing. Race is a social, political, and cultural reality as much as it is experience as a physical one; even without scientific basis, race and racial designation continues to be a social conundrum, and instead of closing the book we should face this predicament. We need consciousness of what race is, means, and how it functions; we can't afford to be unconscious about its stubbornly problematic terrain. Otherwise, in saying we've moved beyond race, we also say that civil rights is a thing of the past.

We hope *Other Tongues* can serve as a place to learn about the social experiences, attitudes, and feelings of others, and what racial identity has come to mean today. Herein you will find an incredible range of poetry, spoken word, fiction, creative non-fiction, as well as black and white artwork and photography that both uniquely and collectively engage, document, and/or explore the experiences of being mixed-race, by placing interraciality as the center, rather than periphery, of analysis.

WHERE DID WE COME FROM?

Adebe DeRango-Adem

Compliments on my exotic looks, as well as questions about whether "brown" might be a suitable category for my phenotype, have, in the course of my life, been a source of both anxiety and critical analysis. And pleasure. When asked where I'm from, I often remark, "Toronto. And sometimes New York. I travel a lot." That always seems to confuse the masses. Thankfully, I'm a writer, and I've been able to find creative ways around these tired questions.

Now, as an editor for this incredible anthology, I find myself at a loss for words … a loss for words at having gained so much inspiration and knowledge along the journey of connecting with women across North America who have understood the need to resist the lure of singularity—and find solidarity culturally, ethno-racially, and otherwise.

Growing up in an interracial family, I always had a penchant for never settling for one thing. As a child, I learned to read by seeing words as faces, each word with a particular expression, personality, and a life. I saw words as living things that could speak, and had a voice. It is that sense of voice that has defined my vocation in the world of writing, and in particular, the poetic medium. As a poet, the act of writing poetry is, for me, a kind of sympathy; it functions by metaphor, allowing you to make connections between disparate things. It allows you to take what's personal to a community level. Influenced by what was also my parents' penchant for the political, I see my drive to write as a way for me to understand the power of language to transcend the superficial description or observation of things, and instead make newness possible in the world.

Charged with the political, *Other Tongues* is also about making connections between the written word and the voice they carry off the page. More than a play off "mother tongue"—a title that I initially saw fit in relation to the multiple languages and cultural codes interracial women speak and live in—to bear an "other" tongue means to believe in alternatives, to speak loudly from the margins and in so doing, prove the margins don't really exist.

Other Tongues was the product of various experiential crossroads: the decision to amplify my writing skills by entering graduate school (where I focused on interracial figures in literature); my resolve to write and publish work on the experience of being mixed-race honestly and with the courage to take it to new lengths; travelling solo between Canada and the U.S. (where *Other Tongues* authors hail from). It is from these various crossings—as a poet, writer, educator and activist—that my sense of self is both deeply rooted and always in-the-making.

We hope this anthology speaks to the personal and communal, with a keenness for aesthetic experimentation as much as political impulse, and from a place that, while largely uncharted, has continued to propose questions about what race really is, how mixed-race fits or doesn't fit into our post-racial paradigm, and how our identities are bound not by essentialist categories, but by the structure of transformation as we travel and endlessly rediscover ourselves.

Andrea Thompson

Born in 1967—from the union between the daughter of a Yorkshire war bride and her Scottish-born Canadian immigrant air-force man, and the son of a working-class Black couple with an ancestry deeply rooted in Canadian soil—it was just before the Summer of Love when I emerged into a tumultuous racial climate.

Growing up in a predominantly white, middle-class suburban Toronto neighbourhood, I was confronted by a culture still fresh from the shock of the civil rights movement. My education on my place in this new paradigm came through careful observation. When well meaning mothers of White friends told me that my brown skin "wasn't my fault," the message of inferiority was delivered as surely as when school bullies called me nigger, or Kunta Kinte. Similarly, when Black kids told me I had to leave my White friends behind, or be forever labeled "oreo," I learned the price of authentication and belonging.

This ambiguous social status collided with puberty in way that left me uneasy, as with the emergence of breasts came a shift in my perceived value. Now my browness made me exotic. Sexy. I remember having a distinct distrust for this shift, and ruminating on the symbol of the mini-skirt, and it's mercurial appearance and disappearance from the seasonal fashion menu. While I appreciated being at least valued for something, I found the objectification implied in this so called positive attention demeaning and unreliable. I knew my value had to come from a deeper, more stable source for it to be enduring and true.

In adolescence I discovered the power of legacy. Through learning the history of the Black side of my family I was empowered. Rooted in the remnants of Lord Elgin's guilt-ridden endowment of land (Buxton, Chatham, and the surrounding areas of Southern Ontario became a haven to escaped and emancipated Blacks who came north to flee the tyranny of the American fugitive slave laws of the mid 1800s) my paternal lineage became an epic tale of endurance and bravery, and formed a context for the emergence of the fullness of my identity.

What am I? First and foremost, I am an artist, which means that all of life is fodder for creative process. Every cerebral impulse and inquiry is an opportunity for integration through the process of inspiration, exploration and refinement. Coming to terms with being mixed-race is an evolutionary process. Like all aspects of selfhood, racial identity is a fluid entity—informed by both the organic unfolding of human individuation and the ever-changing temperament of socio-political sentiment. In the end, we are who we say we are, as surely as we become who we say we can become.

Being an activist means speaking out. Telling our stories and what they mean to us, inspiring others to do the same, and standing together in the face of shame and isolation, as well as in victory and celebration. *Other Tongues* is about finding a centredness in the paradox of our multifaceted humanity; securely rooted to ancestry and the primordial instinct toward togetherness. It is about words as tools for empowerment and the creation of possibility, words as the architects of the beauty of unfolding human potential—both individually and collectively.

If we have a singularity, it arises only in the context of our commonality as mixed-race people, and our proclivity towards creation and re-creation—of our views of the world, each other and ourselves. Reading the stories of the women in this book transformed me in a way that was both private and vicarious, bringing me to a deeper place of solidarity and self-acceptance. There is a place where I belong. It is in the spaces between every word written on these pages. There is room there for you, too. There is room enough for all of us.

THROWING IT ALL INTO THE MIX

Other Tongues provides a rich portrait of the ways in which mixed-race literature, creativity, and criticism, while only having truly recently been recognized, has already taken a variety of forms, and moved across a range of dialogues, discussions and critical perspectives both within and outside the academy. As the newest contribution of its kind, we see *Other Tongues* as an important testament to the shifting aesthetic, critical, and cultural conventions and values attributed to race throughout the twenty-first century.

Instead of defining what women's mixed-race experience is supposed to look like, the anthology's grounding in creativity reflects the desire to find an effective methodology for understanding such an experience. As such, it allows readers to formulate their own anecdotes and self-discoveries as they read. The pieces are meant to be in dialogue with each other, as well as with the reader, so as to form part of an ever-changing and ever-important conversation on a larger socio-political scale. As we create new spaces for expressing what the mixed-race experience is, we refresh stale racial discourse, and make more room for collapsing binary racial theories while remain steadfast for our critical vision—a vision that is by no means "post-racial."

This is because our political stance as editors is to look at if and how women can creatively understand their very subjectivities as subjective, without denying their legitimacy by feeling the need to fit into a single racial box. Like our writers, we see our readers as embarking on their own claims to identity, claims and aims that are both based on social categories as well as our own uniqueness.

THE IMPORTANCE OF SPEAKING OUT

Our agenda is not to define what or how mixed-race identity means, but rather, question if identity categories represent a curb on autonomy, or provide its contours; whether solidarity is necessary for promoting a sense of diversity or if tolerating difference is the best we can do. Talking about identity is as dangerous as it is reifying and necessary; as contestable as it is a question of commitment; authenticity as much about finding one self as it is a concept shaped by social norms. In addressing these questions, we asked the women who submitted work to be considered to make a distinction between issues of race and those of cultural identity.

In *Other Tongues*, there are multiple visions and understandings of authenticity, as exemplified by the various sections we have (see below). Being true that who you really are is always confronting; the difficulty in which knowing one's "true" self—understanding one's relation to oneself—precedes social existence, or if it is possible that one can understand one's existence without having to choose who to be later.

In both scenarios, and in most discourses of identity, the missing link is creativity; by suggesting the above positions to mean that the self is either already fixed or will be fixed is to forget that inauthenticity is less a matter of falling into categories as it is recognizing one's potential for creativity as a source of value for creating your own categories. This also speaks to the distinction between personal and collective dimensions of identity, for both play a creative role in stories of the self.

How does one find their individual voice within communities if the whole idea is to flee mass-based ideas of who we should be? Agency means being able to shape our selves both according to and against labels. Having a voice means contributing to the larger narrative about race in a way that allows individuals to learn from each other's stories. We can only do this is if we share the impulse to speak up and out—and relativism about adjusting that volume is a sure path to falling silent.

Still, the right to speak is still a privilege—language is a boundary and marker of privilege in many of the same ways race, culture, and/or class is. However, our anthology believes that the discovery of a collective dimension of mixed-race is about political solidarity, and expressing regard for the larger racial equity project at hand—that is to say, sharing the experiences of women is, for us, an inevitable part of the sustained campaign for racial justice.

CATEGORIES FOR THOUGHT

As the submissions began to come in, we were struck by the variety and multiplicity of voices and views women shared on their experience of being mixed race. Stories were told by women with a diversity of ancestral, cultural, political, social and sexual backgrounds. Each woman speaks in a unique voice, using humor, anger, sadness, wisdom, insight to convey their experiences. As the book began to take form, we noticed some common themes emerging. Many pieces answered the question "where are you from?" or the more disturbing framing of this inquiry through the question, "what are you?" Through reading through the work, we also found a common thematic thread emerging that reflected on women's experiences of being exoticized, or it's antithesis, being seen as the "ugly duckling." Many women addressed issues of belonging, experiences of being an outsider in both the communities of their racial ancestry, or of being demanded to choose allegiance between one side or another, and to define themselves at the exclusion of half their racial lineage. In creating a structure for these submissions, we looked at these common themes and grouped them together accordingly.

I. Rules/Roles

The pieces included in the first section: "Rules/Roles," investigate women's answers to the question "what are you," and the resulting issues of identity and the direct or unspoken societal request that we choose racial alliances. The desire for mixed-race peoples to self-identify has, for the most part, led to a dichotomy of either/or. Once upon a time, the one-drop rule meant you either identified as Black and dealt with the legacy of dispossession and invisibility attributed to being Black in North America, or you uneasily passed for white. Today, this pressure to choose when self-identifying still exists, and has led to questions of authenticity, belonging, and a desire to simplify the issue by situating mixed-race folks into an exilic space of neither/nor.

All those slashes, dashes, and margins; what do they amount to? Instead of addressing this set of questions, many multiracial activists have taken the celebratory route, insisting on the right to claim a true mixed self that is multiple, relational, and hyphen-happy. Another way of addressing this issue is to consider how, and if, the mixed-race self can be composed of disparate identities in relation to each other, not in opposition to one another, or where "one" identity has to replace another. The nuance is not in what you choose at day's end; it's about the legacy of a haunted racial politics that refuses to account for the experience of the racially ambiguous, to give our experience legitimacy.

II. Roots/Routes

The second section of the book, "Roots/Routes" includes writing and images that pertain to questions of location, immigration, diasporic movement, family, and even hair. Indeed, one of the most interesting way this journey often plays out in the lives of many mixed-race women is through the examination of the politics of hair. How Black women style their hair has long been a paradoxically powerful, yet whimsical symbol of the struggle to understand the relationship between outer appearance and inner racial allegiance. For mixed-race women with Black ancestry, this symbol's power is near explosive.

Many of the stories also discuss the intersection between ancestry and geography. The issue of dual heritage—of being neither African nor American/Canadian, neither fully black nor white—speaks to the various "crossings" of writers whose stories travel across racial, ethnic, cultural, and geographical lines, encountering all types of discourse on miscegenation (or crossbreeding) along the way. The metaphor of the journey emerges in many of the pieces, and indeed has an important place in helping understand the mixed experience. Motifs of exile or not belonging speak to the desire to escape constrictive racial boundaries; self-displacement, journeys outward, and geographical migrations also suggest that while we may have to find a "place" in the world, and a conscious, historical positioning of ourselves within it, our existence is always syncretic and multidimensional, always on the move. Escaping these boundaries means learning to revise the rules/roles we feel born into.

III. Revelations

In this final section, we gathered work that represented a culmination of wisdom garnered from women's experiences—insights and new visions for the future. It is in these pieces where we found women expressing a sense of peace and singularity, as well as a sense of not only coming to terms with the identity of being mixed-race, but finding solidarity and empowerment through weaving their way through the myriad of questions raised by such an identity. In a variety of ways, each women's work in this section represents a sense of finally coming home to the centre of herself.

At first we struggled with the naming of this section, we realized the word "revelations" would have distinct biblical connotations in North America. Our decision to keep the title—loaded associations and all—reflects the perspective we found while reading through the submissions, which is that the theme of spirituality, reckoning, and transcendence represented a thread—weaved through many of the pieces. In this way, this final section represents synthesis, wholeness and a sense of completion. The task for us was not to question personal choices, but creatively explore how mixed-race women assert their identity; a process that often ends not in complete recognition, but revelation. Identity is social, political, material, marked; but there is psychic component of identity that transcends social symbols and phenotypes. There is a part of identity that cannot be staged or fulfill the expectations of other communities; a part of our identities that speaks to the magic of storytelling. Our identities are indeed stories in the marking; narratives authored by us alone and that, whether we are conscious of it or not, can—both delightfully and to our utmost surprise—speak to the question of political solidarity on a more spiritualized plane.

CONCLUSION: FROM RACIAL PASSING TO PASSING THE TORCH

In both scholarly studies on mixed-race, and the attempt to account for the experience of mixed-race figures in literature, the material and psychological conditions of the interracial subject has always resisted conclusion. So too have interracial partnerships continued to elicit resistance from those who refuse social progress. Though the age of racial passing might largely be over, and their literatures no longer in critical circulation, the legacy of racial passing has served an unprogressive starting point for the analyses of the experience of being mixed-race—analyses that have forwarded continued taboos around miscegenation. Still, taboo is a great starting point for new modes of thought; from its radically open fields of debate and exploration, we can finally, enter what were so estranged from.

For some of our featured authors, this meant trying to escape the feeling that we are estranged from ourselves. A motion to do away with the idea that mixed-race folks are always doomed to wander across racial lines. An effort to see the beauty in oscillation; instead of uncertainty, an appreciation of the complex identification at the heart of our "selves." There is much room and a ways to go for mixed-race subjectivities to become a critical discourse. We hope that *Other Tongues* can at least turn up the volume on what it meant to be mixed-race in a historical moment that has continued to demand our silence or invisibility.

While we wished to have included the perspectives of mixed-race women across the globe (an endeavor altogether too large for the scope of this anthology. *Other Tongues II*, perhaps!), we hope the book can both serve as an important contribution to both the literary canon, and mixed-race and gender studies. Our hope is that readers will be inspired by the beauty of stories and poems while be given new conceptual tools for rethinking race, and mixed-race politics, psychology and creativity. *Other Tongues*, asks readers to stop (rather than "pass," as it were) and reconsider what a mixed-race identity means.

I. RULES/ROLES

ANDREA THOMPSON

Enigma

Who I am
depends on which side of my skin
you stand on, in here

it's all neurons firing
synapses telling stories
blood tracing ancestral histories
races blending in veins
truth obscured by memory

inside all is flux and flow
stillness and storms
contradiction – and at the heart of it

just another mammal
wanting to be loved

outside is all vibration
rubbing up against eardrum
someone's mouth pounds out
enigma

my mind tries it on, pins it
itchy like a label on my lapel

and wonders
if the skin over bone
wrapping around this self

distracts
sends the other off

to question, not who I am
but what

Blond

Certainly it was possible — somewhere
in my parents' genes the recessive traits
that might have given me a different look:
not attached earlobes or my father's green eyes,
but another hair colour — gentleman-preferred,
have-more-fun blond. And with my skin colour,
like a good tan — an even mix of my parents' —
I could have passed for white.

When on Christmas day I woke to find
a blond wig, a pink sequined tutu,
and a blond ballerina doll, nearly tall as me,
I didn't know to ask, nor that it mattered,
if there'd been a brown version. This was years before
my grandmother nestled the dark baby
into our crèche, years before I'd understand it
as primer for a Mississippi childhood.

Instead, I pranced around our living room
in a whirl of possibility, my parents looking on
at their suddenly strange child. In the photograph
my mother took, my father — almost
out of the frame — looks on as Joseph must have
at the miraculous birth: I'm in the foreground —
my blond wig a shining halo, a newborn likeness
to the child that chance, the long odds,
must have brought.

SANDRA KASTURI

Mixed

badgers are steady — they remember
even if you don't
their sleek, black and white bodies
they are solid
dense as childhood memory
clawed feet opening up
burrows in the earth
unseen kingdoms

the children of mixed race
have two natures
they belong
everywhere and nowhere
tenuous as water
their ambiguous faces
confusing people
making them hard to place

badgers will rest
under your house
their black eyes sharp
in the twilight
remember
their bi-coloured fur
two sides of every coin
dark and light

belonging
an elusive thing
fence-straddling
never encouraged
even genetically
faces telling all kinds of stories
even the ones
you don't want to hear

pick one

mama?

yes my girl.

i'm indigenous right?

yes my girl.

is poppy?

no my girl.
well —
way back he is.
people'd say he isn't though…
i think.

and uncle?

same thing, girl.

i'm anishinaabe right?

mm-hm.

because your mama is right?

yes my girl.
and her mama
and her mama too.
gaashi.

is papa indigenous?

yep little girl, he is.
from his mom and dad—
walof, pulaar.
although i don't know
if he would say that
about himself.
papa can tell you
where all his ancestors are buried
from way, way back.
you'll get those stories
from him, my girl.

i'm white
and black
and brown
right mama?

yes my girl,
you are.
gdaaw.

i like being brown.

oh my gosh, little girl.
i'm so glad.
it's hard out there
sometimes,
to like being brown.

i know.
especially when
everybody's white.

baby girl?

yes?
there's people out there
that'll tell you
you gotta pick one eh.

okay mom.

no.
not okay little girl.
you don't ever listen
to those people okay?

okay mama.   mom?

yes?

why
would someone tell me
i gotta pick one?

well,
i don't think
someone
would actually tell you
to pick one.
but maybe they would.
mostly,
you'll feel it
in the way they talk
about being
all those kinds
of roots n' colours.
   you'll know.

why would they talk
to make people feel that way?

i don't know, *kwezeNs* (little girl).
maybe it's something to do
with trying to make sense,
maybe it's hard for them
to make sense of. but that's
just me thinking. to know,
we'd have to ask them.

okay mama.   mama?

hmm?

that doesn't make sense though,
does it?
to be able to even pick one?

hmmm?

i mean, how could
i pick You
or Papa
or Poppy
or Auntie
or Auntie
or Nanna
or Grandpa
or Uncle
or Uncle?

hm.
now there goes a good question little girl.

My Sista, Mi Hermana

"You're a beaner?"
"You're a spic?"
"*Hablas español?*"
"*Eres negra?*"
"*Eres morena?*"
"Why don't you speak Spanish?"

My Sista, but I'm here;
And I'm just like you.

Black mamas didn't want me around;
Latina *madres* wouldn't see me.
Never Mexican enough, never Black enough.
Mi abuelita called Mommy a nigger-lover.
Does that make me the nigger?
Cause,
Mommy loves me!
Dad's mom said, "Don't marry that dirty Mexican."
So, he didn't.
Because my colour was different from her;
Mommy cursed all who stared.
Racism from my own people;
The people of my races.

Mi Hermana, pero yo soy aquí;
And I'm just like you.

Was taught to identify myself,
Because society would surely try to label me.
Though, unrecognizable to most;

Including the Census.
Black of non-Hispanic descent;
Hispanic/white of non-black race.
Let me be a colour instead!
"Blaxican Brown," a new crayon to beautify the world.
Both sides say I'm not a real Black girl;
I'm not a real Mexican girl.
I won't deny one for the other.

My Sista, *Mi Hermana*, I'm here;
And I'm just like you.

little half-black-breed

whose skin was not the ebony advertised
on the *Just For You* boxes of hair colour
she stared at in the aisle
of the all White drugstore
whose skin was not the pearl vanilla crème
of the Church Ladies congregating on the
steps after service

(little half-black-breed)
somewhere in-between
warm caramel hot cocoa sun-kissed bronze
these are the colours she was but couldn't see
because all she saw was mud

(little half-black-breed)
one morning she tried to wash the mud away
five year old hands pushed the wooden crate to the edge
of the bathroom basin
pyjama legs stood on tiptoe
as she peered into the mirror

(little half-black-breed)
hair unlike anything else she ever saw
it didn't lie straight and shiny only corked and squiggly
wormed in coils it sometimes frizzed
especially after the rain
nôhkum (my grandmother) always threatened to cut them but she
knew they would always grow back
to swim around the mud face

(little half-black-breed)
she grabbed the bristled floor brush
and dipped it into lukewarm water
beginning with her forehead she
scrubbed scrubbed scrubbed
her cheeks her nose her chin her hands her arms her feet
the mud refused to budge
now it had a pinkish tinge she hated pink
tears began to fall

(little half-black-breed)
she grabbed the bar of soap and lathered it in her hands
she stared in awe as they turned *Ivory* white
down the stairs she went grinning painfully wide
through the living room and into the kitchen
where *moshom* (my grandfather) and *nôhkum* (my grandmother) sat
stunned silence met her smile and *nôhkum* whispered:
what have you done?
Ivory caked face fell, eyes pooled, and she said:
I was just trying to look like (*them*)...

Jordan Clarke, "White Mask," 2010, oil on canvas, 18" x 18".

Jordan Clarke, "Nothing is just black or white," 2008, oil on canvas, 30" x 40".

Roll Call

I became black
at a stop light on north Highway One
just outside of Fort Bragg,
(California not Carolina).
My mother was laughing, distracted
by the antics of my cousin and I —
me eleven, him twelve. We were all laughing,
didn't notice the light had changed.

The horn blast slammed
us chest first
into startled, then easy forward,
left turn into the parking lot,
let relief make way for forgetting.

Don't know how anything so large could be
sudden,
driver's side door torn open —
massive arms
thick and road worn,
dirt stained, jacked up 4 wheeler
truck behind us
one hand
on my mother's shoulder

You better watch your little black bitch"

I could smell his breath
tobacco plaque tangy
from across the front seat

and even then, I didn't know
he was talking about me

Mixed
they called me in kindergarten;
Burnt toast, once
by a boy small enough for me to overlook
without straining my neck

Almost 4ft 10inches,
proud of myself
for fitting into syllables the size of
hardheaded,
stubborn,
impudent.

Didn't know to duck
when grown folks hurled
clipped bullets like
bitch.

Shamed by the way my
back buckled
under the weight of it —
black,
[common] like it used to mean.

The old man
shut the door behind him, left me
[un]touched [tainted]
with the name he'd given me.

***

I became token
learning to finger 8th notes
to Bach and Beethoven.
Conductor taught us all
            Sonatina in D major,
My 12 Bar Blues   rose above the band
even with my instrument at rest.

Nappy ends of my braids
read like sheet music,
Mendocino Middle School band lost their place
caught up in the sullen refrain.

[Minuet]
[Leggiero] *"Do you have any black in you?"* [rest one bar]

I thought she might be joking
but pink cheeks tend
to tattle tale
on the guilt-ridden

[Agitato] *"My dad's a racist."* [rest note]

[Vivace] *"He says that black people
brought AIDS from Africa by
having sex with monkeys—
he says a lot of things—
it's really terrible, but—*

[Crescendo]
I'd never let him be racist to you, though."
[Fin]

I thanked her,
watched relief wash the scarlet from her face,
and took a breath for the pickup note.

***

I became nigger
Two blocks west of Thurgood Marshall High School
in the Bay View.

Call me liar
but I'll hold testament,
this man had a bullhorn
fashioned his front step into
soap box, hawking pejoratives
like mercury tonic

"All you fucking niggers! I will fucking kill you!
Hey you!
Nigger!"

I thought about running
but knew he could chase me down
thought about calling for help
but knew no one would come

I'd like to say it was strength
that kept me rooted
but this is not a poem about heroics—
fist gripped
around bus stop sign post
just to keep from shaking
my only prayer:
for the 44 bus to arrive before
verbal became physical

For ten minutes,
I faced the street and listened
to every reason
why my people are
worthless
dejected
inhuman

And for ten minutes
I thought about each time I'd been called an oreo,
was asked to prove myself, and told I was not Black enough
to understand the struggle—

So for all those still questioning,
here are my final confessions:
I have never had hot water cornbread,
or greens with hamhocks,
have no hotcomb scars,
and the only kitchen I have ever known
was the one where my mother cooked Swiss omelets and bratwurst.

I have never heard a single song by Gerald Levert
and I couldn't do the cabbage patch,
butterfly/tootsie roll, bank head, or soulja boy dance
to save my life.

I learned to recognize my own photographed image
by focusing on the negative space
between my white relatives.
Had to find out I was beautiful
by falling in love with other Black women.

I am
plain fed up
          with being asked
to authenticate something
          I am bound to.

What Am I?

THERE IS A SMALL, tiny window of time in a child's life when they can learn *anything.* This is when they accept anything you tell them as truth. This is when culture is imprinted. Their cosmology, or view of the universe, is sealed in. Their values are not inborn but lifted through observation. They learn about their place in the human hierarchy; in our society this means that they learn their race, ethnicity, religion, and gender. They also learn to believe that these things are undeniable truths.

For example: What is your race? Who told you that? If you are white, Caucasian, or have European descent, how do you know that you are white? What is your proof?

> A. You have phenotypical features that fit the social category of "white."
> B. Your parents also fit this category,
> C. Somewhere along the line there was someone who, using the same definition, called you white.

Now, what if you are white but speak Spanish? What if you grew up in Mexico, are white, speak Spanish and immigrate to the United States? Are you still considered white? Do you know that for hundreds of years, mulatto slaves in the United States have been able to pass as white and free themselves? After the end of slavery, thousands more were able to pass as white and enter mainstream, white society. If you had Ancestry.com® test your DNA and you found that you had African heritage, would you still be white? Or, what if you are like an ex-boyfriend of mine who looked 100 percent white but is actually half-black? Is he white?

So let me ask you: no matter what your race is, how do you know that it's true? Better yet, how do you know that this racial category is not simply made up? Yet race is a living, breathing reality for the 300 million people in the United States; but race is also a construction.

Hence my dilemma.

I didn't know my real name until first grade. I hadn't remembered ever hearing anyone even call me it before my teacher told me. All throughout preschool and kindergarten the teachers would call the roster and somehow, inexplicably, never call my name.

Kids laughing. The sound of gleeful colouring and stacking blocks. I was tiny for my age; in fact I wasn't able to reach and turn a door knob until I was seven years old; now, at age 25, I am only four feet and ten inches tall. So when I tugged on my teacher's dress she really did tower over me. She looked all around the room before she finally found me. "Oh, you're so tiny I didn't see you! What is it?"

"You didn't call my name. My name is Ging Ging."

"Ging Ging?" She scanned the list. "I don't see your name here. What is your last name?"

"Castillo."

"Oh, no dear, your name is Marijane."

"No I am not. I'm Ging Ging."

So a daily routine began where my teachers began denying my identity, though I continued to write Ging Ging at the top of every art project, class assignment and exam. Years later my dad told me that Marijane was my real name, and that Ging Ging was my Filipino name. Of course, because I was too young to understand race, ethnicity, or nationality, I assumed that everyone had two names like me: one "real," and the other "Filipino." The first day of preschool, I talked about it with my little sister Nin Nin. "They kept calling me Lindsay," she said, annoyed. She continued to brush her doll's hair. "They're stupid."

In kindergarten we were forced to memorize and then write basic information about ourselves: our phone numbers, our names, our parent's names, and other simple questions that are enormously hard to answer if you're mixed. My teachers, who were both African-American, assumed that I was black (which I am, and so is my father).

"Race?" My teachers told me to write Black. My friend Hip also had black hair like me, so he wrote Black too. "No," she corrected him, "You're Asian." We looked at each other and laughed. Neither of us had Asian coloured anything- it wasn't even a real colour! "Nationality?" They told me to write American.

"Father's name?" I wrote James Castillo. "Mother's name?" I wrote Pacita Castillo. The teacher came by to check our progress. "You spelled it wrong. It is spelled P-A-T-R-I-C-I-A. Patricia."

"No it's not. This is what my mommy told me. Pacita!" She looked at me with an exasperated expression and pressed on. "That can't be your mother's name. That doesn't exist. Write it again." Now, it was one thing for them to tell me what my *own* name was, but to have the nerve to talk about my mother's name? I was upset, and yelled. "NO!"

She looked at me sternly. "You need to learn to follow directions, young lady. I'm going to talk to your parents about your behavior when they pick you up." I didn't care. When she met my parents she was surprised to learn that my mother's name really was Pacita.

From that day onwards people seemed to be even more confused. When I grew up in Oakland, California there was a tiny Southeast Asian population and there were virtually no Filipinos. Most people's only frame of reference for "Asian" were the Chinese, who looked nothing like my brown-skinned mother and sounded nothing like her heavy accent. So after meeting my parents they discovered two things that had previously been overlooked because they assumed that I was black: that I have a Spanish last name and that my cute baby talk was actually an immigrant accent. Concerned about my future, they sent me home with a letter. "Dear Mr. & Mrs. Castillo, please practice reading out loud with Marijane and Lindsay and refrain from speaking in any language other than English at home, as your children have problems pronouncing correctly."

My dad's eyes were round and wide when he read the letter. Everyone in my dad's family was black as coal, six feet tall (or more), 250 pounds, and spoke nothing but Ebonics and English. Although our last name was Castillo it was pronounced "Cass-ti-LOW" and no one seemed to know that it was anything other than an English last name. Furious, he put our noses to the grindstone and made us read out loud every other night for years. "Stop speaking that animal language to them!" he told my mom, to which she responded, "Shut the hell up."

At this point my race and ethnicity were even more confused. Every Wednesday Mrs. Hicks would come to our class and teach us Spanish. After the teachers met my parents they all assumed that I understood Spanish. They introduced Mrs. Hicks and said, "Oh, Marijane, you know Spanish don't you?" Mrs. Harris, full of enthusiasm, announced to the entire kindergarten class, "your last name is *Cass-ti-LOW*, right? That's a Spanish last name, isn't it Mrs. Hicks?"

Mrs. Hicks nodded in affirmation. "Yes," she made eye contact with me. "*Cas-TI-yo*" she pronounced. "*¿Me entiendes, no? Hablas español. Quizás puedes ayudarnos, tus compañeros?*" All eyes turned to me and waited expectantly. I liked attention, and I wanted to show off. But I didn't understand a damn word she was saying. "What?" I replied, embarrassed. "*¿No me entiendes? ¿Tus padres no te hablan en español?*" I didn't say anything. Everyone looked disappointed and we continued with class. I knew that we spoke another language but I didn't know what it was called. Whatever it was, it wasn't Spanish.

It wasn't until sixth grade that I figured out that I was mixed. It's funny, but I never realized. Once my friend Katy tried to tell me. "What are you?"

"I'm Ging Ging."

"No. You. What are your parents?"

"My mom and my dad."

"NO. Your parents, they look different from one another."

"Of course they look different from each other. They're not brother and sister, you know."

It wasn't until I ran across the yard in middle school and heard kids chant "Mutt! Mutt!" that I was introduced to the reality of living betwixt and between racial categories. That day I slammed the door when my dad picked me up from school and sunk into the passenger seat, teeth clenched and eyes full of tears. "What does 'mutt' mean?"

"It's a dog that has so many breeds that you don't even know *what* it is."

A dog; this summarizes my middle-school experience. I wanted to be a Black girl, with short crinkly hair and dark mahogany skin. I was like a dog that both feared its master and wanted to be its master. Every lunch and in many classes other Black girls would touch my hair, petting me, running their fingers, knuckles, grease, bobby pins, combs, and brushes through it. I was a public petting zoo. "You have *good* hair." They would say, or: "I wish I had long hair like you." Or "You don't do *anything* with your hair. It's so ugly. Now, let me fix it up and it'll look good everyday." I told them that I didn't want to. There were lots of other girls with long hair—it was very common. For example, how about the five Asian girls sitting in the corner, or the Mexican girls over there? Why not bother them? No, because they weren't Black. Because I was a Black girl with hair that was different from theirs, they owned me. I became their doll who they never talked to, hung out with, or did *anything* with other than to mess with my hair. I hated it. I would dread lunchtime and always tried to hide in a classroom or with a teacher. But there were other reasons to hide.

I learned that in Edna Brewer Middle School there were two kinds of Black girls: one half petted me like a dog, and the other half wanted to end my life. They would spread rumours about me, talk about how I looked, and spread general terror. "She fucked all the boys in school," I heard them say loudly about me when I was in a bathroom stall. "She ain't nothing but a ho!" I waited until they left and cried. I hadn't even ever kissed a guy before. In music class it was the worst. I had the entire eight-person terror squad in that class and they would never let up on me. As always, their comments centered on my hair. "That bitch ain't got no real hair. That shit is *fake*." They would laugh. "Look, you can see where her real hair ends and the weave begins. Her hair is only, like, ½ an inch long!" They would talk louder, laugh louder. If people began petting me, they would say, "I wouldn't touch her hair if I were you. It has got *spiders* in it!" They didn't only torture me, but they also followed my sister around school and into any classes where she had a substitute teacher so they could pretend to be in her class. One day the girls spit in my sister's hair. She spent the rest of the day hiding in the bathroom. Another day in music I sat in the front row, furthest from my tormentors. I had felt someone touching my hair, but this was normal and I had long ago learned to ignore it, hoping that the person would get bored and leave.

But then an uproarious laughter spilled over the large room like a tidal wave. Mrs. Griffin gasped as her eyes focused on something behind me. I turned around and saw the bottom part of my braid, detached from my head. The girl had cut off my braid with a pair of scissors and was holding it up in the room for the entire world to see. The laughter didn't die down for 20 minutes. I was livid with anger. The obsession with my hair had to stop.

All of these experiences led me to become very close with my Mexican friends. They never made fun of my mom's accent, or our beat up car, and most importantly they didn't give a damn about my hair. But there were other things to worry about because if you're *prieta*, or dark-skinned, no one thinks you're pretty. But in contrast with my relationship to beauty in the Black community, that was fine with me. I'd take ugly over petting zoo any day. Because Irela, Itzel, Olempia and the two Marias were already dating I always tagged along as the third, fifth, or seventh wheel. In high school I was misplaced in an English as a Second Language class (ESL) for four years because of my last name, but I didn't care because a lot of my friends were in there. By the end of high school my Spanglish was damn near fluent. This added to the confusion about my race. "*¿De donde eres?*" they would ask me, which translated into English, really means the same as "What are you?" They didn't want to know that I'm from Oakland, they wanted to know what my race was. "Well, my mom is Filipino and my dad's Black."

"Oh, so, you have your mom's last name?"

"Well, no, *Castillo* is my dad's last name."

"Is he *puertoriqueño* or something?"

"No, no, he's African-American from Houston, Texas."

"But how come you know Spanish?"

"Well, it's a long story…"

For Black people I was a wad of hair, for Mexicans I was Latino from the Carribean, and for white people I remained Black.

For Asians, my sisters and I were pariahs because we were Filipino. The Philippines is a very poor country and a lot of Filipinos work as janitors, maids, nannies, and prostitutes in China, Japan, and Singapore. Once I went over to my friend Anna's house, who was Chinese. We had walked a couple of miles to get there, but when we arrived they wouldn't let me in the house because I was Filipino. They had no problem with me being Black—for them Black and white people were Americans, but Filipinos were low-class. I had to eat outside on the stoop before walking home alone. Recently a drunk, half-Black, half-Chinese man put a knife to my sister's throat and yelled: "I HATE Filipinos, I HATE Filipinos, I HATE Filipinos!" She called the police and he was put in jail.

So let me ask you the question that everyone asks me and see if you have a simple answer. *What am I?*

D. COLE OSSANDON

Casting Call

Looking for White Girls and Latinas

My acting coach told me to list
"White / Exotic" on my resume.

Casting Call:
Need White Girls and Latinas in the scene.
  Handy that one actress
  can play both roles.

Casting director on the phone cuts me short,
  "Yeah, but do you *look* Latina?"

I ask for clarification.

  "Black hair, brown eyes,
  dark skin, maybe hippy."

Hippy?

  "Big hips. Like JLo or Shakira."
  The only Latinas she knows.

I tell her I have green eyes.

  "We'll put you in brown lipstick.
  Might make you
  look Latina enough."

And then?

  "We'll switch up your makeup,

pull back your hair,
and you can play
the white girl.

It'll be great.
No one will notice."

NATASHA MORRIS

Conversations of Confrontation

my father has always been into black women
no lighter than heated caramel
for he knows "the blacker the berry"
flavour his mother had to acquire

early on my father left, she didn't chase
early on he let another man take his place
relieved from responsibility
relieved of respect

my dad is black
my parents raised me proud
equal among my six siblings
it's only ancestral pigment i lack

wrapped in bleeding colours
researched in my cultural herstory
i heal the gazes of illegitimacy
as if my conception was a sin

for i can't undo my yellow complexion
i can't uproot my semi-straight locks
i can't help be prideful of my heredity
so i don't tolerate that half-breed
pedigree
shit

don't compare me with other "mixed-chicks"
who adopt colonialist tactics

i am conscious of my unfortunate privilege
and feel the unfortunate backlash because of it

resentment is dangerous when fostered in your own community
i identify as a woman of african descent
check the black box when it's presented
and accept the bastard child identity

they say:
girl you so pritty, pritty, pritty
have it so easy, easy, easy
native?
indian?
brazilian?
puerto rican?
asian?
oh?
canadian
yes.
borderless

pale skinned people never ask my origin
BLACK
even though my skin is lighter than some of their own
BLACK
even after the double take
BLACK
but not the regular kind
acceptable

i don't encourage the false attention
for my wishy-washy complexion
for those who worship it
are blinded by its corruption
of unearthed weeds
of self-hate and inferiority
to strangle our children's innocence
is passing on wisdom is your priority?

Q: why would *you* want to dread your hair?
A: to lock in your beauty
Q: why would *you* cut off your locks?
A: to shed the weight of expectations
Q: why do you treat me as your equal?
A: because you are my family, my roots

mi seh, dem weh no have i'
want i'
but dem who have i'
nuh want i'

"i wish i was a little bit lighter"
said the king, who gave up his throne
"i want my baby to have nice hair"
said the queen, turned servant
"i want to be like you"
said their daughter

i don't consider myself mixed raced
but of misplaced biography
i cannot uproot my grandmother's stories
not because she passed away
but because she's too busy
to pass on herstory
forgetting her past unlocks my future's mystery

i can point out the continent
but not the countries within it
not the endless languages
culture, flavours, spirituality
it's what i'm missing fundamentality
where is home?

but there was a time i was absolutely comfortable
head to toe
fearless, round and oblivious
a time where short attention spans had no room for idleness

and all the time to be curious
a time where i didn't feel the cold
because i couldn't pass up the snow
and picking up adult speech to be witty
and i will never forget childhood adventure
of breathing out colour and looking up because
i was itty bitty

ALEXIS KIENLEN

why i don't say i'm white

to say i'm white
is to deny the many truths of who i am
my chinese grandfather,
my half chinese mother,
my blue birthmark,
my chinese middle name,
these high cheekbones.

if i say i'm white
i deny so many facets of my history,
the chinese exclusion act,
interracial love unions,
rice and chopsticks.

saying i'm white
means turning my back
on my ancestors,
an entire nation,
forbidden trysts, head tax, chinese burial grounds,
grandparents who couldn't marry, tea, red at funerals,
incense, chinatowns,
my meaning of home.

Mica Lee Anders, "Confession #8" from the series "Confessions."
Text: I have three identities — one for myself, one for the world, and one you will never know.
I don't want you to see me coming ....

Mica Lee Anders, "Other Female" from the series "Please Mark Only One."

Mica Lee Anders, "MAA and MLA" from the series "You Look Just Like Your Mother!"

The Pieces/Peace(is) in Me

D IARY ENTRY: TUESDAY, JULY 16TH 2009

Today I packed up my clothes, getting ready for my trip back home. Both Bryan and Diana were restless, drifting in out of my borrowed room (actually their room) in a sad silence until my Tía Mireya yelled at them, "*Por Dios mío, deje a mónica empacar en paz!*" "Why don't you both be useful and start on your homework for tomorrow, or else no playing on the computer later on," she added.

The threat in her voice was enough to make Bryan disappear but Diana, the youngest and the boldest, casually leaned up against my suitcase on the bed and stared up at me through her long lashes and honey eyes. Smiling slowly, she patted the top of my already packed suitcase and yelled back, "but mamí, I'm helping mónica!"

"Alright, alright!" I smiled back. "So how about you tell me what homework you are trying to get out of, *mi cielo*, so I can help you with it. I still have some time before my flight tonight and I would love to spend some of it with you," I winked as I took her ten-year-old hand in my 34-year-old one, and walked over to the dining room. I watched her as she unpacked her neatly organized Dora the Explorer knapsack. Even here in Colombia the strong presence of western culture blurs with what's considered traditional, like the simple white tablecloth lying underneath the loud knapsack, probably hand-stitched by one of the plethora of second cousins I have. For a moment I wasn't sure where I was, Colombia/Canada? Lost, I looked at my young cousin's face for an answer, but she just crinkled up the freckles around her nose in question, mirroring my own confusion.

"*Que?*" she asked as she passed me a folded sheet of paper and pushed a loose strand of light brown hair behind her ear at the same time. I turned to unfold the sheet of paper and looked at what seemed to be a diagram. The title at the top read, "*Las Razas,*" "The Races." I stared in stupefaction at stereotypical pictures of people who are supposed to represent what is written as the: "*Caucasiana,*" "*Negroide,*" "*Amerindia,*" "*Oceánica,*" and "*Mongoloide*" races. And then to accompany these pictures to the left was a continuum of classification according to the tone of one's skin. Starting in the top left corner of the page with the specific tone of "Celtic White," the categories worked their way down to the bottom of the page with an all encompassing tone of just plain, "*Negra*" Black.

Startled, I laughed aloud. "What is this? Is this a joke? What class is this for?" I asked Diana.

"It's for my history class," she replied calmly, "I have to memorize the diagram, because there is a test on it tomorrow."

I looked back at the paper, trying to make some sense of it all. *I must be missing something,* I thought to myself. *They can't be teaching race and colour theory this way here in Colombia. For god's sake it's 2009!* But it was actually worse than I thought.

On the right side of the page were photos of the various possibilities of race you could be as a Colombian. Of course the "*desendientes del los conquistadores*" were figured prominently as white, "*Raza Blanca,*" at the top of the page boasting 40 percent of the country's population, followed by photos of stereotypically costumed Afro-Colombians and Aboriginals with much smaller populations of five percent and 500,000, respectively. Finally, a cramped space full of messy looking, half-naked children in the bottom right-hand corner of the page summed up the rest of the country's population, without numbers or percentages, simply as: "*Mestizos, Zambos y Mulatos.*"

The images triggered something in me. My stomach churned and suddenly I started to feel nauseous with inexplicable rage. I looked at my own skin and back at that last photo. I looked up to see Diana doing the same. I searched her quick eyes for answers, one last time, and I blurted out, "What race are you?"

"*Soy Blanca,*" she stared back, without blinking.

Generation Gap (Hawaiian Style)

The tūtū at the lunch counter
has a smile every day
a fragrant gardenia fresh-picked
            from her garden
in her perfectly coifed silver hair
placed
            just so
                        over her ear.

She smiles at my whiteness
admiring the privilege that comes with it
and coos
in English Standard School
            English
with just a hint of local twang
"What can I get for you today, beh-beh?"
Emphasizing *baby* the way my tūtū does
when she's in a magnanimous mood.

I order the usual
to which she replies in a lilting tone,
"Okay deah; have a nice day now!"

My dark-skinned husband
Milo-toned complexion reflecting his full Hawaiian heritage
            and days spent laboring in the sun
receives a wide-eyed stare and tightly pressed lips
she never calls him *baby* or *dear.*

On the street, at the beach, in the classroom
This Milo-toned (not copper-toned) man
is greeted by other young Hawaiians —

    titas with fluttering eyelids and giggles
        all swaying hips and pressing thighs and
        soft kisses on his cheek
            sultry and full of promises
    braddahs with acknowledging eyebrow twitches
        firm handshakes and shakas
        a private club
            with excluding membership

Here it is I who receive
    stares, glares, and tightly pressed lips
    set against the onslaught of colonialism,
    hybridity,
    and a heritage I can neither ignore
        nor change.

M. ANN PHILLIPS

The Incident that Never Happened

I WAS BORN IN Jamaica in 1960, second in a family of four children and only daughter of two mixed-race parents. Born a brown-skinned middle-class girl in a mostly poor black country, a girl in a family of boys, being different was all I knew. Figuring out who I was and where I belonged became my life's quest. When I was growing up race was not an issue to me, and racial differences did not seem to be important to my family. Coming from the incredibly multi-racial family that I did, I grew up seeing colour or race variations as something natural, people were different colours in the same way that some were young and some old. In Jamaica when I was growing up there seemed to be many mixed-race families like mine, with two mixed-race parents who had children ranging in appearance from very light skin to darker complexions. In my family, my younger brother is the lightest and when he keeps his hair short, people assume he is white. My other two brothers have slightly darker complexions than I do, but straighter/more wavy hair. They both look middle-eastern. I, on the other hand, look like a light-skinned black woman, much lighter now after years of living in Canada. I have blue-eyed cousins with straight blond hair and others with dark skin and "woolly" hair. I grew up with the experience and the belief that all families were the same as mine with people of every colour—a true rainbow family.

My mother tells a story that when I was five, and in senior kindergarten, I came home from school one day with my hair braided differently than it had been when she sent me to school. When she asked me what happened to my hair I told her that the little old ladies had done my hair. She was surprised and wanted to know who were the little old ladies at my school. I told her the dark old ladies. To which my mother laughed. Smart woman that she is, she immediately realized that at the tender age of five, I already had a theory of race, which was that you started off young and light-skinned like I was and as you got older, you got darker. In my young mind, the taller darker-skinned girls at my school were not girls but little old ladies. Looking back on the brilliance of my five-year-old perspective on the world, I wonder if racism would exist if we all started off white or light-skinned and got more "sun-burned," "well-done," or darker as we got older?

Was it because I was an upper middle-class "brown" girl from a multi-racial family growing up in a "black" country, that race and class were so intertwined that all I saw was class (and gender) and race became invisible? Or was it that race was really not an important category of classification in my family? It was only when I left Jamaica to go to college in the Southern United States, in the late 1970s, that the realities of the social construction of race and where I fell along the colour line became clear to me. In September 1976, I arrived in Roanoke, Virginia, with two pieces of luggage and my still mostly naïve teenage mind. I was sixteen and was going to study pre-med at Hollins College, a private girl's college. My parents had both come to help set me up. This was the first time I would be away from home and staying abroad by myself for any extended period of time.

My first experiences were very positive and demonstrate the intricacies of the ways in which race and class are interwoven in the U.S. in similar ways to what I had experienced in Jamaica. After registering at the college and going shopping for some essentials, my parents took me to a local bank to arrange my first bank account. As international clients, we were taken to the bank manager's office for an interview. When she informed my parents that I needed to go to the Social Security office before I could get a bank account, my father, a banker himself, asked her where it was located and what was the best way to get there from the bank. It was at this point that this middle-class, white, Virginian woman reached into her purse, pulled out her car keys, handed them to my father, who she had met only a few minutes before, and proceeded to give us directions. We drove her car to the Social Security office and two hours later we were back at the bank to set up my account. There was nothing about this extremely generous and totally "colour-blind" reception that would prepare me for coming toe-to-toe with the colour line of the Southern U.S.

As a shy and sheltered teenager, now fending for herself in college, I was out of my depth. Schoolwork had always been my forte and I continued to do that well, but I missed my parents, my brothers, my friends, the more disciplined structure of the all-girl Catholic high school I had attended, and the much more easygoing, laid-back culture of Jamaica. Race issues were the furthest thing from my mind as I tried to navigate my way through campus life with its maze of new classes, the intricacies of dorm living, meeting other students in classes, and learning all the rules and regulation of this upper-class girls' college. But, for the first time since I was five, race was no longer invisible to me. I slowly began to feel like a fish out of water in this predominantly white, and more upper class than I had been used to, setting. I took that as part of what international students had to deal with. I began to notice that the professors were almost exclusively white and the few blacks worked in places like the kitchen. I started to pick up on the places where blacks were not present when I went into town and even noticed that on my floor in the dorm there was somewhat of an inadvertent colour divide, with the international students, who were mostly women of colour and black women, in most of the single rooms on one side of the hall, while the occupants of the double rooms were mostly white "Southern belles." Slowly, the dynamics of the colour line began to seep into my consciousness.

A few months into my first semester, I was sitting in the dinner hall with a group of international students. One of the other freshmen/frosh had mentioned going for a walk in the woods behind the college. At that point a senior student turned to the group and told us that we should never go walking in the woods alone because there were "hillbillies" there who acted as though the civil war was still going on and if you were black they might shoot you because they thought you were a runaway slave. Her statement dropped like a lead balloon among those of us who were relative newcomers to the college, but the others did not seem to be surprised. This nugget of information swirled around in my head for days and soon expanded into something that began to reshape my race consciousness. I had studied about the American civil war but knew only a very little about the subsequent history of lynchings. I had very limited knowledge about the civil right's movement, but I had heard about the Klu Klux Klan. I had grown up watching the *Beverly Hillbillies* on television but only saw them as laughable and ignorant "country bumpkins" not as potential "nigger-killing" racists. "What if there was a war between blacks and whites?" my young mind questioned. "Which side would I be on? What would happen in my family? How would we deal with it?" There were no answers for these questions.

The incident that was to colour my consciousness for many years to come took place several months later. I had gone to a movie at the campus theatre and was walking back to my dorm late one night with a few other students with whom I had become friends. We were chatting as we walked down the hall. When I reached my room, the message someone had left on the memo board tacked to my door jumped out at me as if the words had leapt off the board and punched me in the face: "GO BACK TO AFRICA, NIGGER!" The words re-ignited the energy of fear that had been living at the back of my mind since I first heard about the gun-toting, black-hating "hillbillies." I read and re-read those words. I was not from Africa and had never been there. I wondered which of my dorm-mates was so ignorant as to not know the difference between Jamaica and Africa, and why me, I wondered. I was not the only black woman on the floor and by no means the darkest.

My friends walked with me to the room of the senior international student on our floor. We told her what had happened. She came with us to see the writing on the door. At her suggestion we walked along the entire hallway looking at all the memo boards. One other woman had similar words on her board, a black freshman from St. Lucia. We knocked on her door to see if she was in and she was. She had been studying all evening and was not aware that anyone had vandalized her memo board.

This became a major incident on our floor. The residence monitor facilitated a meeting with all the students to discuss what had happened. It was the minimum the College needed to do. Maybe it was educational for the girls who wrote the hate mail, but it did not help me. I was in shock and too shy to really express my feelings. I was angry, with nowhere to vent my anger. But mostly I was afraid. Afraid of being in a country that no longer felt safe; afraid of other girls who knew nothing about me but who felt it was their right to tell me where they thought I should go, when my parents were paying no less (by virtue of my private room) than their parents for my education at this prestigious college. My innocent, naïve mind died when the "Hollie Collie Dollies" saw only my blackness, or was what they feared the traces of whiteness beneath my brown skin? They, like the "hillbilly" neighbours we had been warned about, felt the need to lash out at something/someone they considered to be less than whoever it was they considered themselves to be.

When the girl from St. Lucia and I were invited to a meeting of the black students association, I was surprised at their level of anger and unprepared for the suggestion that because we as black students had been victimized, the black (male) students from the local Virginia Military Institute were willing to come to Hollins College to march in protest, with their guns, as a show of force. Not having grown up in the U.S. during the racial tensions of the 1960s and '70s, I was totally unprepared for this. As a mixed-race Jamaican girl from a multiracial family it seemed to me that the question I had wondered about when I learned about the "gun-toting hillbillies" was now confronting me. "What if there were a race war, which side would I be on?" I asked myself again as I began to feel the pressure of the other angry girls at the meeting who suggested that we respond to this racist attack with a show of force.

Sometimes I still wonder if I made the right decision when it was my time to speak and I said, "No." No, I would not be responsible for having a group of black boys with guns come as a show of force because of something that had happened to me. No, I would not want to be responsible for what might happen to those black boys, because where there are black boys with guns there are sure to be white boys with guns. In the end, the decision was made by everyone at the meeting to say "no" to black boys coming to fight racist actions and racist words with a show of guns.

Was that the non-violent way, the cowardly way or the peaceful way? I am not always sure. I do know that when the appointed day came and there was no march, no show of force, no boys with guns, there was a part of me that was sad, a part of me that felt cowardly and knew that deep down inside I was still angry and even more so, I was still afraid of being caught in between two sides I felt deeply connected to. But there was also a part of me that thought maybe my role as someone who is in-between is to find a different way—the middle way.

In the Dark

M Y FAVOURITE COLOUR IS brown. I know what you're thinking. Brown? Really? Not blue or purple or even a sunshiny yellow?

Nope. It's brown. I love a deep, dark mocha. The colour of slightly milky Darjeeling tea, the shade of walnut oak, the rich texture of a Hershey's milk chocolate bar. I favour, hands down, a sip from steaming hot cocoa to apple cider. I love the colours of autumn—the yellows and oranges and penetrating reds—but I prefer the hue of the crinkly, dry brown leaves long after they've expired from their branches.

Despite our one-quarter European heritage (we are also one-quarter Puerto Rican and half Indian), my brother and I have dark skin. We are both brown as brown can be. In the summer, we are even browner—a trip to the mailbox and back might colour us a shade or two darker. There are no genetic hints of our pure Austrian grandmother who still pronounces "th" like a "d" due to her thick accent. Depending on the setting, most people assume we are one hundred percent Indian.

When I look at myself in the mirror, I take great pride in the image of brown before me. I have always loved being brown, despite the occasional insults it attracts. In youth, I was asked more than once, "Are you brown because your dad shit on you?" Of my parents, my father is the brown one. My mother, a mixed Puerto Rican-Austrian, favours her relatives in the Alps.

Then there was the ever so popular, "Why don't you just go back to your tribe?" to which I was forced to explain that my father was from India. As in, the country. Or, I've been told to take my hiney back across the border, no doubt something a classmate would have heard from their anti-immigration parents. I have been called the N-word by children too young to understand its jarring significance.

Though their comments and actions were less obvious, when I grew older, people still had issues with my brownness. I never got parts in plays for characters that were traditionally white. When kids started "going together," my friends kept suggesting that I couple with the other Indian or Asian or African-American boys in the class, not the adorable white Scandinavian. Parents acted justified in their spoken discrimination, as if their hipness to multiculturalism exempted them from the invidiousness of racism. Adults often proclaimed in a complimentary yet condescending tone that I spoke flawless English (the only language I've ever known), and asked whether I've ever eaten typically American dishes such as meat loaf. My senior calculus teacher seemed surprised if I ever got a B on an exam—the other brown kids scored in the high 90s without opening a book.

My brownness has even projected political turmoil. At the height of Desert Storm, I prematurely fled the Wendy's counter before picking up my baked potato and side of chili, because the men behind me were casting such evil eyes at my back while angrily cursing about "those fucking A-Rabs." As soon as I reached the door to the restaurant, they bust out laughing while yelling, "Where do you think you're going, *Darkie*?" I was shaking so badly by the time I got to the car, I could hardly fit the key in the ignition.

Then there was the delight of travel post-9/11. On one particular trip, I was flagged as a security risk on each leg of the flight (both going and coming), as well as at the ticket counter itself. No matter. I had highly entertaining conversations with all the other brown, shoeless passengers who had also been singled out. On two other trips, my oldest daughter, who at the time was still in size three diapers, took her turn at being felt up by a magnetized prod. Even though she was just a brown, drooling infant, she was still required to do her part to combat The War on Terror.

None of it—the harassment, the biting commentary, the humiliation of being picked on—has ever made me wish I was white. If anything, my disparate treatment solidified my brownness as the driving force of my identity. I wouldn't have had it any other way.

I married a man who is half Hispanic and half German. He is significantly lighter than me, but still possesses a healthy olive glow to his skin and tans well during the summer. In other words, I did not see him as a threat for the genetic erasure of brown skin in my children. I figured, after mentally calculating the percentages of brownness versus whiteness in our combined make-up, our offspring might be lighter. But I knew they'd turn out a little brown. They would never "pass" for white.

Jaya, who was born six years ago, came out just as brown as I am. It was plain to see that in the making of our lovely daughter, there was no dance of light and dark chromosomes. Jaya's flesh absorbed all of my mocha. There was no dilution of melatonin whatsoever.

Two years later, my second daughter, Surya, was born. Oh, she was just as beautiful in every way—the perfect embodiment of ten fingers and ten toes. Except that she was very light. At first, I didn't lose hope. Some babies are born lighter, and then steadily darken as they get older. Perhaps Surya's tan-ness was dormant and would appear fashionably late.

But a brown tone did not metamorphose. Surya was and is white. There is a slight peachy undertone to her silhouette and her cheeks blush a lovely rose hue when she plays outside in the heat. But there is no shadow, no tan, no darkness, no brown. If I were to outfit Surya in a Lederhosen and ship her off to her Austrian relatives who still reside in Linz, she'd fit right in. My one-quarter Austrian genes, my half German husband's genes, chose to remain dormant in our own physiques. But in our second daughter, they ripened and flourished. Every sign of brown ethnicity-- Indian and Hispanic—has eluded her.

I'll be honest here. Surya's skin colour has caused me some distress. Not because I don't think she'll look good in pastel colours, or because I now have to be extra careful about sunscreen, or because she'll likely have to wear foundation to avoid looking pale.

I worry that Surya won't empathize with the life experiences of her brown mother and sister in a society that still favours the "fair." That she'll attribute any injustice that Jaya and I endure to a host of other factors, but never, particularly in situations where it's obvious, to our colour.

I worry that because Surya is white, Jaya, in this world where beauty is defined by whiteness, will not think that she's as beautiful. Or worse, that Jaya will not feel as valued. That while Jaya will have to avoid playing near the tire swing because of the rotten kid who told her to go back to her own country, Surya will continue to romp around as she pleases, without noticing her sister's pained face. And I worry that Surya will have a luxury that her sister will never have—of recognizing only the most obvious manifestations of racism, while ignoring its toxic subtleties.

I fear that light-skinned Surya, as an insecure pre-teen, may hate me for my colour and its burdens. I worry that she'll go through the brief yet painful phase I once did, where I was embarrassed by having a parent of a dark skin colour, and carefully, publicly, aligned myself with the lighter parent.

I'm afraid, too, that Surya won't feel as connected to her brown ethnic background because she doesn't look the part—that she'll be dismissed by Indians and Hispanics as a "wannabe." That she'll feel silly wearing Indian bangles or *salwar kameez* on her white skin. I worry that Surya won't own her desire to take Bollywood dancing lessons or attend Diwali celebrations. That in a conversation with another Hispanic, she'll hide her Latina heritage and her love for rice and beans. I wonder if she'll be perceived as some sort of multicultural poser. An ethnic fake. An individual who can avail herself of the vibrant cultural traditions of her dormant brownness, but then escape its inherent discrimination.

And if Surya benefits from all of the good of her background, and none of the bad, will Jaya resent her?

Or for that matter, will I?

While I had my brown brother by my side, Jaya won't have a brown sibling to confide in when she faces the hatred of others. I worry that, because of this, she will feel isolated and alone. I worry that Surya won't be able to come up with the quick comeback to a racist taunt, the way my brother once did for me. After all my brother was a partner in my brownness. My ally in ethnicity. My first line of defence in discrimination. He was my system for support against racism. I worry that Jaya won't have this in her own sibling.

Perhaps my fears about the girls' difference in colour are exaggerated. Perhaps I'm too sensitive, too suspicious of the actions of others. Perhaps I play the race card. I don't know. I still maintain the hope that the world is a better place. That the perception of a person is not a consequence of his or her colour. But my careful eavesdropping of conversations in school hallways, at birthday parties, and on playgrounds, belie my optimism. In a few years' time, maybe less, the girls will know that their respective skin colours matter, and in very different ways.

Or, perhaps *I* am the one with the problem. Perhaps, because of my own prejudices, I see Surya as a child that lacks the exoticism of my brown, instead of the evidence of my equally important Austrian bloodline—the Kristnooks and Gouslash, the native expressions that punctuate my Oma's conversations. Perhaps if I release my partiality to brown, when I look into Surya's eyes, I will rediscover a whole other side to my rich heritage, one that my brown colour affords me the chance to ignore. Because Surya is not only my lovely, light-toned daughter, but also a daily reminder of our dozens of relatives in Austria who either grew up or fought during World War II, the great-grandmother who delivered babies in the Alps, the Great Uncle who became a nationally known soccer coach in Europe. Surya is the confirmation of the rest of my wonderful heritage.

Nevertheless, my wishes for my daughters are the same. I want them to grow up to be sensitive to others. I want them to speak out against injustice, acknowledge when either they or others face discrimination. But above all else, I want them to be sisters who stick by each other despite the fact that their differences in colour will likely afford them diverse life experiences.

And I want them to love the colours of the skin they were born in. Just as I love my own.

ananse vs. anasi (2007)

saf and i have a boston tea party
tossing crates overboard
a declaration of a manifesto
"the mixed politic"
light versus dark versus oh just

set theorize
my curves on a venn diagram place
where the one set
tastes of grandma's lamb chops
and the other
granny's salty bake
a union
the chocolate au lait in our porcelain
the ass they all wanna rub
and oh tuck your shirt in
they can all see that underwear

yea we the neo mulattas
well maybe
er maybe not
cause sometimes we're cubans
or ethiopian jews or something

i really don't know how to
pick and choose
this free ride
shake your hips
sample shades
appropriate

pass white/s
sidelines

who are you
i haven't seen you around at all
i've worked my ass and
played my role

(we laugh
cause there's a hundred versions
of that)

who are you
please
  huh
come on
who are you
knotty curls
oh
come on
there's no kinks in there

oh
come on
i grew up in the country
calgary   nobleton
stampedes and chickadees
old wooden fences
lining around the salty dawg road stop
with cmt over electric circus
isolated by the notion that

we weren't kinky
an ideological shift
it was frazzled
it was humid
it was frizzy

sooo i was a puffball
and she didn't know product until 12 or 21
and we spent at least most our lives

squeezing our hair into tight ponytails
the tagline of the script
sighing for relaxation
and flat iron brushes
frizziness fried
sooo wanted that

  and she well
she gelled
like totally
the age of clueless
and hilary
curls that squirrel
never moved
just to keep up this image
of how safe you want to be

sometimes it's united colours of benetton
american apparel and
maddox jolie-pitt and
jasmine du-bois and

other times
it's symbolic logic
powerpointing post/colonialism
the one drop rule
miscegenation
her sister vision
always threatened

(sometimes
all i can do
is hurt
for those reality tv makeovers)

dry
an after shot
since

it ain't this
singe

it ain't that
burn

(just try to
brush
and blow dry)

AMBER JAMILLA MUSSER

Contamination

T HE GROUP OF CHILDREN is gathered around the white sink looking intently at the small clump of red in the sink. It is my blood that we are watching, blood from my mouth, blood from the loss of a tooth. This spectacle has come about as an experiment of sorts; we are watching to see if what I expel will be dark (darker than others).

It is hard for me not to feel this insistence on my difference, my darkness, as a form of contamination. I feel like a foreigner, an invader, a threat. In some ways this is true. Technically, I am a foreigner, I am not a native of anywhere. I have lived in eight different countries only two of which count me as a citizen. This is part of globalization, this is part of modernity, but I feel like its seamy underside. My existence offers tangible proof of the sullying of various bloodlines; it evokes histories of colonialism, conquest, invasion, and pain.

***

I can see the ways in which my parents' union plays into certain historical scripts. Some want to believe that my (white) father is my (black) mother's saviour, that their marriage saved her from the Caribbean and poverty, and that she should be grateful for her lighter, well-educated children, children that are certainly better off for his (white, colonialist) intervention. In short, her (black) bloodline has been helped by his (white) contribution. Others want to believe that my (black) mother seduced my (white) father. Once she touched him, he was gone; her blackness corrupted his (white) bloodline.

My brother and I are the light brown branches off of my father's white Swiss-German and British family tree. In family photographs, no one says that we look like anyone except one another. Statements about the lack of resemblance are a joke. How, after all, could we be similar? The difference is obvious. It renders us opaque—what else could one need to know? Similarities—love of language, love of science, love of dancing—remain unseen. We are symptoms of our father's rejection of what was supposed to happen, of whiteness, of normalcy. We are reminders that he wanted something else, something more; reminders that he left middle-class America in his twenties for an adventure, that he was filled with curiosity about difference, that he met my mother along the way, that he chose to forge an unexpected path. Forever marked by his deviation, we cannot be assimilated.

My brother and I are the light brown branches off of my mother's black Caribbean family tree. The tree itself is multi-racial, multi-cultured, and multi-national with roots in Scotland, Africa, and the Caribbean and branches in many different cities and countries. Visually, my brother and I belong to these people; we are the contemporary mirrors of faces and people long gone. Yet, there is difference of a different sort; it is almost intangible, but it marks us as foreign. Amounts of money that we can spend without difficulty, cultural references, and education place us in a different world. They are the legacy of my mother's choices. My mother, the only girl in a middle-class island family, left when she was 20 for education, for adventure. She left a poor island nation so that she could become educated, become cosmopolitan, become experienced. Her story is the familiar immigrant story, it is the story of her brothers, it is the story of her cousins, and it is the story of many other middle-class islanders. The sameness of the story does not homogenize the experiences, does not offer familiarity, it just reinforces the different ways to be.

***

It is from this fabric of history and personal experience that I emerge. Against cultural anxieties about mixing and the privileging of purity, I experience myself as the embodiment of contamination. I wonder if I am a darker version of my father, perverted by colour, less innocent, less able to take leaps of faith? I wonder if I am a paler version of my mother—somehow less: less dynamic, less exotic, less dark? In this twisted mathematics, black plus white have somehow become something that is less than either one alone, not quite one or the other. And so I feel like blackness and whiteness are indefinite limits that I can never truly reach. I will never be or feel *authentically* one or the other.

Pairing authenticity and race is inappropriate. What could it mean to be authentically black or authentically white? I know that both are constructs shaped not by genetics, but by histories, geographies, power inequalities. This is not to say that these concepts operate without meaning, without effect, without affect. Based on my appearance, any claim to whiteness that I might attempt to make would fall under the category of absurd. Despite the potential validity behind the claim, society would not permit a brown girl to say that she is white. Effectively, this separates me from half of my family. Affectively, this denial creates a void, a sad sense of un-(w)hol(e)liness.

Race started to become important in high school when my family moved from the Caribbean to Boston. I was aware that I was perceived as different and I was aware of race and racism, but I felt separate from all of that. I thought that these issues could not apply to my multiracial family. And then I moved to the United States. We had family in Massachusetts and visited most summers, but it was only when we moved here that it actually mattered.

I went to a private school with few students of colour and classification of all types was of paramount importance—black, white, rich, poor, athletic, artsy—ambiguity was not tolerated. A classmate of mine said that my skin was too dark, my hair too curly, and my eyes too brown for me to be anything but black (even half-white). And so I became black. The other students of colour welcomed this addition to their numbers, and I was happy to have company.

Assimilation was not perfect, however. Being foreign (though technically American) added a layer of strangeness and alienation. In these adolescent attempts to understand identity, to understand blackness, I did not relate to its cultural referents—jokes about liking fried chicken and watermelon and hip hop— and my personal history felt divorced from tales of urban blight and Southern roots. The only conclusion that my brain could make was that I was not truly black. I was on the outside looking in. I felt like a voyeur.

As I grew older, I grew less resistant to the label. I figured if people were going to treat me as though I was black, by default that made me black, regardless of my feelings about the matter. I was either going to receive the benefits or the burdens of this identity regardless of my own fraught relationship with it. Sometimes this feels like an alien designation, sometimes I wish I looked more ambiguous; I do not always recognize myself in the identity.

Once, on the main street of a small town, I was called a nigger and my reaction to this was instant and violent. Immediately, I distanced myself from the term, "but how could they be referring to me, I'm not, I'm not like *that*," then I was flooded with shame—did my desire to distance myself from this term mean that I felt that I was better, different from other blacks? Finally, I realized that that was the type of insult that was meant to divide, meant to instill fear. Still, the resultant schism between self and identity felt like more than that, it felt personal.

Once, I was called a Caribbean doll; though it is more accurate to say that the man purred that I was a *muñeca caribeña*. I was 13 and it was late and I was out getting ice cream with a friend and he was older and I was scared, shocked, excited that someone found me appealing. In that moment, and the ones that followed, I inhabited a seductive body, a threatening body, a body culled from fantasies of race and place. When read as a colour, when read racially, my body does not feel like it is mine; it is a space for others. It is a space where some project their fantasies, fantasies about being seduced by difference, fantasies about boundary crossing, fantasies of otherness. I am someone's Caribbean doll, African queen, ghetto princess. My body exists as temptation, as fetish, as separate from me. My body is a canvas; I am a blank page, opaque, inscrutable. They do not desire *me*, only my difference, and this difference sometimes feels like it devours everything, everything real in the entire world including me.

Sometimes it feels as though my self owes a great deal to this identity. Sometimes being identified as black has conferred privilege. Having minority status has made me a desirable commodity in the era of multiculturalism. My skin expresses difference; *I* represent diversity. Sometimes this identity feels like a liability, a burden, a falsehood, a performance. After all I'm only half different. It's all about context.

And so, what to do with this difference? What to do with this feeling? I feel like a threat, a contamination, not necessarily to the rest of the earth, the rest of the population, but to myself; my identity is threatening to annihilate my self. My identity is larger than me, larger than life, but all I want is to be: be myself, be genuine, be authentic, be....

LIBERTY HULTBERG

A Mixed Journey from the Outside In

L ATELY I HAVE NOTICED that I am in style. I keep seeing people that look like me on television, in magazines, on billboards. Skin cashew-crème, light green eyes, tightly coiled hair that appears to be somewhat ethnic. Racial ambiguity. It's the new thing. Maybe advertisers know that people are uncomfortable with ambiguity and will stop and think, *What is she?* I might have asked the same question years ago, baffled with seeing my features reflected in images, but I have learned to be critical of visual representations of race.

Perhaps I am hyper vigilant about these images because, for me, being mixed has never been about a diverse blend of family cultures and experience—it's been all about appearance. Literally. In 1981, in the rural Midwest, I was adopted by white parents who thought they were getting what they had requested: a white baby. Instead, they got the baby of a white mother and African-American father. The child was fair-skinned, and darn well might have continued to pass, had her hair not grown out. When I was accused of having an Afro on the playground I thought, *what is an Afro?* When a scary-looking man accused me of being a nigger and threatened to come after me one day, I thought *what is a nigger, and how do I get rid of it?* My parents said these comments were not indicators of my heritage, but were simply born of country ignorance (they considered themselves city people). I was white, they assured, because that's what the social workers had said. Well, that was good, 'cause that's all I saw around me and all I knew how to be.

Sure, I'd *seen* Black people. Like many kids from the sticks, television helped form my imagination of the *real* world that existed beyond my cornfield-fortressed town. I don't remember noticing that on the evening news all the criminals seemed to have dark skin. I don't remember thinking anything was wrong with all those rap music videos on MTV (Music Television) and BET (Black Entertainment Television) showing Black women shaking their booties, fake straight hair swinging down their backs. I did not consider the prevalence of certain images of Black people problematic. I did not see myself in these images, nor would I have wanted to. I had no evidence that these images did not, in fact, reflect reality. And I had no evidence that they pertained to me.

My adoptive mother always had trouble taming my wild curls. She'd cut short to my head, and a cycle began: I would cry and protest that she let me grow it long, it would grow into an Afro, someone would call me a nigger, and I'd relent to cutting it again. Eventually I found chemical relaxers and began relaxing it religiously. I noticed that when my hair was straight my life was easier. When my hair was straight I didn't as often get the question I couldn't answer: *Where are you from? What is your background? What are you?* No more did people mistake me for being Black when I wasn't.

People had wanted, it seemed, evidence of my racial heritage, because I did not look like my parents, and my hair indicated something dangerous. But that's the thing about adoption—it suppresses evidence. Most people have their parents and other blood relatives for evidence. A birth certificate that verifies their parentage. Children adopted into closed adoptions do not. Their birth certificates are amended—their original parents' names are replaced by the names of adoptive parents. Sometimes locations and dates are changed as well. These omissions allow for the white space in my case, for social workers to bend the evidence and pretend that I was white, verbally guarantee to potential parents that I fit their desires.

At age 19, I requested the few small pieces of evidence I was then legally entitled to from the adoption agency: non-identifying medical history information about my birth and biological parents. There it was, in black and white: *Father: Black/American.* I thought it must be a mistake. I told my parents. They thought it must be a mistake. Then, when I made contact with my birth mother, I wrote to her that my hair was ferociously curly and I hoped it looked like hers. But she responded that her hair was straight. *The reason your hair is so curly,* she wrote, *is because your father is Black.* Hadn't the adoption workers told us that?

After reading this I leaned in close to the mirror, trying to see this terrifying new truth, in my fair skin and hazel eyes and curly, curly hair. Could I see the possibility? My still and silent reflection gave no answer. I knew not what it meant to be Black. So, I pulled my hair back, and left the country to study in Holland.

I stayed there for months that fall, through the Christmas season. I thought I had escaped until the holiday decorations emerged. In Holland Santa was called Sinterklaas, and by his side were black elves with huge red lips. I eyed them with a sinking horror. The elves were called "black piets," my Dutch classmates explained, and they were Sinterklaas' helpers.

But why, I asked with a hollowness under my voice, did their faces looked blackened, like they were painted? A simple reply: The piets delivered the presents, and the soot from the chimney covered their faces.

But that didn't explain the lips, huge like swollen wounds and so red. Images were everywhere. On greeting cards, on television. Yet no one seemed to know the reason for the lips. No one seemed the least disturbed. The images haunted me, taunted me.

One day I stood staring at these elves in a window display. Their heads were either bald or covered with a hat. The small statues were trying to tell me what was wrong but I couldn't quite understand. Was it because they were black? But they weren't black like their skin was black but like they were white people who jumped in a pool of dark ink and glossed their lips in fresh blood because it's all just hilarious. Like some sick parody.

Like me. They were just painted black on the outside, and on the inside they were something else. It was, I'd realize later, a type of minstrelsy I saw in those figurines for sale.

As I stood there and my eyes softened focus, I saw my reflection in the glass, concerned eyebrows, sun lighting my pale skin and tight bronze curls with roots long and kinky as ever. *The reason your hair is so curly is because your father is Black.* Again, the images gave no answers and I walked away.

I returned to college in a Midwest city determined to embrace this new knowledge of my roots, to understand on the inside what I was on the outside. Which meant no more hair relaxers. I found ethnic salons. I made efforts to be around real Black people. I learned to mistrust media images of people of colour. I learned to sniff out exoticism and tokenism. And, slowly, I coaxed my hair back to life.

At the restaurant where I worked customers always engaged with my hair. *I like your hair,* they would say. Or, *Are you mixed?* I would nod, owning this carefully. It was okay now because at last I had answers. I had evidence, my birth mother's word. My hair.

I noticed that often white women and Black women had different ways of asking. White women: *Is that natural, or a perm?* As though they wanted to know how to get my curls. Black women: *Which relaxer do you use?* As though they wanted to know how to get their curls looser like mine. Sometimes I hoped I had the best of two worlds, though most of the time it felt like I didn't totally fit in either one.

As I experimented with various natural hairstyles I revelled in this new freedom, the one area that allowed me access to something that had been withheld my entire life. I often shared my new hair conquests with one of the restaurant managers who always complimented my hair. One day I told him I planned to get braids like one of the other African-American servers named Melanie.

"Um, no," he said. I frowned.

"Since when are braids not allowed? Melanie wears them all the time."

"It's different for Melanie."

"But why? My hair will do that too."

"Honey," he said. "I love you but no." He turned back to the expo station to slice a pizza just out of the oven. I lingered like a small persistent child.

"But why?" My voice shrank inside my throat.

He said, "It just wouldn't look right."

Many moons later it dawned on me what he'd really meant:
You're too white.

It was then I realized that crossing the colour line for an adopted person of mixed heritage raised in white culture was not like jumping a fence from white to black, from ignorance to awareness. It was more like walking a tightrope.

The rest of the world has been confused about it too, when it comes to adoption. Laws have vacillated on whether to account for race in adoption for decades. Black kids make up the majority of children in foster care waiting for families. Some say it's not fair to make a mixed or Black kid grow up in an all-white home; others say it shouldn't matter. When I read accounts of white parents adopting Black children using the rhetoric of "colourblindness," I cringe. Unless they face up to what the world *really* is, they won't be able to transcend it. Ignoring something and pretending it isn't there doesn't make it go away. Even the ability to do that is predicated by privilege. I hope these parents teach their children to be critical of media images and dominant representations of race. Better yet, I hope they raise their kids amid cultural diversity so they look to those images as reality.

Today it appears the "mixed" look is all the rage—I see images everywhere. Kellogg's cereal commercial. Ipod print ads. Dove soap promos on the Web. This is not a tragic mulatto, in fact it seems the images are positive. Maybe these multiracial models are meant as a happy emblem of racial harmony. Perhaps this is progress, and these images indicate more awareness. Still I remain carefully critical. I hope it's not a way to meet a diversity quota without going "too Black." I hope it's not just a new kind of minstrelsy.

What Are You?

YOU WILL HEAR THIS question 9,652 times in your life. No more. No less. While you are certain your mother was asked on several occasions what exactly your ethnic background was before you could talk or even walk, you will not remember this question being part of your life until you turn nine years old. It is around this time that your grandfather, Manuel Renillo, a miniature man with a felt fedora and tiny eyes behind large glasses, will die.

PACIFIC ISLANDER

You liked your grandfather a great deal. He smelled of dust and sugarcane and before he died he allowed you to play with the enormous fishing nets he cast in the Pacific Ocean all those years prior to his arrival in the United States.

At his funeral, people from both sides of the Pacific will pack the cathedral downtown. At first, you may find it odd that you have not seen half these people before. Eventually, this fact will seem quite normal. Families fight and form rifts over things as minor as stolen inheritances or deciding whether or not to put the old man in a comfortable assisted living home. Cultural clashes, you will decide, seem to fit well into this realm of feuding. Ultimately, you come to terms with the fact that petty grudges are part of any normal familial bond. Even if these grudges are completely asinine and brought about by racial prejudices by one side of the family to the other. Whatever you do, do not to stare at these brown men and women from California you are just now encountering. Instead, marvel at them—these people your grandmother calls *arrogant assholes* and your mother refers to as *our Filipino side*.

Things at the funeral will get awfully strange. People will line up before the casket in a never ending trail of black clothing and tissues moistened with snot and tears. Jumping up and down, make yourself tall enough to see the casket for short bursts at a time. During one of your jumps into the air, see that people are kissing the dead hands of your grandfather. Just when you think that only crazy people are wilfully partaking in this disturbing action, your mother yanks your arm, pushing your tiny butt toward the casket. While keeping your eyes shut to avoid the sight of death in your face, pucker your pink lips. As you finish, you will feel a tug on your black baby doll dress.

"Do you know who I am?" A woman with dark eyes behind tiny silver glasses will ask. Nod; wanting to explain that she is one of those people, the arrogant assholes or the Filipino side, but catch it before it comes out.

"I am your Auntie Marta from the Philippines, your Lolo's sister," she will continue.

Nod again, thinking this is crazy talk, but notice how she calls your grandfather Lolo—something you thought only you did. Try as hard as you can to imagine your grandfather having family other than you, your grandmother, and your mother. Try imagining your Lolo as a little boy in a jungle land, falling asleep to the sounds of a million buzzing crickets and the roaring whir of the ocean.

"Your name is Lucia, right?" she asks, handing you a piece of butterscotch candy from her purse.

"Yes," you will finally say, "but everyone calls me Lucy."

"Oh, I see Lucy. You have very pretty pinay eyes. Did you know that?"

"No, I didn't," you will answer.

"You are a Filipina, Lucy."

There will be silence, then church whispers behind your black hair, and a cold chill from the open cathedral doors snaking up your neck. In ten minutes your mother will snatch you back from Auntie Marta. You will never see her again—not at Christmas, not at your grandmother's funeral, not even at your own wedding. Still, from the moment your Auntie Marta asked you this question, nothing will be the same. You are a Filipina, someone once told you.

Remember this forever.

HISPANIC

Two years later in fifth grade you will take a standardized test to measure your abilities with mathematics, writing, reading, and filling in bubbles with a pencil. For some reason, the instructions call for you to fill in your ethnicity or racial background. Read through the options very carefully while flicking your pencil eraser toward your mouth. The choices are as follows: White (not Hispanic), American Indian or Alaska Native, Asian, Black, or African American (not Hispanic), Native Hawaiian or Other Pacific Islander, and last but not least Hispanic. Scratch your head. Though you do not cheat on spelling tests or anything like that, desperately look to your classmates' papers for answers. Take a mental note of what ethnicity bubbles they have filled in. Think this will somehow clue you in on your own ethnicity. Autumn Estrada, the big-mouthed girl next to you whom you always assumed was some sort of Latina, has definitely filled in "White (not Hispanic)." Eric Roberts, a short black boy with green eyes, has bubbled in "Hispanic." Scrunch your eyebrows together and mouth to yourself *What the heck*. Raise your hand.

Your teacher, Mrs. Shook, approaches your desk in her high-waisted navy blue slacks and kitty cat sweater. Her greying blond hair is twisted into a bun with pink chopsticks. She will smell of apple spice and fruit roll-ups.

"I'm not sure which bubbles to bubble," you tell her.

"Pick only one, sweetie," she says and her pointy index finger, topped off with its aquamarine-coloured fake nail, will graze one bubble—the Hispanic bubble. Feel accomplished. This is, after all, the bubble you were originally leaning toward. Think to yourself, *I knew it! I knew it!* Let out a sigh of relief until your pencil lead snaps in half. Raise your hand again. Ask permission to sharpen it. While walking to the pencil sharpener know with 100 percent certainty that you are now in the Hispanic bubble, even if you have only coloured in half of it. Life seems simple in this bubble.

On the walk back to your desk, take note of the posters plastered across the walls of your classroom. In between ones that read *Enthusiasm Inspires Greatness* and *Bully Free Zone* notice the one which reads—*Do I Dare Disturb the Universe?* Sit down, take your test, eat animal crackers for a snack after you have finished. From this day on, always bubble-in the Hispanic bubble.

EASTERN EUROPEAN

At nineteen, you save and save. Your godmother has a second cousin in Madrid with two girls your age. In order to visit them for a summer all you need is three thousand dollars and a passport with a horrendously washed-out photo. Work cleaning houses with your Auntie Elsa in the afternoons after your Tuesday/Thursday classes to make extra money. Stash this money in a savings account at First Bank and do not touch it until you reach your goal amount. It's easy work and only mildly strange when one of the men you clean for lounges on his plush leather couch while you sweep up day-old pizza crumbs from the oak hardwood around his fat callused feet. But it's worth it. Europe is calling your name. It is saying, *Lucia Christina Renillo Sobieski, come to the fatherland of two, if not three, of your nationalities!* You must heed this call.

One morning before your first class of the day, you will stop off at the bank to make a deposit—a twenty-five dollar cheque which your Polish grandmother mailed from Minnesota for your twentieth birthday. After depositing the cheque into your savings account, the teller hands you a receipt with your account balance on it—a balance you have been working toward for a year. Feel like crying tears of pure joy, but in place of those desired tears run home and search Expedia.com.

Upon arriving in Madrid, notice that your godmother's cousins are well-to-do, and much to your discomfort and the universe's constant jesting, they even have a Polish cleaning lady named Krystyna. Do not act unnatural about being the cleaned instead of the cleaner. You will treat her in the same manner you wished to be treated while cleaning up the filth of others. Meaning, stay out of her way and discreetly walk about the flat in every room but the room she is tidying.

One day, you walk in on her wiping crystal bowls with a white dishtowel in the dining room. She will ignore you. You will consider ignoring her but, ultimately, you end up sitting at the end of the glass dining room table. Her blond hair will be pulled back in a ponytail. Smile, say hello, do anything but watch her clean in silence. She will smile back and this is when you feel it—this unmistakable urge to tell her that you are the same, that your people are her people, that you two are cut from a similar Eastern European cloth. This is when you will tell her in your best blended versions of English, Spanish, and some Polish curse words you have picked up from your grandmother that you are also Polish. Tell her how your grandmother immigrated to the United States in the 1950s, tell her how you eat kiełbasa whenever you visit St. Paul, and ask her how she really feels about the stereotype of your people being too stupid to screw in light bulbs.

Feel silly when, despite your attempts to connect on a cultural level (no matter how basic and flawed it may have been), Krystyna does not laugh, smile, or seem to care at all. She will look at you, continue wiping down the crystal bowls, and say *hmmm*, the international sound of *I do not care*. And, to be frank, she does not care. It means nothing to her where your family members originated from. All she knows is that you are an American, and she is not. You will remember Krystyna as the most memorable person in the entire country of *España*.

OTHER

You are on your lunch break. You are tired, mildly irritated with the long line at the bank, and worried about whether or not you left your curling iron on at home. An attractive blond man in shirtsleeves and black slacks standing behind you in line at the First Bank will study your ass and hips for five minutes. His eyes then will venture up to the fish-eyed security mirror where he will spot your face—oblong with a bluish hue over your already strangely pale skin. Your eyes will throw him off. He will think that they seem slanted or exotic. Do not be frightened by this word *exotic*. Remember it is not reserved for topless dancers or rare parrots found in the Amazon. This word applies to you now. You are exotic. You, like the Moluccan Cockatoo, are a rare find. Accept this.

As the line slowly moves a foot and a half forward, make the grave mistake of dropping your bank slips to the floor. His arms will drop to your papers like thousand pound weights are attached to their sides. You also will drop to the floor to gather your things, as to not seem in need of his assistance. On his way up from the grey-patch carpet, his head will bump yours. He will laugh wildly. You will also let out a laugh in-between rubbing your black hair and moving your eyeballs in wide circles inside their sockets. *What an idiot*, you will think.

Now here it comes. Do not act offended or taken aback. After he says hello, smiles, and sticks his smooth well-moisturized hand out to yours, you see that look in his eye. You will know this look anywhere and you tell yourself that it is that same look he got when studying for the SATs back in high school. Notice as his blue eyes move back and forth from your somewhat thick lips, the somewhat flat bridge of your nose, and your somewhat *exotic* eyes for several seconds. This one is a guesser.

"You're not, uh, Hawaiian are you?"

Do not laugh at him. Do not tell him that the closest thing you are to Hawaiian are the Dole pineapple chunks you ate for breakfast. In your past, there were times when you felt gracious at these moments. You would correct people at this point, telling them *No, I am actually not Hawaiian*. Then you would search their features and think of your own—wonder what it is they see in you that they do not see in themselves. Maybe your high cheek bones, maybe your dark hair, maybe your thick lips, maybe your black eyes. Whatever it is, it is the difference between you and them. While thinking this over, the attractive blond will grow impatient. Decide that he is truly not that attractive.

"You're part Thai, aren't you? You know, you sort of look like my sister's friend back in high school. Really exotic features like you. She was Thai."

Smile out of reaction but retract that smile instantly after you see that the teller before you has closed his window for lunch. Now only one teller is open. It can be estimated that this man will stand behind you in line guessing your ethnicity for at least another ten minutes. This is almost unbearable for you to imagine. So far, he has not moved away from the coastal areas. Alaska is most likely next.

You know you must answer him or he will never shut up. You look him dead in the eye, "I'm part—"

"Native Alaskan? I knew it!"

Just as he interrupts you, close your eyes, and when you open them, refocus on the newspaper in his hands. It is the *New York Times* and everything about it seems ordinary except for one tiny insignificant headline: On Ethnicity, Check Outside The Box. Apparently, you read below the caption, the U.S. census is now allowing multiethnic responses to be given.

"Did you read that article?" you ask, pointing to the paper.

"Oh, no," he says looking down. "Not yet."

Study his face for a moment, but not for too long. He will take silence as a cue to continue speaking. Because you do not want that to happen, you speak. "Guess this means it's no longer one girl, one box."

Laugh like a crazy person at your own joke. Tip your head back, smack your hands across your thighs, and let out a hugely exaggerated sigh. When you have exhaled fully, laugh again, and again, and again. The attractive blond man in shirtsleeves and black slacks will not ask you anything after this point. In fact, he will leave. He will gather his bank slips, fold his paper over, and head out into the sunlight.

The joke's almost over, you think to yourself, *but not quite.*

On Being Brown

EACH TIME I AM asked to think about who I am, I am compelled to consider what it has meant to live for over three and a half decades as a woman of mixed racial parentage. In my pondering, I remember a Creole proverb: "Tell me who you love, and I'll tell you who you are." Remembering this, I return to my usual conclusion: my identity is nested in my family—both my family of origin and, now, my family of choice.

Historically, race was conceived as a matter of biology, of blood and bloodlines, of drops and dilutions. Although we now realize that race is, as Henry Louis Gates, Jr. has suggested, a "trope of ultimate, irreducible difference" (5), rather than a biological property, metaphors of race continue to suggest a link between race and genetic heritage. They continue to link race to reproduction and reproduction to race. This view of race, then, becomes complicated by people of mixed parentage. It becomes complicated by interracial romance. It becomes complicated by families—even those like mine. I am a woman born of matriarchy. I know so little of my father that I may as well know nothing. My mother has offered, several times, to answer any questions I may have about him so, over the years, I've asked a few. This is how the conversation goes:

> Tru: Where did you meet him?
> Mom: In college.
> Tru: What was his name?
> Mom: David.
> Tru: How tall was he?
> Mom: About 5'10".
> Tru: Where was he from?
> Mom: Toledo, Ohio.
> Tru: What did he study in college?
> Mom: I don't know. I do know that he ran track, though.
> Tru: Did he ever know I was to be born?
> Mom: No.

Such is the extent of my knowledge of my father, aside from the fact that he was/is black. So here I am, a brown-skinned woman who was raised by her white mother and grandmother—one of the brown-skinned white girls, as France Winddance Twine calls us, we brown girls raised in white families and predominantly white communities. Although I can relate to the experiences Twine describes, I am not entirely comfortable with her term because it seems to assume that white and black communities and cultures are necessarily separate and discrete, rather than overlapping in significant ways. Moreover, it assumes that people of colour living in "white" communities are white, which clearly flies in the face of experience. Nevertheless, her discussion of the unique position of brown girls raised in white families is insightful and relevant, allowing a window into at least one realm of interracial experience.

As is often attested to in contemporary culture, children of mixed-race unions are far from uncommon. Yet, unlike this current cultural attention would have us believe, they are nothing new to the history of the United States. As we know, the rape of black female slaves by their white masters during slavery was a rampant practice. The resultant offspring were racially classified as black, since children followed the race of their mothers during slavery. However, the one-drop rule, which defines those who have at least one black ancestor as black, has been in effect at least since 1896 (if not before), when the Supreme Court ruling of *Plessy v. Ferguson* instituted the era of "separate but equal" by declaring that a man who was one-eighth black could not sit in the whites-only section of a railway car. Thus, according to social definitions, which are still strongly influenced by the one-drop rule, I would be classified black; the "race" of *my* mother means nothing.

Still, this white mother of mine and my family of origin were definitive in shaping my understandings of race as well as my own identity in terms of race. I do not (unfortunately?) remember much about the racial details of my childhood. And I do not recall any instances, other than those rare occasions I mentioned above, when I contemplated or inquired about my father. Yet my cousin Mel, it seems, remembers facts about me that I don't. She remembers, for instance, that as a child I would stand in front of mirrors, pondering what features I had inherited from my unknown father. She wonders if perhaps my desire to succeed, indeed to excel, stems from a sense of lack because of his absence. Subsequent consideration has led me to believe she is both right and wrong about me. Although I didn't feel the need to make up for a perceived lack due to the absence of a father in my life, I did feel the need to be perfect, knowing somehow that those of mixed race have been seen as tragic and pitiable in the eyes of many. Concurrently, I felt my mixture to be a symbol of the union possible between blacks and whites. As a child, I self-importantly felt my presence in white communities was a symbol of the racial progress that might occur if people would recognize the fallacies of race.

Perhaps because my childhood was one surrounded by white people, I always imagined myself marrying a white man. I was raised in predominately white communities, grew up attending predominately white schools. When my family went to church each Sunday, I would notice that mine was the only brown face around. For some reason, this made me feel different in a positive way—unique, special. I lived with and loved white women, my mother and grandmother; thus, when I thought of the people I loved, I saw white faces. Marrying a white man in my early twenties, I still contemplated whether or not I was marrying inter-racially. Did my brown skin and my husband's white skin make us an interracial couple? Was my "white" upbringing the equivalent of white ethnicity, and did it therefore bar our marriage from the interracial realm? Since race is so often made synonymous with culture, I often suggested that our marriage really wasn't interracial at all. Skin colour does not make race. Or does it?

For the fact of my upbringing is not recognizable on the street; it isn't something one can pinpoint definitively in the cut of another's clothes. So, walking about with my young husband, I would encounter glances and speculate about the monologue filling strangers' minds. In the conservative, Southern city where we lived, I began to perceive hostility, real or imagined, that filled me with anxiety and anger. Suddenly unwilling to hold his hand in public, I would nonetheless complain to my husband about the irony of people thinking we were an interracial couple. Instead of defending the right we shared to hold our hands together, I fought the perception that I was black.

That fight always seemed problematic. I didn't feel like rejecting blackness, but I also didn't want to be pigeon-holed into a racial category. I wanted to use my existence as a comment against the usefulness of race—or at least against the assumptions and stereotypes that accompany it. While I held as a motto the determination to bond based on causes, not colours, I still recognized the power-ful and useful bonding that can take place based on race, on colour. Yet I didn't have bonds with other brown people. I had to consciously forge those, and in so doing, I've questioned my own sense of self.

This questioning, of course, didn't change me overnight. In fact, the ques-tions didn't really begin until intimacy set in. By that, I mean that I continued to maintain my challenge to race and to others' assumptions of me within my new eclectic community. When seated among black and white people discussing race, I would be sure to ask where they thought I belonged, and I would be sure to assert my own sense of belonging. If they joked of white and black caucuses within the group, I would joke along, saying that I'd either have to be a caucus of one or be the drifter between the other two.

Yet after I divorced and met the man to whom I am now married—a man who, like me, is of mixed parentage—I began to feel my affiliation shifting. Earlier naïve, I had allowed myself to believe that my white mother, my white husband had shielded me from racist attack. At the same time, I imagined the fact that my "interracial" marriage would make me an object of racist attention and scorn. I loved white people, not because of their whiteness, but the fact that the people I loved were white made me feel an affiliation to whiteness. The lack of black folk in my life was the initial fuel that fed my crusade for interracial harmony.

Now, though, married as I am to a man whose brown skin matches my own, I feel a stronger than ever affiliation to other people of colour. He and I have coined a term to describe ourselves as not-black, not-white people—Brownies—and have given this appellation to other people of colour and interracial couples as well. We celebrate the sight of Brownies in predominately white neighbourhoods; we applaud to ourselves the interracial couples with their Brownie children; we encourage Brownie-owned businesses. Our term is playful, reminiscent of the "Brownies" girls clubs that function like the Girl Scouts. At the same time, our term is meant to connect us to other people of colour and to anti-racist white folk. It is not meant as a co-optation of Latino culture or a synonym for Latino, although we claim affiliation with many Latinos. As Richard Rodriquez writes, "A Chinese or an Eskimo or a Countertenor could play this role as well. Anyone in America who does not describe himself as black or white can take the role" (125). For Rodriquez, "brown is a reminder of conflict. And of reconciliation" (xii). Likewise for my husband and me. Our brownness is a symbol of our mixture, of the fact of love and commitment between his black American father and white Italian mother, the fact of the link made between my white American mother and my black American father. Brown is the reality of our skin and the ambiguity of our features.

Brown, too, expresses an understanding that we are subject to racist attention. I have lost, so to speak, the bliss of ignorance. It's not that I hadn't realized that racism and discrimination exist; it's just that I'd been able before to slough off that waiter's bad attitude as a bad day, the frowning looks when I entered an establishment as squinting in the sun's glare. Now, though, I notice that the waiter seats my husband and me in a cave-like corner or near the noisy kitchen and that he smiles at other customers. I notice that the frowning looks follow us beyond the sunlit open doorway. Walking into an all-white establishment with my husband, I no longer feel the sense of being shielded as I did with my first husband. Now, he and I are singled out together in our brownness, an experience that allows me to feel a bond stronger than ever with other people of colour. Now, it's not so important to me that people understand the fact of my mixture. It's not such an imperative that I ontologically demonstrate the contradictions of race. More important now is my place in the struggles against the experience of racism, of unjust treatment based on colour. This, then, provides me with a link to my absent black father, to the probability of us facing similar experiences in the world.

For the first time in my life that I can remember, I have developed an interest in learning more about him than the few miniscule facts my mother is able to provide. I have felt curious about the possibility I may have siblings. I have been interested in knowing my father's successes and failures and the implications colour has had on them. These are, however, passing curiosities. More important for me is the fact of my brown husband, the brown daughter we now have, the life we lead together, and our place in relation to other brown people and their struggles.

Strangely, the fact of my brownness, the reality of my superficialities, has taken on a new importance, despite the fact that my history and my family have always been paramount to my identity. It is as if I have come to terms with the fact that the way people see me is, after all, important; my skin says more about me to strangers than I will ever be able to tell them otherwise. I know they do not know the fact of my mother's whiteness or the relative absence of black presences throughout my childhood. Previously, though, these were the very things I demanded that strangers not take for granted. I wanted my existence to force people to halt their assumptions, to detour from their own experiences onto the avenues of difference. Now, it seems, those goals are weakening in priority if not in importance. More pressing now is that fact that the city in which I live was not too long ago named the most racist in Florida. Devastating is the fact that African-Americans have twice the infant mortality rate of Caucasians. Paramount is the reality that there are more African-American males incarcerated than in institutions of higher education.

These realities, I know, have nothing to do with my brown skin, and they are of concern to all people who fight for justice, regardless of colour. But my brown skin and the experiences it has allowed me have increased my awareness of these realities and have brought them closer to home. Too, my brown-skinned husband, and the challenges he has faced as a man of colour have sharpened my awareness of racism and its insinuations into daily life.

According to my cousin Mel, I studied myself in mirrors as a child, looking for my black father. When others looked at me, I insisted that they see my white mother. Now, when I look in mirrors I see my own brown face, and this is what I expect others to see. There is more to me than my skin, of course, but it is within this brown skin that I engage the world.

Works Cited

Gates, Henry Louis, Jr. "Writing 'Race' and the Difference It Makes." *"Race," Writing and Difference.* Ed. Henry Louis Gates, Jr. Chicago: University of Chicago Press, 1985. 1-20.

Rodriguez, Richard. *Brown: The Last Discovery of America.* New York: Viking, 2002.

Twine, France Winddance. "Brown Skinned White Girls: Class, Culture, and the Construction of White Identity in Suburban Communities." *Gender, Place and Culture* 3 (1996): 205-224.

MICHELLE LÓPEZ-MULLINS

One for Every Day of the Week

I LEARNED MY SPANISH accent in elementary school when the other kids asked me to read the Spanish side of the flyers in our cubbies. Never mind that I didn't understand *what* I was saying, as long as I had the accent, the kids bought it.

I wasn't the only kid in class with a Hispanic last name, but I was the only kid with a hyphenated one. *López-Mullins.* For some reason, the pairing of *López* and *Mullins* made me the official translator as if *López* meant "enter Spanish phrase here" and *Mullins* meant "and the English translation is:"

When I was five, I asked my dad if he was black because I'd never heard of a "Hispanic" or "Latino." I figured my dad was too dark to be white; ipso facto he *must* be black.

"No!" He said, taken aback. "I'm Hispanic! I'm Peruvian!"

Oh. Oops.

That was all nice and good for him, but what was I?

My mom grew up on the top of a beautiful West Virginian mountain, my dad in the gorgeous central highlands of Peru. I knew my mom was white. Through a recent development, I knew my dad was Hispanic—a word that I forgot at least twice before it finally stuck. What did that make me? I decided that made me both and that being both made me cool.

In kindergarten, everyone was everyone's friend and I became aware of the "Asian kids" as well as the Hispanic kids in my class. The world was my oyster. The biggest problem I had was when a kid decided my hair would look better orange during art class.

In first grade, things started changing. When my blond-haired, blue-eyed mother dropped me off at school, things suddenly stopped computing to the other kids.

"That's not your mom!" a kid said one day.

"Yes it is!"

"No, it's not!"

"Uh huh!"

"Uh *uh*!" He crossed his arms and threw out his greatest weapon. "Your mom has yellow hair and you have brown. She's white and you're not and she's got blue eyes and you don't so she's not your mom."

Well, this amazing piece of logic had me terrified. *Was* my mommy…my mommy for real?

I asked. She said yes. I believed her. And why wouldn't I? She *is* my mommy, after all.

In third grade, a little boy called me Chinese. At the time, I didn't know my great grandmother on my dad's side *was* Chinese. I just knew the little boy had called me something that I wasn't in a mean way and that meant he didn't like me. I never really cared about cooties, so even though he was a boy it really hurt.

"I'm not Chinese!" I said.

"Your eyes are Chinese!" he said. *"Chy-neeze!"* He proceeded to slant his eyes and carry on in ways that, if we'd been any older or more educated, would have dubbed him a racist.

In middle school, kids started questioning my motives.

"Why do you talk like that?"

"Talk like what?" I asked.

"Like black kids," my friend said.

"I talk like me," I said. It seemed like a valid argument. Just because I liked Destiny's Child and used slang some of my friends said they got off of BET (Black-Entertainment Television) did *not* mean I was trying to talk like *anybody*.

A girl cut in front of me in the lunch line once and when I told her to move she whirled around with that "bitch please" look we all learned about around then. "You can't tell me what to do, white girl!" she said. I guess "bitch please" wasn't the only thing we were learning about back then.

A year later I learned exactly how complicated my ethnic background really was when my mom started looking into our family tree. "You're German, French, Irish, Cherokee, and Shawnee on my side," she said. "And you're Peruvian and Chinese on your dad's."

People asked, "Hey, so what *are* you? Like, what are your parents?" within minutes of meeting me. I guess my face held too many different characteristics for them to compute. They wanted to know *what* my parents were, not *who* they were or *where* they came from. "Human" was the only answer that came to mind. If they wanted a different one, they could rephrase the question.

Eventually, people wanted the real answer. Needless to say, I appreciated that approach much more. Then again, I felt bad bogging them down with all seven. So, I tended to say, "Oh, I'm a lot of things. My mom's from West Virginia, my dad's from Peru."

If they asked me to elaborate, it was all fair game and they usually left wide-eyed. In all honesty, I didn't feel any real loyalty to *any* of the groups. I was me. I didn't grow up in Peru, China, Germany, France *or* Ireland. Nor did I grow up with the Cherokee or Shawnee, *or* in West Virginia. I am Michelle López-Mullins and I grew up in Takoma Park.

Since then, I've learned a lot more about the social constructs that box us in based on culture or appearances.

My culture is me—what I do, what I believe, what I enjoy doing—*not* what "white" or "caramel" people do. My favourite food is unagi sushi because eel is finger-lickin' good. I listen to music in English, Japanese, Hindi, French, and Spanish—just to name a few. No, I don't always know what they're saying, but that doesn't mean I can't Google a translation nor does it mean that it isn't beautiful.

People ask me, "Isn't that confusing for you? Not being able to *identify* with anything?"

The greatest gift my parents gave me is the knowledge that I don't need to choose a label for myself in order to define who I am and what I can and can't do or enjoy. Yeah, it sucked when people tried squishing me in the wrong box, but I feel I have a very solid identity because of that. I like what I like not because they fit some made up social idea of what people like me *should* like, but because I simply like them.

I saw the stages of ignorance we went through from a different perspective, one that realized how wrong and messed up it was. I saw the stages alone, with no Cherokee/Chinese/French/German/Irish/ Peruvian/Shawnee kids to cling to and generalize others with.

I just have friends.

I couldn't be happier.

GENA CHANG-CAMPBELL

Savage Stasis

I am an agent of racial destabilization
More than a metaphor
Far beyond a symbol
I trouble social mores
Containers and conceptualizations
Of identity.

I am a mirror of society's fears
Hopes and dreams
I embody
Much more than the edge
Of a page
Or polity.

I bring controversy and corruption
To the nation's table
I cannot align with you
Nor you with I
Seas of misunderstandings
Bar our solidarity.

The story's been told
A thousand times before
Yet the tale and my liminality
Hold fast
Like tears to my cheeks
Denying our future.

M. C. SHUMAKER

The Half-Breed's Guide
to Answering the Question

DEAR READER:
Thank you for your interest in, *The Half-breed's Guide to Answering the Question*. Below is a sample of just a few of the techniques I can teach you in dealing with the constant harassment of explaining why you look the way you do, speak the way you speak, and other issues when it comes to not fitting into the racial norms of society. Feel free to apply any of the below techniques to your daily life but understand, I cannot be held accountable for any legal ramifications that may occur from finally sticking it to the man. (For information on *The Half-breed's Guide to Sticking it to the Man* please refer to the form on the back of this pamphlet for more information on ordering.)

Sincerely,
The Half-breed

Welcome! If you are reading this you are probably sick and tired of hearing "What are you?" or what I like to call, "The Question." Annoying isn't it? Getting harassed in the grocery store, library, study group, and public restrooms by curious strangers wondering why you look the way you look, speak the way you speak and act the way you act.

Before you become frustrated enough to get your DNA tested and the results tattooed on your forehead, I have a solution. Listed below are five of my one hundred sure-fire responses to The Question that will guarantee people will leave you alone, or at least think twice before asking The Question.

I. THE OBVIOUS

When asked, 'What are you?', state the obvious and leave it at that. For example, I am a human, a female, and an American.

Therefore, when asked, I might answer; human, or female, or American.

This is a personal favourite.

It is just as obnoxious as the inquiry in question.

II. THE MOCKINGBIRD

This technique requires a bit more effort. For every question asked, answer said question, then ask the other party the exact same question.

Usually, they will take the hint and stop. If they don't, continue as before, answering their question and asking them the same question.

III. HEAR NO EVIL

Sometimes, you just have to ignore a stupid question. Ignore their question. Act as though the words were not uttered. If they repeat the question, continue to ignore it.

This works best in group settings, such as parties and other social gatherings involving groups with more than two people.

IV. THE HULK.

It can be hard to hide how you really feel about The Question. You aren't always going to be pleasant. Get sarcastic. Get rude. Get loud. The Hulk is not a polite technique nor one I recommend unleashing on a regular basis. It tends to lead to a call to local law enforcement. Please, make certain to have a friend who can supply bail.

V. NOTHING BUT THE TRUTH

Sometimes, it's just easier to answer the question honestly. Just tell them what you are. Yes, it's degrading. Yes, you are giving in.

But we haven't hit that age where a person who doesn't look like the socially acceptable racial norm can walk around without being interrogated about their background. And until then, I will continue to use technique number five. When it is revealed I am half Cherokee there is shock. Shock to learn that we exist outside of a reservation, a sexist costume, or a tasteless insensitive fashion trend. If my honest answer to The Question helps them to realize that we exist and live and feel like everyone else, that is good. Maybe it will make them think twice before they decide to be a sexy native for Halloween, or sport a "tribal" band because it is in fashion.

If more people realize that the race, the heritage, the ethnicity they read about or see in a film belongs to real people and is not just here for their amusement, that is a step in the right direction. I can be troubled for a few minutes to explain why I look the way I look, talk the way I talk and act the way I act.

KAY'LA FRASER

My Definition

In an image obsessed society
that is dominated by rules and categories,
I find it difficult to pinpoint where I belong.

You see

My parents come from different backgrounds.
My mother is white.
My father is black.
So what does that make me,
other than damn fine?

Am I blite or whack?

Now I haven't quite decided that
and I'm not sure if I want to place myself in column A or B.
Why can't I choose none of the above?
Why can't I just be me?
Why does the colour of my skin say more about who I am
than the words I speak, the choices I make or the friends I keep?

I've come to realize that people can only see as far as their closed minds allow.
And while I am not one for labels,
I decided that it was time to brand myself,
(in keeping with tradition and the spirit of conformity of course).
So I present to you,
my definition.

I am not white or black or any shade in between.
I am the prism that light penetrates and radiates through to unveil colour.

I am a marshmallow that has been toasted over a fire to perfection,
with all the warm sweet goodness in the middle that coats your fingers
and you lick off slowly with satisfaction.

I am the burning desire you feel during a passionate kiss
that leaves you breathless and wanting more.
I am the "ah" sound you make after a cool drink on a hot day
and I am the soul of the fire that keeps you warm on a winter's night.

I am that intimate wish you make on the brightest star.
So when you see me, you don't see colour, but the cosmos surrounding
    your heaven.

I am the stuff dreams are made of.
The fairy dust flight plans while you sleep.
I am the youthful spirit you embody when you laugh out loud
and joy captures your heart.

I am energy in motion.
A hope. A whisper. A dream.
I am part of an endless cycle and I am a dying breed.

I am beautiful. Complicated. Creative. Passionate. I am alive and hungry for life.

I am a priceless piece of art that breathes,
intricately arranged with style, depth and honesty
sculpted and composed in such a way that makes my flaws seem perfect
    and intentional.

Or perhaps I am merely an animal
that seeks not to be named, trained or contained.
No collars around this neck
so throw your bone to another doggie
because this bitch belongs to no one.

You see, I am a woman. Someone's daughter. A mother. A lover. A friend.
I am a living, breathing entity, like the sparrow, the mountains and the wind.

You feeling me? It's clear.

I am like you and you and you and you sir.

I am not a Mulatto, a gelato or any other kind of auto.
Not a Heinz 57, mistake or a mutt.

So when you see me with your mind,
when you look past these social constructs and misconceptions;
when the shades dissolve and fade and your vision clears,
you no longer see the colour my skin,
but the life, potential, the being that exists within.

Pop Quiz

WHAT IS YOUR BACKGROUND? Your question is met with silence. Does that make you feel a little uncomfortable? (Just asking). I am Canadian. But I am not sorry.

I've met you before. Many times, actually. You ask me what my background is before you ask my name (Erin). You want to solve the formula (E = ?) that stands, taller, or shorter, before you.

I find myself slightly stupefied when I hear that question. When I was younger, I was never sure if I knew the right answer because I knew the question was wrong. I struggled with what you expected to hear. The order (mother/father, father/mother) mattered. Now I just struggle with you. I wonder what gave you the authority to ask me. We clearly do not belong in the same school of thought.

I began to realize I could "pass" for whatever I felt like saying on any particular day. You would accept whatever answer I chose. If this is a test, it is flawed. If I am a teacher, I am also flawed. There have been many times when I did not want to teach you at all.

You study me. I am a subject that you want to paint. Maybe I am just a paint-by-number set. Without colour, until you are told how to fill it in. I've learned that no matter how I position myself, my background always stands in the foreground. You stare, deconstructing me. Searching my face like it is a map of the world. Placing foreign features. Pinpointing differences. Exoticizing.

I am often asked to define myself using numbers and percentages. I am tired of being split. Analyzed. Scrutinized. Prodded. I am much more than a map or an equation or a hybrid. Existing language only allows me to use divisions, fractions and amounts to express who I am to you. Yet numbers are not accurate. I need a new vocabulary.

The truth is, I am not a "half" or "bi" or "multi" human being. I have always been whole.

I am 100 per cent mixed.

Final answer.

I hope that answers your trick question.

II. ROOTS/ROUTES

Melanomial

Shaken early to my root.
Stem of selfage met with pseudospeciation —

that psychic scorcher
survived as a seedling: the basic dicots
of language fucked up —

Black diverted through slavery
into white, the plump leaf
of whiteness
watered on red corpuscular water,
pumped by whip-accelerated
red muscular pumps.

Two four-and-one-phalanged
limbs — one might
make right, another one is almost

tsuj
tfel
ereht

Des noyeaux
sans conditions, sans habits
dans mon petit doigt
gauche.

Now the hypertrophied
solar panel
of the bright leaf

casts a shadow
over its own understory.

The whole stalk bends
with the weight
of the white leaf in my
right-leaved mind.

My whole life,
a wrighting:
trying to write the gentle stakes
to prop and train
our culture towards a fairly
balanced lighting

before its pale and heavy fruit
tears from the soil
its own body's root.

JONINA KIRTON

half-breed

are we not all two halves?
father, what half did you give me?

mother, i do not feel
white, i know you tried
i feel mixed, neither here nor there

father, where are you? *he never says*
the stoic indian, misunderstood, silent watcher
mother, christian woman birthed a stoic indian who
does not understand her place, feels neither here nor there
mother's home is church, father's home is no more
his land gone, spirit trapped in routines of time
keeping up with mother, christian woman
as the world measures her purity against his lack

of innocence leaving me

half-breed, neither here nor there

Margo Rivera-Weiss, "Inca/Jew," ca.1998, woodcut, 6" x 8".

Open Letter

dear half-bloods,
half-castes,
half-breeds,
cross-breeds,
miscegenates,
alvinos,
cabres,
castizos
cholos,
chinos,
creoles,
dustees,
fustees,
griffes,
mamalucos,
marabouts,
mestees,
mestizos,
misterados,
mongrels,
moriscos,
mustafinas,
mustees,
ochavons,
octavons,
octoroons,
puchuelos,
quadroons,
quarterons,
quatralvis,

quinterons,
saltatros,
tercerons,
zambaigos,
zambos,
and for all the others who passed —
tell me
who failed you?

ADEBE DERANGO-ADEM

Prism Woman

every turn seems a wearing away, smoothing my sides
  down
washed up on the shore always hesitating, burning. this river a sight,
  the streets still yonder, still the rotting ship,
glimpses of the barefoot earth masked in ancient
armour, still the water unquenched with blood, prisons
of the body. I am a woman of many sides and sidelong looks,
  my angles are alternating
in shape and sharpness provoking the edges
where most of us choose to reel back. I cut myself
and others out and in without siding with anybody,
my sides always chasing the curve
of a dream. besides, which side of a river is right
and which left if it runs through a sterile earth,
an earth still stumbling on old blood myths
waiting for us to choose against the Veil
and try walking on those waters whose asides
are barbarous laughter. it is all a lacy mixture
of two sides and no side, an outside
  I learn to live in.
it is an exilic paradise I can pass through,
bleeding across the invisible and coloured lines
those strange divides and feral fields where I was born
and reside and resist.

NATASHA TRETHEWEY

Southern Gothic

I have lain down into 1970, into the bed
my parents will share for only a few more years.
Early evening, they have not yet turned from each other
in sleep, their bodies curved — parentheses
framing the separate lives they'll wake to. Dreaming,
I am again the child with too many questions —
the endless *why* and *why* and *why*
my mother cannot answer, her mouth closed, a gesture
toward her future: cold lips stitched shut.
The lines in my young father's face deepen
toward an expression of grief. I have come home
from the schoolyard with the words that shadow us
in this small Southern town — *peckerwood* and *nigger
lover*, *half-breed* and *zebra* — words that take shape
outside us. We're huddled on the tiny island of bed, quiet
in the language of blood: the house, unsteady
on its cinderblock haunches, sinking deeper
into the muck of ancestry. Oil lamps flicker
around us — our shadows, dark glyphs on the wall,
bigger and stranger than we are.

NATASHA TRETHEWEY

Miscegenation

In 1965 my parents broke two laws of Mississippi;
they went to Ohio to marry, returned to Mississippi.

They crossed the river into Cincinnati, a city whose name
begins with a sound like *sin*, the sound of wrong — *mis* in Mississippi.

A year later they moved to Canada, followed a route the same
as slaves, the train slicing the white glaze of winter, leaving Mississippi.

Faulkner's Joe Christmas was born in winter, like Jesus, given his name
for the day he was left at the orphanage, his race unknown in Mississippi.

My father was reading *War and Peace* when he gave me my name.
I was born near Easter, 1966, in Mississippi.

When I turned 33 my father said, *It's your Jesus year — you're the same
age he was when he died.* It was spring, the hills green in Mississippi.

I know more than Joe Christmas did. Natasha is a Russian name —
though I'm not; it means *Christmas child*, even in Mississippi.

MIRANDA MARTINI

The Drinking Gourd

Three Tales

When the sun comes back, and the first Quail calls,
Follow the drinking gourd;
For the old man is waiting for to carry you to freedom
If you follow the drinking gourd.

RUFUS

MY JOURNEY COULD BEGIN in several places: it could begin with the 1910 exodus of between one and two thousand Blacks, who escaped the Jim Crow South by emigrating to the Canaan Land, Heaven, also known as Canada; it could begin 48 years before, with six-year-old Rufus, my great-great-grandfather, being kidnapped along with his two brothers from their Arkansas home and taken to Texas by slave traders. The story goes back farther still than that, but I suppose the real beginning—and ending—is with me, nine or ten years old, and my grade five class' First Nations study project.

At the end of the unit on First Nations art and culture, we were asked to write our own First Nations legends. I wrote about how the night sky is a beautiful woman who wears a cloak of many colours when she goes out walking, and how it shifts in purple and orange and becomes the Northern Lights. I loved the sky stories best, because they belonged to everyone. You don't see much of the Northern Lights in Alberta, I'll grant you, but everybody in the world looks at the stars. In those days, I was beginning to consider myself something of an aficionado of world mythology. I think I lived more deeply searching the sky for the story maps laid out there than I did on earth.

Our next assignment was to share a legend that came from our parents. My parents both grew up in Bowness, a district of Calgary nestled against the Bow River that used to be its own town. Now, there are so many suburbs stacked like shingles way out in the Foothills, Bowness is almost considered a "city centre." But in my parents' minds it's still dusty and rural, with the river valley and train tracks for its playground.

My father's stories all began the same way: "I grew up in a grey house with a blue roof, and I had three brothers—Nic, Liv, and Ben. And we had three pets—Sirius the dog, who was black as night; Nosey the bunny, who was white as snow; and Smokey the cat, who was grey as a puff of smoke." The stories were word-perfect each time, and soothing as a litany. My mother's stories were different. They tended to be longer than they at first appeared, because time and an interweaving cast of characters attached them to one another. You pulled one end of the scarf from my mother's pocket, and out came yards and yards of story.

She was the third-oldest child in the family but the oldest girl, which meant the *de facto* caregiver and second in command to her mother, my Nana. She was—is—also the primary storyteller. It was my mother who first instilled in me the knowledge that I was half-Black, and that my ancestors had emigrated from the States in 1910 to found communities in the "Last, Best West," the prairies of Alberta, Saskatchewan, and Manitoba.

I knew I was half-Black years before I was even aware of differences in skin colour. My mother, never one to miss an opportunity to tell stories, is the pre-eminent historian of Alberta's Black pioneer community. My knowledge of the 1910 exodus goes back further than I can remember. I also knew my father's parents were German and Franco-Italian. It didn't seem all that complicated growing up. My maternal cousins, most of them half-Black as well, varied in colour from "darkish-white" (a phrase I coined to describe my own shade at around the age of three) to the creamy coffee brown of my mother, aunt and uncles.

The concept proved difficult to translate to others. When I was a little girl, my best friend overheard one of her parents refer to me as half-Black. She spent the next several months wondering which half of me they were referring to. When no one was looking, she would examine my arms, legs, neck and face for some sign of my blackness. She eventually gave up looking and assumed it was the part of me that was covered by clothes.

It was my half-Black-ness that led to the difficulty with the assignment. I could write only one myth, which meant I would have to choose between a story from my mother and one from my father. If I elected to tell one of Mom's stories, it would have to be that of my great-great-grandfather Rufus, but where to begin?

In 1862, when he was six years old, Rufus and his two brothers were taken from their home in Arkansas to work on plantations in Texas. Rufus was unaware that, as he was entering captivity, the Civil War was raging around him. The family Rufus worked for saw no need to tell him when the end of the war finally came. He had been a slave for four years when he overheard that the law had set him free. Shortly after making this discovery, he hid in the field until he was sure all of the inhabitants of the house were out of doors working, snuck into the house to steal onions and a few scraps from the kitchen, and made a dash for it.

Too old and feeble to chase a healthy, work-hardened ten-year-old, the master sent Red, the snarling family dog, after the boy. The master had forgotten that Rufus had raised Red from a pup, and the two friends made their escape together. When he was 18, Rufus returned to Arkansas and found his mother and aunt still living there. He found his younger brother Billy by chance many, many years later, at a travelling circus show.

Isn't that perfect? Couldn't it be a page out of the *1001 Arabian Nights*? I'm not sure why I decided in the end not to share it. My best guess is that I was afraid Rufus' story was too complicated, that it had too many layers and would take too long to adapt for a grade five-level laminated picture book. Part of me wonders, though, if I shied away from it because I felt it wasn't mine to claim; that Rufus, wanderer, adventurer, was too far away from my world, which was small, and sheltered, and darkish-white.

By grade five I was already awakening to the fact that my mother told one story and my skin another.

JOHN

My education from that point on was, consciously or unconsciously, bent towards finding a point of entrance into my self. The next foray into my mixed-race identity was a grade seven culture studies project. I made cornbread, and wrote a paper about how the slaves in the U.S. took the worst cuts of meat (the only cuts they were allowed) and used them to make button bones, the pungent and sticky dish of tiny, meaty back rib tails. The cornbread smelled at home in my kitchen when I baked it, and the button bones were already a part of me—they had been taken straight from the best meals of my childhood. Button bones meant family, noisy joviality, a hot cramped kitchen. Button bones can now be purchased at Safeway. They're no longer dirt-cheap because, well, it's pork, and because white people eventually caught onto the decadent nature of ribs slow-cooked in barbeque sauce and brown sugar. I gave up pork, after an ill-timed screening of the film *Babe* and the discovery that an adult pig can play Pong. Still, from a distance I see a little bit of myself in those foods.

For the next unit—language—I researched urban ebonics. I was fascinated to learn that entire English sentences can be translated into ebonics and be almost unrecognizable. "For example," I wrote, "Instead of 'I'm going home,' say 'I'm coppin' my trill to my pile of stone.'"

What am I doing? I thought, even after Ms. Elliot gave me an A+. It felt a little like bringing a cool uncle to school on Parents Day. I don't know if what I was talking about was real to someone else, but it certainly wasn't me I saw in there. Even though I was twelve years old and not yet well-versed in the ethical issues associated with white scholars going into Black ghettos to "document" their lifestyles, I instinctively felt that the assignment was cheap, exploitive. I needed a new story.

So, I tried again. In grade eight I went back further, to cowboys and ranch-hands, some of them freed slaves who found their way to Canada from the South. I gave a presentation on John Ware, the cowboy, the great Albertan legend—one of the only true legends to come out of Alberta. It's believed that he was a slave in South Carolina; after the Civil War, he ended up working on a Texas ranch and came to Alberta on a cattle drive in 1883. Once he was introduced to the Big Sky Country—the clear blue eye that hangs above the Rocky Mountains and the golden sea of prairie grass rippling over the hills—he started to wonder if a Black cowboy might do better to settle here than in Texas.

He stayed, and the rest is breathless tourism pamphlet fuel: He was never tossed from a horse! He could lift an 18-month-old steer clear over his head! Like Davy Crockett or Robin Hood, he has taken on the character of the land to become something more emblematic than human. The myth-starved little girl I still was responded to the larger-than-life stories that were tied to his legacy.

I say he fell in love with the land; he stuck mainly to the vast rural expanses and rarely travelled into the city. The travel time between urban centres is about three hours minimum. In John's time, it was more like two days, if you were in a hurry. In the countryside, John was free to roam about and feel the pull of the Big Sky all around him.

When John was forced to do business in Calgary, the weight of being a person in the world, a Black man at the turn of the century, came rushing back to drag his solid form to the earth. He was one of the city's most lauded men; his funeral was the best attended in the young city's history, but to his death he was known "affectionately" as Nigger John.

"Did his Black friends call him that?" I asked my mother when I came across this tidbit. I was at the dining room table researching my report while she was cooking dinner.

"Oh, no. Of course not." She made a characteristic face, pursing her lips and looking into the middle distance. I immediately felt it had been a stupid question. After all, those were different times. No doubt his white friends assumed he didn't mind, or else they thought so little of it that they imagined he never thought of it either. It was just his name: Nigger John. They couldn't know that he heard what every other Black man hears: Worthless John. Brainless John. Third-Class Citizen John.

I think that was the moment John Ware's legendary life lost its glamour for me. The truth is, no hero's legacy is entirely without taint. Rancid thoughts have the power to infect even the most hallowed memories.

An old boyfriend of one of my cousins was around my family a lot a couple of years back. His desperate desire to be Black himself caused him to spend as much time around my family as possible. One of the first times he was at my parents' house, he noticed a picture taken of my sister and me one Halloween. My sister, a genie, was smiling her serene smile, her cheeks perfect pink apples in a golden face. I was a princess for the third year running, and my golden hair made an angelic frame for my round blue eyes and little pink lips. (It would be eleven years before I started dyeing my hair a deep, dark brown.) The natural light of the picture caught everything just right. We looked like a couple of dolls in our plastic costume jewellery, holding onto each other and grinning. "That's got to be the whitest thing I've ever seen," the boyfriend laughed, snorting. The picture still sits in the same place on the side table in my parents' living room, and I can still see on it the speck of shame from that moment.

I would have loved to claim John Ware for my mythology, my extended family, but Nigger John kept getting in my way. What no one knows: I secretly crave to be Nigger to someone; to have the word thrown at me, or anything that would ignite in me a righteous fire, that would let the Black part out, give it reason for being. I hate the desire—I cringe to feel its presence in me—but it's there for all that. I imagine vivid scenes in which I'm coolly chewing out some faceless, ignorant bigot for a comment that slipped out in my presence. *Playing the race card*, I believe it's called.

Outside of my elaborate fantasies, I'm hardly that hostile. I rarely have reason to be. The most I have to deal with is the occasional cousin's boyfriend, or else having to explain to my incredulous Australian roommate that *mulatto* means mule: half-donkey, half-horse. I don't deal with "racism" as it appears in Public Service Announcements. Instead, I defend and re-defend my territory in the fracturing world of racial categorization to people who are just as Franco-Italian and German and English as me.

I'm not great at dealing with these situations. When my roommate, a cheerful redhead, saw the discomfort telling on my face, she quickly defused her comments, laughing and hugging me. "Don't be offended," she said. "I'm just jealous I don't have your beautiful tan."

My skin. The emblem of either my whiteness or my Blackness—or just my Otherness. In the eyes of an observer, I take on whatever Other they want me to be: Latina, Filipino, Italian. A few weeks ago, my mother and I went into a church in downtown Calgary to ask for directions. The man who greeted us at the door asked if we were Portuguese. Normally I'd put up my defences at such a question, but I got the sense that the man wasn't about to ask us what island we were from. When my mother told him we were Canadian, he didn't look embarrassed; only a little sad.

"No? You look like you Portuguese, or Latina, you and your daughter. Pretty girl." He sighed and led us to a phone booth. It turns out he was a recent immigrant from Portugal and had very few contacts here. Perhaps he was hoping that we'd be able to hook him into some sort of community. I felt sorry in a way. In a lot of ways it would be easier for me—and other people—if I "passed," if I pretended to be Latina or Italian or Portuguese. Some community where my deceptive, chimerical skin would be an unquestioned VIP pass.

But I can't pass, can't even approximate; I can only be what I am. And what I am, as I realized in grade eight, doesn't allow me to share hardships or skin colour with my ancestors, for good or ill. I decided that John Ware's story wasn't mine after all. It was close to me, but it wasn't inside of me. He was like the evening star: the more earnestly I reached out for him, tried to be a part of him, the farther he seemed to retreat from me into his distant realm of make-believe, of steer riding and steer lifting and never being tossed from a horse. His story wasn't the home I'd been expecting.

Better to let the dead rest.

THE GOURD

My mother read an early draft of this piece and said I had gotten only one thing wrong, when I said I didn't share my skin with my ancestors. "Haven't you seen pictures of Grandpa? He was exactly the same colour as you."

How could I have forgotten about my great-grandfather? George Smith had nappy hair from Africa, the "bad" hair, as Nana calls it, but he was extremely light-skinned and endured glares and looks of pity or confusion when he was seen sitting with Coloureds in restaurants.

This reminder, plus a quick refresher in American history, brought a hundred other similar examples crowding into my mind. Rosa Parks, herself light-skinned, wrote in her memoirs about how her grandfather's straight hair and light complexion allowed him to pass for white. He used this to defy Jim Crow etiquette, shaking hands with white men and neglecting to address white acquaintances as "Mister" or "Miss." The Incognegros, figures in the early Civil Rights push, also famously used their ambiguous nationality to do dangerous work for the movement. Rufus, the escaped slave, was of mixed race, another *mulatto*, but this didn't protect him from being enslaved for four years.

Of course, I'm not the same person I might have been if I had been born one or two generations ago. Is anyone? There's no Civil Rights movement for me to join these days, and I don't always share skin or experience with my ancestors, but their memories are mine by right. Three generations after Alberta's first Black communities moved to urban centres and the wild pioneer story came to an end, I can only identify my family with the voices that whisper their stories to me. I listen intently and scribble things down when I can, but I'm not a perfect scribe. I'm too much of a dreamer; I'll always want to mix my history with myth and high adventure to make it more palatable.

But sometimes history needs no embellishment. When slaves sought the freedom of Canada, they sang a song called "Follow the Drinking Gourd"—ostensibly a Spiritual, in fact a detailed map of the Underground Railroad. The refrain instructed them to travel in the direction of the North Star, the bright one at the tip of the Drinking Gourd. There is a reason humans have always looked at the stars. For the escaping slaves, they made a bridge to home, one that went on forever and ever into a rarely-illumined dark. I take great comfort knowing that for all of the great chasms between us, we—John Ware, my mother, my great-great-grandfather, and approximately two thousand African-American emigrants—we are all looking up, together, at the same map to freedom. This is the beauty of the stars: they are, in a sense, everyone's home.

JONINA KIRTON

Reflection

white woman perfectly coifed
        apron, dress fit for an outing
standing guard by the perfectly
    clean
        oven
          like a picture
            from a 1960s' Home Ec. book
smile   big for the camera

        hardwood floors
          polished
(to a bright sheen)   looking glass of the home
    the reflection
by which we will be judged
neighbours must   never
             know
        the   breaking
    dishes thrown
        holes in walls
    quickly filled (cover up)
scrub clean, trim every piece
    of your body (cover up), your body (cover up)
Comb your hair
    you look like
        a dirty little Indian.
whitening cream rubbed with brutal force
    as if to rub away, *cover up* the dirty truth
        Mom, the church lady married
        an Indian and

Dad *the Indian*
betrayed the picture   (of the white woman)   unravelling
in the background four children
are being cleaned, primped and properly clothed

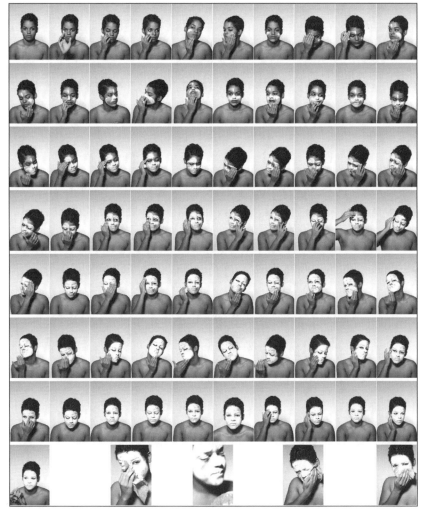

Cassie Mulheron, "Untitled" White Sequence, "Whiteface vs. Blackface Series," 2009, 16 x 24, digital photograph.

Cassie Mulheron, "Untitled" Black Sequence, "Whiteface vs. Blackface Series," 2009, 16 x 24, digital photograph.

GAIL PRASAD

Mapping Identities

EACH TIME I LOOK at a world map, I can't help but recall the world map that was drawn on the wall in the hallway outside of our school gym. I must have been about ten years old at the time. It was during the late '80s when multicultural education was being promoted heavily in Canadian schools. A teacher circulated through classes one afternoon to take pictures of students who came from other parts of the world. We were asked to volunteer if we wanted be photographed for our school's multicultural map. Students' photographs were then pinned up on the world map for display and strings were attached from each photo to a pin that represented our school in Toronto.

In retrospect, I'm positive that the school-wide initiative to map students' points of origin was intended to celebrate the school's multiculturalism. It was a way of showcasing the diverse cultural heritages that were represented in the student body. A dilemma arose, however, when I volunteered to be photographed for the mural. The teacher took a polaroid shot of me against the hallway wall beside the school gym and then she asked, "Where are you from?" Naturally, she wanted to know where she should pin my picture on the world map. When I explained that my father was from India and my mother was Japanese, however, it became unclear where I belonged. Since the map already had a photograph of a student from India, it might have seemed a reasonable compromise to put my photo on Japan. But, she was clearly uneasy with that option. I didn't fit neatly into either category.

There were no other children in my year who had parents from two different visible minority groups. No plan was in place or even any language available to talk about the possibility for someone to have *multiple* points of origin. In the end, a "real" Japanese student must have been found as I was given my polaroid shot to take home at the end of the day. I learned that day that I did not belong on our school's map of the world.

Literally and metaphorically, I took my mixed (up) identities home from school that afternoon.

AMY PIMENTEL

Whose Child Are You?

The boy looks like you, a random woman buying produce
but the girl … is she, woman drops an apple
your daughter?
She takes after her father

My mother wants me to meet her friend
but the girl … is she … her eyes search for some resemblance
She takes after her father, disappointment lingers in mother's voice
People say we have the same smile

Her eyes search for some resemblance
from my black curls to my mother's straight blond hair
People say we have the same smile
Mother's blue eyes search for recognition

Past my dark curls and her straight blond hair
Whose child are you? Eyes ask at the grocery store, ballpark, and dance studio
Mother's blue eyes search for recognition
My fingers find familiarity in my father's brown hands

Whose child are you? People ask at the grocery store, ballpark, and dance studio
The boy looks like you,
My brown eyes find familiarity in my father's face
People ask my mother, *is this your daughter?*

LISA MARIE ROLLINS

From the Tree

I

my mother did not know
her voice was sometimes yellow like
the pain of her brush
she wrestled through my curls
needles on my forehead

she explains why she has blue eyes
is white
and my skin is brown
she brushes and murmurs
it may be "apples and oranges"
but it's all fruit

but today I am falling
further than an apple can ever roll
the air between ground and branch
separates my birth from my childhood
birth mother from mother
birth father from father

sperm and egg light years away from
goodnight kisses, bedtime songs
walks to school, kisses on scraped knees
broken hearts

if I hit the ground sharp enough
this descent between trees

may redraw the rumour of my birth family
across my spine.

II

my birth mother's name appears
typed mimeograph style purple
on these court papers

blocked out government secrets
leaves of information
held as far away
as branches will grow.

my history is out at limb's end
I stretch my arms wide-wide
pulling shoulder muscles
over-extending legs to reach sapling seeds
only to discover she does not want
to be reminded I am alive.

I clamour for truth
only find pieces suitable for the chainsaw
of umbilical cords cut
tossed inside toxic bins
without even blood taste on her lips
or a red line drawn across
my forehead.

it can't be good luck
her missing my naming.

all I know is
my name belongs to her
somehow
it is still lost
in between these spaces
in between roots entwined
with blood, tears and flesh.

My sister's hair

Is like cooked *saimin*
pale blond
curled strands
tangled into each other
but soft and supple
like Kealia waves
pounding surf
shore breaks
tumble cross soft sand
in winter
and the tūtūs ooh and aah
call her *blondie, blondie*
soft sing song voices smiling
with such love
while at school
the Homestead kids
tease
eh barbwire
eh tumbleweed
eh egret
eh haole
her face masks all emotion
but when we grew up
she moved away
to the U.S. east coast
as far away
as she could
without leaving the country

come home
I tell her on the phone
no reason she says
her voice masking
any emotion
but I know why
the echo of those schoolyard voices
linger
decades
later

I, too, hear the drums

1975, KINGSTON, JAMAICA

MY GRANDMOTHER IS BRUSHING and plaiting my hair. She brushes it so hard that the brush hurts my scalp but I know she is simply trying to brush out the knots and the curls. My hair cascades down my back but I don't think it's beautiful. Beauty is the hair of those American TV women in the programs we get at night, straight, long, wispy hair, the type that falls into your face and you toss your head to get it out your eyes. I ask my grandmother how come her sister has blue eyes and is so fair skinned. She tells me that when they were growing up, they would visit their cousins in the country. Their cousins were practically white. The girl, Daisy Rose, would give my grandmother's fair sister the best dolls and my darker grandmother would get the dolls with the missing legs and arms. My grandmother laughs gleefully about this; she's simply telling me a story, a fact, and it doesn't bother her.

"Daisy Rose was one mean girl," she laughs. Even at my young age, I sense the injustice. I get mad. I tell my grandmother that I'm angry and that it was terrible of Daisy Rose but she shrugs and laughs it off.

"Daisy Rose was just a stupid girl. There are lots of people like that. Where would I be if I let that bother me?"

I look at my grandmother and I see why this doesn't affect her. Of all her siblings she seems to be the favoured one, the smart one, strong, ambitious, wise, and beautiful with a strong dose of common sense. I am in awe of this woman.

1978, KINGSTON, JAMAICA

My friend Anastasia has cut her long, dark, thick, unruly hair. She is sporting a pixie cut and it is miraculous to me that her once wavy hair is now straight. She looks cute. I want the same cut, the exact same cut. My mother takes me to her hairdresser, Ann. Ann has been straightening my mother's hair for years, setting it on rollers and giving her American magazines to read while she sits under the dryer and tames her tight curls. My hair is long, wavy and wispy, light brown with blond highlights from weekends at the beach. I don't mind seeing it lopped off and fall to the floor. I don't want to sit under the dryer, my hair pulled tight in rollers anymore. That is not freedom. When Ann is finished, hot tears of shock and anger burn my eyes.

"You don't like it," she purrs. I shake my head. My mother tries to console me.

"It looks cute," she says. "Tell Ann thank you."

"Thank you," I murmur. But when I get into the car, I explode. "I hate it. I'm never going back there. I'm growing it again. It's an Afro," I scream and release the tears of anger. Gone are the blond highlights. This new hair on my head came out of nowhere. It is dark and coarser and curly, very curly. It feels alien on my head. This is the beginning of a love-hate relationship with my hair that goes on for decades, from extremes of relaxing it to tame, cutting it crew cut short during pregnancies, bathrooms filled with products to defrizz, detangle, decurl and now, in my 40s, to volumize and frizz and curl. "Anastasia has different hair from you. It's straighter," my mother says.

I can't answer because I'm crying so hard.

1982 OR THEREABOUTS

The Greatest Invention Ever—Hair Mousse.

1984, AMERICA TO JAMAICA

My family return to live in Jamaica. I am distraught. I have an American-Puerto Rican boyfriend who I think I'm in love with and although we promise to write letters and to be in love forever, I know this isn't true. It can't be. We will be miles apart in culture and distance. I promise to stay a virgin and return to America as soon as I can. But when I get off the plane with my 16-year-old body dressed in American clothes with a slightly punk edge, my hair cut in a bob, a big blond streak in the front, I am elevated to a status that I've never known. This is a new Jamaica where I am a goddess. My golden brown skin is sought after. I am bathed in glances of longing and admiration. This sudden fame is abnormal. I've gone from being a spic, a nigger, a number, an other, to a princess. I am no longer laughed at and ridiculed for my hair, my skin, my accent. I have now become what I thought I could never be. Popular. Rich white girls, Jamaican old money, glare at me. Black girls treat me with contempt. It's fine. I'm surrounded by hundreds of other goddesses, that fusion of DNA that churns out the most exquisite beauties. Someone, a man, said to me once, "You brown people all look alike." I was surprised. Never have I seen such diversity. You're wrong, man. We can have brown eyes, dark like ackee seeds or yellow like the eyes of a wolf. Our eyes can be midnight blue to pale grey, forest green to mint. Can be slanted, almond, round. Our noses, Nubian, Greek, Roman, snub, hawk, retrousse. Our hair, never mind colour now, can be kinky as the blackest woman or straight and thin as the whitest one. Our skin shades are like an artist's palette, from milky white to chocolate. We goddesses play a game, parading around each other, sometimes forming lasting friendships, others times spreading wild gossip about each other, stealing each other's boyfriends, fooling our parents about where we're going while we live our young lives in hedonistic nirvana, at beaches, parties, movies, plazas.

1986, TORONTO, CANADA

I am excited to be in Canada, 'foreign', as we call any white country. Excited about new beginnings. If you stay too long on an island, it gets stale. My parents drop me off at York University. I chose York only because a guy I liked was going there. A friend of mine chose York because it has the highest population of blacks, the Canadian version of Howard. This is where I taste my first bit of anger. Someone calls me a black cunt because we have a disagreement at the fast food restaurant where I am working to earn a little extra money. I decide I have to be black. I seem to have little in common with white Canadian girls who go beer drinking as a hobby and head to the ski slopes for March break. I have to try too hard with them. I head to the Caribbean Student Association where I am told that I cannot join. It's a club for West Indians, I am told.

"But I am Jamaican. I was born in Jamaica. I am West Indian."

The guy I'm speaking to is Dwayne. I know this because someone in a red, green and black t-shirt walks by and greets him with the fist to fist, 'respect.' Dwayne, tall, muscular and black, also donning a t-shirt with a Bob Marley face spread, has that typical Torontonian-Jamaican accent. I can tell it's been cultivated. Has this jackass ever even been to Jamaica? He tells me I don't sound Jamaican. I've heard this many times before but usually it's said with interest, surprise. People assume I've been living in England. No, people! I went to London once for two weeks, hardly enough time to acquire a British accent. But this coming from Dwayne, is accusatory, angry. "I'm from Jamaica," I insist again.

"Prove it, he says. Can you hear the drums?" I am taken aback. I feel slapped in the face.

"Were you born in Jamaica? I ask.

"No, but I can hear the drums."

"I can hear the drums," I say, "but I don't need to wear my culture on my t-shirt. It's in my blood. Screw your association." When I walk away, I think, what fucking drums? He wasn't in Jamaica for the brain drain, the political riots, the empty supermarket shelves, the senseless murders where we all knew people who died. He was in rich North America learning how to be Jamaican second-hand.

I spend four years at university never once attending the Caribbean Students Association. I feel strangely disconnected to any race. White guys treat me like an exotic fruit, some are brave enough to taste, but mostly they wrinkle their noses. Black guys like me eventually, when they discover I really am Jamaican. Their line is always, "You don't look Jamaican." When I hear this, I too put them in a special category. Ignorant. They say this same line to my Jamaican friends who look Chinese or Indian or white. These are the people who don't know Jamaica at all, don't know its rich history, know nothing about the many immigrants who set foot on Jamaica's sandy shores, don't know our motto is, "*out of many, one people.*" Yeah, ignoramus, screw your association.

1995, TORONTO, CANADA

I get a job. I finally get a decent job that doesn't include serving drunken pre-adults or lecherous old men. I am teaching English as a second language at a small private college outside of Toronto. I spend my days teaching not only language but Canadian culture. It all goes smoothly until I take them on a field trip in Toronto and they see a white girl lip-locked in a passionate embrace with a black boy. They are around seventeen, maybe more, who knows these days. Then they see an Asian girl holding hands with a black guy. They gasp at these couples and tell me it's not right. Black should be with black. All races should stick to their own. I take a deep breath and try to explain apartheid. I try to convey that their views are wrong, out-dated, and totally dislocated from this new land to which they have come. My students are all from India and no matter what I say, I cannot change their views. I think, "Oh no, my children will go to school with their children. Why come here then? Why use Canada as a hotel for its freedoms while keeping yourself in a prison?" At first, I tell myself it's just their upbringing but I get mad when they tell me they don't like black skin colour, they don't like black hair, and they bring their fingers up to their head and make a disgusted face. They don't see me as black because I look like them. When our arms touch, my skin is no different from theirs. It's my hair that is different and even then, they don't see it as "black" hair. I notice this. I don't look black so people feel they can say anything. I am mad, mad when they see a blond-haired girl and tell me she is beautiful when I see that she is just a plain Jane. I get mad that they don't see that the blood of Africa runs through their veins, that their DNA contains the genes of those first people who set foot out of that continent. I get mad that they've brought their "us" and "them" mentality, that they don't see that one big bang explosion created us all. This anger makes me weary and I wonder how those great men of history kept fighting for justice through all the dissension.

2002, TORONTO, CANADA

I get married to a mixed-race man and we produce two more mixed-race people for the world. A boy who is darker than the girl, his hair is thick and curly. His skin colour is like honey, golden reddish brown. The girl could be white, creamy, except for the giveaway hair, wildly curly from roots to ends, a fuzzy pale halo around her head. To me, they are mesmerizingly beautiful. People will ask them, what is your background, where are you from, what are your parents, is one white and one black, what are you really? They will have the trouble of explaining the whole thing. Or, maybe not. Maybe the world will be a different place and Canada will be that country of indeterminate race. In 20 years maybe Canada will be such a mixed-race country that no one will bother with these questions; inane questions if we think of the bigger picture. But we're human. We love to see what's different.

This country where we all make our home is rich in resources, especially water. Maybe the world will war with us for it and this country of indeterminate race will have to stand as one. I hope so. Not for war. I hope we will learn to stand as one.

MICHELLE JEAN-PAUL

Learning to Love Me

AS A BROWN-SKINNED girl, I have received many messages over the course of my life, some covertly and others very directly, that I am undesirable. As a child, my world was presented to me through two very different lenses. One was the reality of a Black, Catholic, francophone Haitian man and the other was that of a White, Mennonite, German speaking woman. Neither of my parents' realities reflected my own and as a result, these two distinct lenses resulted in my developing a divided view of the world and of me. I was fortunate to have four sisters but we were each so embroiled in our own struggles with identity that we weren't much support to one another.

For the longest time, I struggled with the idea that I am two different people. It began with my mixed-race identity but, over the years, I have come to realize that there are two very distinct parts to my personality. For a long time, I thought that this almost schizophrenic quality to my character was a good thing, but as of late I have come to understand how detrimental my divided perspective of myself has been. I don't believe that any one quality is tied to my Blackness or my Whiteness but I do believe that the dichotomy presented by my racial identity is the reason for my inner conflict.

I grew up in a white world with few positive examples of Black women in my environment. But even if there had been, in my teenage years I was very attached to the notion that I was neither Black nor white, but somewhere in between. I felt isolated and believed that no one could understand my realities. I know that my parents did their best in raising us. I can only imagine how difficult it was for my white mother to raise her brown daughters. She struggled to care for our hair. Her frustration became mine; I hated my nappy afro. As a child, it didn't seem to matter if my sisters and I were wearing earrings, pink dresses and standing in the women's restroom, some ignorant person always wondered if we were boys. This taught me that my difference was a deficit. It taught me that I was not perceived as an attractive woman. My hair became a symbol of my undesirability. I often wished to have long, straight hair like that of my friends. I also wished that I had a mother who could braid my hair. I admired the little black girls I would see on occasion whose plaited hair was like a work of art. Once my father's family moved to Winnipeg from Haiti, I would look forward to the rare opportunities to get my hair braided. While I would still get teased by my classmates about my cornrows, they made me feel beautiful and feminine.

As a young brown-skinned girl, I believed the negative messages that were being sent my way. I believed that I was not as smart, as beautiful, as deserving as my white friends. I was so wrapped up in myself that I could not understand that the people I was letting hurt me were just acting out of their own insecurity. Somewhere along the way, in spite of all of my struggles with my identity, this insecure girl grew into a vibrant, powerful woman. One who works hard and always pushes herself to be better. But the 12-year-old version of me never went away. I manage to hide her yet every once and again, she appears. Her appearance always brings self-doubt along with it. She doesn't feel deserving of the accomplishments or accolades that come along with the adult version of me. Slowly, I am unpacking the layers and making peace with the 12-year-old version of me. This reflection is only a small part of that process. I now realize that much of her self-doubt arises from her perception of her physical self, namely her attractiveness.

I find that many of the insecurities that I have carried into my adult life are related to my race and specifically to my hair. I can't recall ever agonizing over my caramel coloured skin. For whatever reason, I could accept that difference as it was who I was but I always felt that I would be more desirable if I could just get a handle on my hair. In my teens, Black women began to appear in the mainstream media with more frequency but even they had long, beautiful, flowing hair. I thought that a relaxer would solve my hair dilemma but quickly learned that even though my hair was straight, it still would not move like my friends' hair. I ended up wearing it pinned up for the next eight years of my life. Around the same time that I began relaxing my hair, I began to develop a real interest in boys and hoped to have my first real boyfriend. Boys would talk to me, flirt with me, and tell me that they liked me, but they always ended up dating my friends. This continued into high school. Guys would call me, write me notes, and confess their feelings, but again, they always ended up dating my white friends. Although it was never stated explicitly, the message became very clear to me on a subconscious level. As a brown-skinned girl, boys would lead you on when no one else was watching but, at the end of the day, they would always walk away with a white girl on their arm. Caramel skin and nappy hair were not attractive. In university, I began to feel that Black men weren't interested in brown-skinned girls either. I grew extremely self-conscious about my hair when pondering the possibility of dating a Black man. I worried that his mother or his sisters would mock the fact that I didn't know how to handle my hair. In my heart, I felt that no man would find me beautiful because beauty equalled whiteness. I had several experiences with men that reinforced that idea to me. The most poignant was when a boy who I had been friends with since high school, and had shared a secret romance with, told me after he had loosened his lips with alcohol that he was still surprised at how attracted he was to me. He went on to explain that he didn't find Black women attractive with their wide noses, large foreheads, and weird hair. He had finally named the issue that I had pondered for years. And almost a decade later, I am still carrying the heartache that came with his confession.

Growing up as a brown-skinned girl, I always wished that I belonged to one world or the other. I often wished that I was Blacker so that I would have full membership into a world that I felt society associated me with, but I did not entirely belong to. At some point along my journey, I realized that I could not control my physical appearance so I worked tirelessly to control the things that I could. I shied away from activities that I did not excel in because it was important to me to be perceived as one of the best in the things I participated in. And even when others expressed their delight in my abilities, I still felt as though I had to be better than I was.

I have learned a lot from the 12-year-old version of me. For the longest time, I hated her because she represented my weakness and I try to present myself as unflappable. I tried to understand her so that I could conquer her but all I was doing was pushing her further down inside of my soul. I am learning to love her. I am learning to feel grace for the girl who doesn't feel deserving of the love she desires so she accepts love as and when it was given to her. That part of me is broken and sad and lonely. That vulnerability also made me into the powerful, beautiful woman that I am today. By getting in touch with that side of me, I am understanding that I do not need to define myself as part Haitian, part Mennonite; part English speaker, part French; part Black, part white. The conflicting sides of my personality are just the evidence of my humanity. I can be the sinner and the saint, plain and exotic, powerful and pathetic. All of these qualities and all of my experiences are part of my authentic self. This is a lesson that I will continue to learn over again throughout my lifetime and it is an essential one. It informs the lens through which I see the world and through which I will engage with my environment. I will always carry within me the young, brown-skinned girl who felt as though she was undesirable. And I will be better because of her.

A Conversation Among Friends

AFTER THE TWELVE-STEP meeting wrapped up, they all decided to go to Ginger's for a bowl of soup. Irene in particular was adamant about the soup. They had to push three tables together in the steamy restaurant to accommodate the six of them, and once they'd placed their orders at the counter, they pulled off their coats and seated themselves: Daniel at the head of the table, Antony and Colleen at the foot, and all the other girls in between.

[*Irene, to Jennifer*] I'm surprised they have wonton soup here. I didn't even know that.

[*Jennifer, trying and failing to grasp a sushi roll with her chopsticks*] It's Pan-Asian. They have everything here but the kitchen sink. I'm going to get a fork.

[*Michelle, to Daniel*] So it raises the whole question of how honest I'm being. I mean, I like him, but do I really like him enough to have a serious relationship? Even though that's what he wants?

[*Irene*] That's the temptation to people-please. It seems to make them happy to give them what they want. But does it?

[*Michelle, nodding, her tight curls trembling at the apex of her head and her earrings flashing as they swing gently against her neck*] You mean maybe he senses my heart isn't in it.

[*The server comes and sets a plate of vegetarian cold rolls in front of her.*]

[*Irene*] I love your shirt.

[*Michelle*] It's Indian silk; I got it in Kensington.

[*Irene, gesturing to her own cotton sweater, already dotted with spots of grease*] That's smart of you not to order soup—it's hard not to splatter it all over yourself.

[*Jennifer, eating with a fork now, to Michelle*] So what's this about your man?

[*Michelle, sighing*] I don't know. Maybe I should just break up with him instead of playing games.

[*Daniel, folding his arms across his chest*] That might be the kind thing.

[*Irene, to Daniel*] Aren't you eating? The food is really good here. You should try the soup.

[*Daniel*] No, I have to watch my figure.

[*Irene laughs, faces front again. Michelle is sitting directly opposite. Irene's fiancé, Antony, is eating fried shrimp two seats away as Colleen murmurs to him about the meeting*] The dating game, huh?

[*Michelle*] Yeah, it's hard. I don't want to be another bitter black woman.

[*Irene*] What does being black have to do with it?

[*Michelle*] You know, it's that much harder. There are too many of us out there, not getting what we want and getting bitter about it.

[*Irene, waving her arm dismissively*] Well, that's women in general. I don't see that there's anything to be especially bitter about as a black woman. I don't even identify with that.

[*Michelle*] The last guy I dated was this Rasta, and he was the nicest, most gentle guy you could ever meet, he wouldn't hurt a fly, but whenever we used to walk around late at night, people would stare at him. One time we were in Rosedale after dark and the cops stopped him because he matched someone's description. That's what I mean about bitter.

[*Irene, trying to catch Antony's eye*] Well, that can happen.

[*Michelle, snorting*] He's like six-foot-five with dreads down to his ass. What description did he match?

[*Daniel*] They say that happens a lot. I have a friend in L.A., and he used to get pulled over constantly just for being black and driving a really nice car. And I mean, he's as gay as they come, he wears a bow tie, he's just prim and proper.

[*Jennifer, making a face*] That's L.A. I heard they really packed the police force with blacks and Hispanics after the Rodney King thing, but I don't think it helps. Cops only see blue, isn't that what they say?

[*Irene*] The fact is, that's L.A., not Toronto. I've never experienced racial prejudice here. When I was a kid, people used to throw words around if we were fighting, but that was thirty years ago.

[*Antony*] But you don't really date black men.

[*Irene*] That's not true! I dated two, long before I met you. I date who I happen to meet and have things in common with and connect with.

[*Colleen*] How did those relationships work out?

[*Irene*] Well, one gave me herpes, and the other one is my BFF to this day.

[*Antony*] You mean Marvin? He's not even black.

[*Irene, with irritation*] He's from Kerala. He might as well be black; God knows a cop wouldn't be able to tell the difference if I didn't even know for the first two months.

[*Michelle, making finger quotation marks*] Well, anyway, we are living in a "white supremacist" society.

[*Irene, pushing her empty soup bowl away*] How can you say that?

[*Daniel, getting up*] I think I will have some green tea after all.

[*Michelle*] You can see it everywhere. I mean, in my program, there's this unspoken understanding that I'm only there because of affirmative action.

[*Jennifer*] I thought you were studying midwifery.

[*Irene, making finger quotation marks*] Thank you. I mean, if we're going to go with stereotypes here, isn't that a profession they'd assume you'd be naturally good at? "Birthin' babies?"

[*Michelle*] No. There's this subtle hostility. It's like I'm just the wrong colour to fit in.

[*Irene, shaking her head*] I mean, that's something my mother used to tell me, and I didn't believe it then and I don't believe it now: that I'd have to work twice as hard to be accepted. It's just not true. If anything, I've gotten more opportunities and more acceptance because of being mixed.

[*Michelle*] That's because you're well spoken…

[*Jennifer*] I would never know you were black if I heard you on the phone.

[*Irene*] Exactly. But then when people meet me, it's not like they say "oh, sorry, we didn't realize you were black, you can't have the job." It's the politically correct thing to do, to hire me.

[*Michelle*] You shouldn't have to get by on that. It shouldn't have to be like, you're exceptional or something, just to get hired. I bet people are surprised by you once you open your mouth. You're very articulate, and they're not expecting that.

[*Irene*] Good! I like surprising people.

[*Jennifer*] I think what Michelle is saying is, you shouldn't have to be the exception that proves the rule in these people's minds.

[*Michelle, leaning over to Colleen*] I'm sorry for leaving you out of this conversation!

[*Colleen*] No worries.

[*Michelle*] Is there meat in that?

[*Colleen*] No, it's just their house curry tofu with noodles. It's really good.

[*Michelle*] You know, I was reading about this phenomenon in the States called "black rage." It actually causes heart disease. All these people are dropping dead.

[*Irene*] I heard of that, where you eat the meat that's been killed in an un-ethical way, and you absorb all the rage and fear the animal felt before it died. Is that because of the meat-heavy diet they eat down there? I mean, it hasn't stopped us from eating meat, right?

[*Anthony shakes his head.*]

[*Michelle*] I don't know about that; I meant rage against your quality of life. It's like, imagine living in the ghetto, knowing you're never going to get out, seeing the devastation all around you … it's no wonder you're gonna want to kill people.

[*Irene*] But really, when you look at some of the problems in the ghetto, whose fault are they?

[*Michelle*] It's easy for you to say. You grew up where, in the Annex? With a white mother? You have no idea what it's like to live in the ghetto.

[*Irene, hotly*] Neither do you.

[*Michelle*] You're right. I had a white mother who was able to provide me with the best things in life because she had a really good job.

[*Irene*] Well, my mother didn't. I grew up poor in a pretty rich neighbourhood and it sucked, but it didn't make me put a cap in anybody's ass.

[*Michelle*] I've heard some of your story. Your mother didn't have a clue what to do with you, did she? There were no black influences around you. You lost your culture.

[*Irene, pointing her chopsticks at Michelle*] Okay, what I want to know is, if I'd been raised solely by my African-American father instead, why wouldn't anyone be saying what a tragedy it was that I missed out on all that rich Italian culture? It's because you see me as black and you think I don't act black enough. But I don't identify as black or Italian. I'm just Irene. And to give her credit, my mom did whatever she could to educate me about my history.

[*Jennifer, laughing*] But I bet she didn't know what to do with your hair.

[*Irene, patting her bun self-consciously*] No, she didn't. She brushed it with a dog brush. She thought I'd be a traitor to my race if I put a relaxer in there. She just didn't know what she was talking about, so as soon as I could, I bought myself a box of Dark n' Lovely!

[*Michelle*] But don't you feel there's this part of you that's just…missing?

[*Irene*] Only when I visit my relatives down in the States—it's a whole different mentality in the South. They would disown me for marrying Antony, so the prejudice goes both ways.

[*Michelle*] I'm not saying it doesn't. I'm just saying the whites are in power, so what difference does it make if we're racist to them? They don't even care.

[*Irene*] That's a really poor excuse for prejudice. This isn't the Deep South of forty years ago, this is Toronto, for God's sake. There's no conspiracy.

[*Daniel*] Well, as a Jew, I can say that—

[*Irene*] And anyway, in Toronto it's usually an African culture, or a West Indian culture, and my black half is neither. So how could I relate?

[*Michelle*] You could learn.

[*Irene*] Why? No one tells white people "you should embrace your culture and celebrate St. Paddy's or Robbie Burns Day or Guy Fawkes Day, or else you're a race traitor." All this identification is what separates us. Like I should be a certain way because of my race. Isn't that the whole thing we're supposed to be getting away from? Making race matter, and forcing people into some kind of mold?

[*Michelle*] But race does matter. You're living in a fantasy world if you think it doesn't. Just look at the language we use – 'black' has such negative connotations. It means everything bad in the world.

[*Colleen*] Except when it comes to budgets. That's where my people really take a hit, and yours are singing.

[*There is a moment of silence.*]

[*Colleen, rolling her eyes*] In the red? In the black?

[*Jennifer*] You're Native? I didn't know that!

[*Colleen*] Métis. I have my Status Card to prove it.

[*Michelle*] Métis, I thought that was a derogatory term? Like mulatto?

[*Jennifer*] Now there's something I think we can all agree on: I hate that word. It used to come up all the time when I was escorting. All the ads were "mulatto this" and "mulatto that" and I used to call myself a mulatto too.

[*Michelle*] Why did you? If you knew it was a slave term?

[*Antony*] I didn't know it was a slave term.

[*Irene, elbowing him*] Yes, you knew that. It means a cross between a horse and a donkey—a mule.

[*Jennifer*] That was just an industry term everyone used. I'm a total Heinz 57, but because I'm pretty dark skinned, I had to say mulatto. If I said black, they would think Grace Jones.

[*Michelle*] See what I mean? That's what we're up against. A single drop of black blood makes you black—and undesirable.

[*Antony*] I never even see it. Irene's always saying 'so and so is black' or whatever and I just can't tell. They look completely white. Like Hootie.

[*Irene*] That's the one-drop rule, that's Deep South stuff again. That went out with the Jim Crow laws.

[*Michelle sniffs*] You're living in a dream world. It's alive and well down there.

[*Irene, ticking items off on her fingers*] Do you think I'm denying it happened? When Antony was born, we didn't even have the vote. People were killed and lynched and spit on and beaten and they had dogs sicced on them just for eating at white lunch counters. I've read everything Richard Wright ever wrote. I've read *Nigger* by Dick Anthony and I've read *Black Like Me* and I've read *Soul on Ice* and a whole lot more. I've seen the documentaries about SMCC and the Panthers and everything else. But ultimately you can't isolate and blame and wage war, it's not the answer.

[*Jennifer*] Calm down, no one's talking about a war.

[*Irene*] I'm just saying you can't keep blaming history for the problems in the black community. My dad grew up poor in Alabama, but that's not what made him a drug addict or a bank robber, anymore than my upbringing made me a drug addict.

[*Michelle, shaking her head in wonder*] You really think that if a person grows up in the ghetto with no father, trying not to get shot as he goes to a substandard school every day, watching his friends sell drugs and go to jail, that it doesn't psychologically affect someone? You're all about the bootstraps, aren't you?

[*Irene, calmly*] Yes, I am. It's the only way. Clarence Thomas had a point.

[*Michelle*] He's a war-monger. He's a perfect example of what's wrong with America.

[*Irene*] You're thinking Colin Powell. I said Clarence Thomas. The one with the Coke can. Or are you too young?

[*Michelle*] Clarence Thomas was a pervert, an Uncle Tom, and a right-wing Republican.

[*Antony*] You say that like it's a bad thing. Anyone who can make good use of a Coke can is a hero in my books.

[*Irene and Jennifer explode in laughter. Daniel smiles and shakes his head. Colleen looks confused.*]

[*Antony, to Colleen*] You were a pothead mostly, right? Pop cans make great crack pipes.

[*Colleen*] Oh.

[*Irene*] I would seriously put a bullet in my head if I walked around thinking about how held-back I was or wondering what people were thinking of my skin colour. I'm paranoid enough!

[*Michelle*] You just made the case for black rage.

[*Daniel, draining the dregs of his tea*] Well, it's been a slice people, but I have to get going, it's past my bedtime.

[*Antony*] I agree.

They gather their things, pull on scarves and hats, and step outside into the freezing night air. Daniel hugs Michelle, Jennifer, Irene, Colleen, and Antony. Jennifer hugs Michelle, Irene, and Colleen, and shakes Antony's hand. Irene puts her arm through Antony's.

[*Michelle*] I can't believe I brought my bike. I'm going to freeze.

[*Irene*] Well, safe journey home.

RACHEL AFI QUINN

The Combination of the Two

IT IS TRUE WHAT we have been telling you about this experience of being mixed race: that us mixed folks often share in common the malleability of our racial identities; that we know what it is like to be racially indecipherable; that we have experiences in our communities in which we are exoticized for our racial difference. I have spent much time looking inward, trying to make sense of this, this mixed-race phenomenon. Am I really mixed and not black? Why can I choose this identity for myself, and the black women who came before could not? I try defining mixed race for those around me, as a social construction that emerges in the late 1990s—one attached to a movement spearheaded by white parents of non-white children. I ask, why now? I am suspicious of mixed race even as it says something about my identity and my experience in the world that other categories do not.

I teach the concept of mixed race to North American college students who live in worlds in which they have come to believe that race is something fixed, and that racism will go away if we just don't talk about racial difference. I wonder, as a mixed-race person in front of the classroom, whether students see me as a special teaching tool, speaking on my lived experience. My authority from years of research on the subject gets trumped by the fact of my biography, by how I look and how they interpret me visually. Like other people of colour in academia teaching about the experiences that shape who they are, I become native informant for the predominately white communities of higher education of which I am a part. I am ill-prepared. I have been told that I am "different than the rest" in many, many uncomfortable ways. Over the years, I have learned that my experience being racially-mixed is not so remarkable as it once sounded growing up in a southern city then divided between black and white, or while attending predominantly-white private schools. There are more and more and more of us. And we have always existed. It was when I finally really started to travel outside of the United States, at age 20, that I began to notice that my race kept changing on me. In each environment or context I put myself in, my identity seemed to change to suit the needs and understandings of other people.

Growing up in North Carolina I am a black girl as my white playmates struggle to understand why my mom is white and I am not. I know no other children like me, at a time when white mothers in the South have just begun to identify their non-white babies as "biracial." I am at college when I finally find classmates in varying shades of brown that, like me, have grown up in white middle-class communities; collectively and politically we begin to identify ourselves as "mixed race," sharing a common experience of being racially misinterpreted. I find it fitting that on my junior year abroad I am Brazilian to the Bolivians I meet; I do not look American to them. Though back on campus I am African American when my classmate, in search of solidarity during a class discussion about race, assumes that because of my colour we see eye to eye: "You're black, you know what I mean."

When I travel to West Africa to get to know the paternal side of my family, however, my Ghanaian Auntie speaks to me of African Americans with such disdain that I quickly understand that to her I am not one. According to my father I am an African like him, yet somehow I am simultaneously a white woman in Africa, catered to because I am so transparently a foreigner. To the many Ewe children who see me throughout the Volta Region of Ghana, I am indiscernible from the blond Peace Corps volunteer that they once knew and so they call me by her name. That year, when I travel to northern Niger I am a Tuareg, my height and colour inviting desert Africans to speak to me in Tamashek. Later, in Spain I am met with the sexualized gaze of men who liken me to the few African women they see on the streets selling their bodies; I am unwelcome at some Barcelona cafés because I look North African. As an American, working in the non-profit world of San Francisco, I am one of few black program coordinators and so I am seen as an ambassador of cultural diversity. In my daily life, however, white strangers assume that I lack education or a position of authority at my work and black children tell me that I "talk white." As a mixed-race person, I am often one of "us" and one of "them" simultaneously.

My experiences of racial fluidity, and my interest in writing about it and studying it by talking to other people in bodies that like mine are marked by blackness, but have some room for movement depending on context, has brought me to Santo Domingo, Dominican Republic. After living much of my life in worlds in which I was a minority, as a black person (in the U.S.) or on occasion as a "white" person (in Ghana), it is quite something to be able to settle in to city life surrounded by people of varying shades of my colour. The majority of Dominicans are mixed heritage of African descent, like I am, but over hundreds of years. If I keep my mouth closed, if I just follow the group, I don't stand out here. For the first time in my life, I can pass. Dominicans listen for my accent; when I don't understand or stumble in my speech they ask, "You're not from here, are you?" They want to know if I have family here, if I might be one of those many children of the Diaspora who comes back. I am not. In a way I am one of the ones who comes forward. In studying the history of the many peoples brought to the island of Hispaniola over the centuries since Columbus first landed here, I can see that my own heritage of Ewe and Eastern European Jew is represented in the mix. "And that's why I look like I am from here," I tell friends, taxi drivers, the guys who sell me fruit on the corner, everyone who asks—and everyone does. Out in the open, I feel like I am hiding. I can walk down the street and people don't look twice at me. But I am not Latina, I am not Dominican, I am not one of them, I explain. "Well, now you are," say my new friends. "When people ask you where you're from just say you're from Los Jardines, the neighbourhood you live in." It is a rare feeling, this fitting in, and I want to hold on to it. But I can't.

Going out to a lesbian night club in Santo Domingo, there is not a white woman in sight. None. Only women of colour, every shape, every hue, every hair type. We are all brown. I notice my feeling of relief in this context. I identify with the group in some imagined way, as if my own affiliation with whiteness has somehow disappeared, as if we all share an experience of being mixed and of being black too. For the first time I visually blend in in a queer space. A new friend later tells me that I was drawing attention from her peers that night, not for my height but for what she referred to as my white facial features that people here find so attractive. She says, racism is so deep here that while blackness in women is more desirable than whiteness for its hypersexualization, certain European features are highly admired and sought after. "The combination of the two is appealing to most Dominicans," she tells me.

"Sounds familiar," I tell her. It is this theme that I keep studying, writing about, thinking about, chasing. Only now I am thinking about it in a Caribbean city.

Had I really thought it was just about hair in the Dominican Republic? No. But hair straightening is such a common practice here that over time one starts to believe that nearly all Dominican women actually have straight hair—because they do. You succumb to the mythology of it just until a sudden rain, when women start racing for cover, or wrapping their heads in plastic shopping bags to walk back from the corner store without getting their hair wet. Or, you become disillusioned about the cooler month of May because as rainy season arrives your friends are less willing to hit the streets with you, for fear of getting caught in a downpour and wasting money spent that week at the neighbourhood salon. Hair matters. I wear my hair in a short, puffy Afro of sorts, which is somehow increasingly acceptable because numerous pop stars now wear their hair this way. Just two years ago, this style was not nearly as common. I remember. Men on the street were happy to let me know they didn't like it, that "going natural" wasn't okay. "Comb your hair!" they shouted in my direction.

"Were you just in here a few weeks ago?" the woman at the Payless shoe store asks me. It had been more like a month, and I had just stepped in the store for a second looking for shoes that might fit my extra large feet. As it turns out, a lot of Dominican women have large feet. "I thought so, she said, I remember your eyes." (How strange that she didn't remember my feet!) Such comments make me uncomfortable, seem invasive somehow yet are so commonplace here, so constant. The Dominican Republic was the first place I heard that there was anything at all different about my brown eyes, now suddenly it seems I have *ojos de miel*, "eyes of honey." I hear this phrase again and again from people I've just met. There is something about here, this spot on the globe where I have landed, the closest I've ever been to looking like those around me. Why did I expect that this context might make comments about difference disappear?

I notice difference too. I always have, but where I come from you aren't supposed to remark on how dark that woman's skin is, or how fair that man is, how fat that child is becoming, or that their eye shape makes them look of Asian descent. Not so here. Here you give them a nickname that best represents this predominant feature: *Negra, Gringo, Gordo, China*. When my Dominican host sister and I look into a crowd of teenagers on our car trip to *el campo* we both notice the same thing. But she's the one who comments on the teenager with the startling grey-blue eyes. They are in sharp contrast to the copper colour of his skin and his thick curly hair pulled back under a baseball cap. It is as if these eyes were someone else's, mistakenly given to him. But it is the Dominican Republic, and brown-skinned people who don't have brown eyes do not necessarily warrant a modeling contract. Still, they receive praise and attention for it, for being born that way. Just like light-coloured children born into dark-skinned families have, all throughout the Americas for centuries.

"It could be the opposite," I point out to her. "It could be that kids like that get rejected for not looking like everyone else. It could be viewed as unattractive—or scary, even." But we know that is not the case. We know because we have seen models on billboards employed for their contrasting features, their "mixed-race look." Driving along the road, any road in the Dominican Republic during campaign season, one can literally pass hundreds of billboards and signs with faces on them in a matter of minutes. Blond Dominican politicians with icy blue eyes or other European-identified features are certainly the most striking. These images dominate the landscape, gazing out over the people in the streets who they aim to represent, who do not look like them. They share neighbourhood spaces with the headshots of these politicians, often photo-shopped with finer noses and lighter skin so that they might look like something they are not.

In the last few weeks I have been told four times that I look like Rita Indiana, the queer Dominican rising star who mixes Afro-Latino rhythms with alternative stylings. Her increasing popularity in this context has become so fascinating an anomaly that I have begun studying her as obsessively as her fans do—but for my dissertation. While our smiles might be similar, I don't look like her. She has curly hair too, that she wears short, but it isn't black like mine. At six-foot-three, she is a good five inches taller than me and that much skinnier, at least. Long flowing pants make the woman look as if she is standing on stilts. Maybe these men are keying into my gender performance as something like Rita's, a boyishness or femaleness different than the rest. She is a-typical, that is certain. But she is white, as white as Dominicans can be. I am not her colour, not even close. As these remarks about my being her likeness continue, I am reminded that no matter where I am, I am a shape changer—and I see myself quite differently than do the people around me. I have often felt that being mixed race has meant I carry a secret: "I'm not what you think I am." I have only recently come to accept that I have never been what people think I am. And no matter where I go to next, I never will be. Already, I never ever am.

Laura Kina, "Loving Series: Elena Rubin," 2006, charcoal on paper, 42.5" x 34".

On the Train

FOR WHAT SEEMS LIKE forever, I am on a noiseless train in a colourless land-scape. But then we are out of the tunnel and there is noise again, and there is colour. A woman's voice announces that we are approaching Ehime. It is about two towns away from Kochi, my destination.

On one side of the tracks, there is a large yellow field of grass. It should be green, I think, but it's yellow. It's been a hot summer. On the other side, there are the mountains. They are in the distance and some low clouds obscure their shape, but their peaks reach out above the haze. The train is humming now and I have a headache, but I can see the mountains so I know I am okay.

The man beside me is a *gaijin*, a foreigner. He is American. The lady across from me is Japanese and their daughter is like me, *happa*, half. She is speaking Japanese to her mother. They are chatting about what to have for lunch when the father breaks into their conversation.

"Speak English," he says.

His daughter stops talking. Her mother smiles. "Yes, Saori, practice your English."

They are putting on a show for me. But Saori doesn't want to play the game. She starts playing with her dolls instead.

"That's a pretty doll," I say. Saori looks up at me. She squints at me, annoyed. "*Kirei ningyosama*," I say in Japanese. She nods while keeping her eyes on her doll.

The father turns to me and smiles. "Your English is great," he says. "And your Japanese too."

"Thanks. My mother is Japanese."

I can see the mother watching me, sizing me up. I am a grown version of her daughter.

"Saori refuses to speak English," the father continues. "She hasn't been to the States yet but one day she'll come with me and then she'll be sorry she didn't study harder."

Saori keeps her eyes down but she can understand her father. She wishes he would stop talking. "*Kanojo no okusan wa nihonjin, Saori.*" He has meant to say that my mother is Japanese, but has used the wrong word, substituting the word *okaasan*, mother, with *okusan*, wife. His wife corrects him gently, but he is embarrassed. Saori smiles and her father stops talking. We all sit back in our chairs. I stare back out at the mountains.

It's been a long time since I've travelled alone in Japan. The last time was about ten years ago. My mother returned to Kochi from Vancouver, the city where I was born, for her father's funeral and I followed about a week later. When I arrived there was no talk of my grandfather. We stayed in the city at my aunt's for a few days and then went into the mountains where my grandfather and grandmother had lived, where my mother grew up.

***

My mother grew up in an abandoned primary school. The first time I saw it, I remember thinking that it seemed so flat, just one level with low ceilings. There were six rooms. My mom had eight brothers and sisters. There was a stream nearby and they had chickens. On the hot summer nights, the kids slept on the floor, pressing themselves into the cool wood and soft tatami. In the winter, they pulled out the futons and slept close together.

I remember spending a few days there, the last time. I was terrified in the middle of the night. And I remember being particularly afraid of the outhouse. I would wake my brother and tell him to stand outside the door. There seemed to be so many noises in that house, in that clutter, and the silence of the outside world in the middle of the night was too much to bear alone.

***

The man next to me on the train is sleeping. The girl across from me, Saori, is staring at me. At first, I try not to meet her eyes and look down at my jacket, adjust a button and shrug my shoulders to stretch. But then I turn and look at her, at her smooth skin and high forehead, her small mouth and round eyes. And she looks at me. We have the same skin. And she doesn't blink. Her mother breaks the silence.

"What are you doing in Japan?" she asks in Japanese. "Do you live here or are you just visiting?"

"I used to live here but now I'm visiting. My grandmother lives in Kochi."

"Oh, Kochi … famous for *yuzu* juice. It's a very nice city."

I smile and nod. I am quieter in Japan, somehow at a loss for words, partially mute, nodding and smiling. I am self-conscious about my Japanese, about inadvertently offending someone by not using the honorific verbs or correct grammar. I can understand the words of those around me but often struggle for a response.

"What will you do in Kochi? Is your mother there?" Her hands are folded in her lap. She seems more at ease now that her husband in asleep.

"Yes"

"And your father?"

"No. He's in Canada."

"Ohhhhh. He is Canadian."

"Yes, and Jewish." I don't know why I've added this piece of information. And the woman doesn't seem to know why either.

"Oh, Jewish," she says. She smiles an empty smile and sits back in her chair. It's a signal that means the conversation is over.

***

"Where are you from?" the man selling snacks on the train asks. He is curious, trying to make conversation and practicing his halting English. It is clear that I am foreign here, even though it is the country of my birth. And it is a question I have heard often in various incarnations: "What's your background?" or "What are you?" There are many ways in which I could answer these question. I could give my name, my age, my place of birth, but usually the person asking the question doesn't want to know any of these things. In my mind, this man on the train melts into the many people who've asked me this in the past. They look at me with curious eyes and want to know about my unusual features: slightly slanted eyes, olive skin, jet black hair. Over the years, my answer has varied. The possibilities would roll off my tongue: Half white, Half Jewish, Half Canadian, Half Russian, Half Japanese. And their responses would also vary, sometimes surprise, sometimes a nod, often they would tell me their own background. "Oh, I thought you were Native American, like me." Or "I thought maybe you were Chilean. My neighbour is from Chile." And sometimes, "I knew you were mixed," like they had just won a contest. To the man on the train, I simply respond, "My mother is Japanese. I was born here," and I smile and he smiles back.

In Judaism, one's mother must be Jewish in order to be 'officially recognized' as Jewish. Because it was my father who was Jewish, I didn't count. And although I was born in Japan, I was not granted citizenship because only my mother was Japanese. From both sides, stranded. When I was 18, I decided to convert to Judaism. My mother was supportive, but she insisted that if I were to have a mikvah I must also start taking Japanese lessons. I'm not sure why she thought these two things went together, or that they somehow balanced each other out. Balance was something both my parents strove for. Balance was important, they explained.

So, I met with the Rabbi. I studied the Torah. Even though it was years ago, I remember these little things well: I remember choosing my dress, black with delicate flowers. I remember the room at the Beth Israel Synagogue. It was larger than I thought it would be. It was in the basement with a large, round tub. Three rabbis waited outside, keeping their ears pressed to the door to make sure I was saying the blessings. With one hand outstretched for balance, my eyes looking down, I stepped into the cool water. In the next room, it sounded like people were talking backwards. I closed my eyes, said the blessings, and let the water inch over my chin, my cheeks, my eyes, my forehead. I was under water. The water was shallow and in a moment I lifted my head. Another blessing and then once more under the water. This time, I opened my eyes.

The water was clear and I could see my hair swimming around my face. The third and last blessing. And then water in my eyes. I opened my mouth just a little, expecting the taste of chlorine, but there was none. It tasted like nothing: flat and cool.

***

We stop in Ehime and some passengers leave and others get on. The family I'm sitting with stays on. A young Japanese man sits further down the aisle. He has yellow hair and blue contacts. If eyes are the window to the soul, I imagine his soul shrouded in a blue shadow, heavy under the weight of trying to be somebody else.

Another man sits sideways in his seat, twisting so he can look outside as the train departs. He's making faces out the window at someone, a girl, I guess. He scrunches his face and then laughs, and then sighs, unaware of me watching him. He keeps scrunching and laughing, and sighing until we go into a tunnel and the girl is gone. By the time we exit the tunnel, he is already reading his newspaper. I wonder if that girl is still smiling. I settle back into my seat.

"Hello," Saori says.

"So, now you want to talk English," I say.

She smiles. Her father is still sleeping and her mother isn't sitting in her seat.

"How old are you?" I ask.

"*Kyuu-sai desu.*" Nine.

"You're so tall for your age," I say.

"*Un,*" she says, using the nasal sound that means "yes" in Japanese. She gets up from her seat and stretches, then walks past me and down the aisle.

***

Of the few days we stayed with my grandmother, I remember most the sounds. Everything seemed louder there. The insects were loud, the floor creaked, and even the sun seemed to be screaming. It was unbearably hot.

I remember waking up one morning and hearing sounds coming from the kitchen. My grandmother sat on the floor, next to the low kitchen table, wearing her green and grey, thin robe. At first I thought she was laughing. But then I could see her face, the redness in her cheeks and eyes. She looked broken. She leaned against the table and called me to her.

"Don't leave this place. Your Mom wants to leave." I sat next to her. She was so small, maybe four-foot-eleven. At twelve, I was already taller than her. I didn't know what to say. I wanted to go back to Canada too. I didn't want to stay here with the hot sun and noisy insects. I wanted the cool grey of the Vancouver sky and the easy sound of my father's voice. I wanted to breathe into the crisp air in the night and marvel at how it would turn into steam. How luxurious it seemed, to breathe hot, white air into the dark cold. I wanted home.

"Home." I swallowed the word so that my grandmother couldn't know that this small house in Kochi could never be my home. The word slid into my stomach and settled there. In Japan, it is the stomach that is the seat of one's emotions, not the heart as it is in western cultures.

I sat with my grandmother until she stopped crying. She rocked back and forth on her knees, calming herself down. I couldn't say anything to make her feel better and she knew it. She got up and put on the kettle, and started to tell me a story.

"You know, you have an auntie that you never met," she said.

"Hmmmm?" I looked down at the floor, tracing the scratches in the wood with my fingers.

"Her name was Kayo. She was eleven when she died. You look a lot like her."

I stopped. Everything. I stopped tracing the scratches in the wood. I stopped being aware of the heat. That was the first time anybody had ever said that I resembled anyone on my Mom's side of the family. I looked up at my grandmother and let out a long breath and she smiled.

***

A different man is sitting across from me on the train. He is looking around and nodding as he reads the advertisements overhead. Up and down. I can't tell if he is crazy. He nods in agreement with all the ads and then continues to nod as he looks around the train, while not really looking. He nods at the doors and the windows, at the rails, and the handles. He ignores the people and nods up at the ceiling. His movement is so rhythmical I find myself nodding too. And I watch him and nod as we hum towards Kochi. Now I wonder who it is that is crazy, the two of us nodding, or the rest of the train staring straight ahead.

The woman's voice comes back on the speaker. She announces the next stop, Kochi. I look out the window and a city has sprung up around the train. It's so bright outside and even though the train is comfortably air conditioned, I can imagine the heat of the sun pushing down on my back. One day, I think, I will have a staring contest with the sun and I will win. For now, I blink and stand up, gather my things. I step off the train and it seems as though the cherry blossoms have bloomed overnight.

Coloured

WHEN I WAS NINE my parents decided to immigrate to Canada. My stepfather's brother was a doctor in Alberta and he sponsored us to come over. We arrived in Canada at night in August, 1974. My stepfather, who had arrived before us, picked us up and drove us to a rectangular two-story building that had two balconies on the front. An outside light illuminated the green front lawn. I remember looking at my mother and asking her if we had got rich because we now had a lawn. It took a month of school to dispel the illusion.

We had moved into the basement suite of a four-plex. I didn't care, we had grass and, after living in a London tower block, I loved it. The novelty of my English accent quickly wore off on the other kids at school, especially when they found out where we lived. Most of their families owned their own homes and we were living on a poor street in a poor area. Like most immigrants we owned next to nothing.

It's not that there weren't friends or acts of kindness by many people, it is just that as human beings we are more easily shaped by our negative experiences. Our survival instinct means that we are influenced more easily by the bad things that happen to us than by all the good things put together.

When do we first realize that skin has a colour? It happened to me when I was four years old playing on the swings with my brother. It was summer and the city playground was busy. Moms sat talking on benches, it's easy to make friends, to strike up a conversation with strangers when you have children in common. It was hot and I was thirsty so I ran up to my mother who was sitting and chatting to one of these playground acquaintances.

"Mom, I'm thirsty," I said. She gave me that look.

"Sorry. Please may I have a drink?"

Manners were important. You got into big trouble for not remembering your manners, especially in front of strangers. The woman got up and looked me up and down, appalled, and almost spat the words: "She's coloured" at my mother and then walked away. It was an era when white women like my mother were just not expected to have brown skinned children. I did not know my father, and it was the first time I realized my mother and I were different. When I went to school I got called nigger, coloured, and half-breed. By the time I was seven, every wish on my birthday cake candles or falling star, was for white skin and pale-coloured eyes. It seemed to me an unfair act of fate that I didn't look like my mother who is translucent pale Irish white with green eyes and red hair. I don't look a thing like her, except for her freckles. Both my brother and I have bands of them across our noses and cheeks, incongruous on our brown skin. We got lucky, my mother is so covered in freckles that I used to tease her that she had brown skin with white spots.

My mother's words to describe my brother and me were "half-caste" and "coloured." She tried to comfort me by telling me that I was half white and that made me as white as the next person. She never tried to comfort me with the fact that I was nearly black. She had the prejudices of her time and yet she stepped away from them to love my father. I grew up angry at my mother for choosing my father. There were so many white men, why did she have to choose him? She was living in London, England in an age where people still put signs on their doors that said "No Blacks, No Irish." I was both.

History looks back at the "permissive" sixties, but forgets that it wasn't so permissive between the races. She loved my father so much she would have done anything for him, and she did. She had two children out of wedlock, a second sin. My father was a nurse from Mauritius, a small country in the middle of the Indian Ocean that most people have never heard of. He had dark brown skin, brown eyes and his thick, curly black hair was just like mine. He was the oldest of seven children and he shouldered the responsibility of setting a good example for his siblings, of taking care of his relatives and adhering to their strict Hindu customs.

My mother was born and raised in a small village in County Claire, Ireland. She saw enough Catholic hypocrisy and alcoholism to swear her off Irish men, alcohol and religion for the rest of her life. Perhaps she rebelled in her own way by falling in love with my father. He left her when she was eight months pregnant with my brother and I was thirteen months old. I never met him. When he left, he destroyed their letters and pictures, all evidence they had ever been together. I have one picture of my father taken with a group of other staff members at the hospital where he worked. I look like him, my brother looks a lot like him, but both of our skins are a milked down version of his darker brown skin.

My mother married my stepfather when I was six. She won't say why, though when pushed she says it was a love match. I think it was a colour match. I think she felt that, after my father left, my step-father's brown skin would hide her mistake and validate our existence in the eyes of the world. From the day they got married she told me that we were now half Pakistani and half Irish. It was the first time she told that lie, but not the last. That is how she now presented us to the world.

I may not have looked white, but I wasn't black enough to be black either. I went to a Catholic convent day school in London until I was nine. Half of the students were black, the rest white. The only two exceptions to this were my brother and me, who were mixed race. My stepfather's Muslim culture was more alien to me still than anything I had experienced so far. I felt more at home with the black and white kids in my school who at least spoke with the same East London cockney accent that I did, than with the various Pakistani "cousins" that came to the house. My stepfather's presence in my life made me feel even more alienated from the world, another sign that I didn't belong anywhere.

My being mixed race was more revolting to some than if I had been all black. As a young girl I sat across from an educated white man in Alberta, while he told me why what my parents did was wrong and that I was a freak of nature. Like a donkey and a horse mating, I should be a "sterile" mule. Other people also told me that the races shouldn't intermarry because their children look wrong. The thing about being of mixed race is that there are plenty of ways for people to hate you. Most people can't tell what mix you are, all they notice is the colour of your skin. So if they happen to hate Mexicans, First Nations, Pakistanis, or any race that has brown skin, there is a good chance their prejudice will extend to include you.

My mother worked hard and kept her head down. She believed that as long as we didn't get above ourselves, we would be fine. She was of a generation that deferred to educated people, doctors, teachers, and policemen. She knew she wasn't as good as them, the problem was that she also deferred to everybody else. She would walk away from rudeness and prejudice, and her advice to us was the same. Don't talk back, ignore them, and walk away.

I walked home from school with my head down, I spoke as little as possible. But inside I was filled with anger because I just wanted to be ordinary. I wanted to belong, to fit in, somewhere. Coming to Alberta had just added other layers of difference. I was now a foreigner and immigrant as well as mixed race. No one spoke like I did. I could not swim, ice skate, or ski. In an inner city London school that doesn't matter, nobody else can either. In Calgary, to me, all the kids seemed rich and able and white. I was the only brown child in my grade five class and suddenly there were no black kids. I saw my first black children, two boys, in junior high school. This was the prairies.

Some of the kids didn't even learn racism until they met me. I was the first brown person that they'd met and it didn't matter to them that I was half anything, only that I wasn't all white. Mostly I was called paki, sometimes nigger, with the added new insult of being told to go home, back to where I belong. I had no idea where that was. There was little physical violence, bullies didn't need it. We were already intimidated. My mother said, sticks and stones will break my bones but names will never hurt me. She was so wrong. It was the taunts, the name-calling that did the real damage.

I remember the day I raised my head and realized that times were changing. I was fifteen, all legs and long curly black hair. A boy who had called me names when we were children whistled at me from across the street. He knew who I was and he catcalled me not paki or nigger, but "Hawaiian princess." It didn't make me feel better about myself, it just added another layer. Now I also learned bitterness.

I couldn't wait to leave the strict Muslim household of my stepfather and I moved out on my sixteenth birthday, the first day I was legally allowed to leave my parents. My stepfather didn't talk to me for the next three years.

Over the years we had been in Canada, ethnic minorities had immigrated to Calgary by the thousands, and people intermarried, I was a visible minority no more. By the time I graduated high school, nobody was calling me names anymore. As I went on to work and university, it has seemed to me that the only one who knows that I am mixed race, that my skin is different anymore, that it isn't white or black, is me.

Western Canada grew up and so did I. There wasn't a single watershed moment, no sudden light bulb of understanding. The anger and resentment that had been so much of my life growing up and had shaped me simply dissipated over the years. I grew up and travelled, got married and had children. Surprisingly to me, my husband is white. He has blond hair and pale blue eyes. We have six children, and only one of them has my brown skin, my oldest. When she was three years old I pointed out that her dad has white skin and compared his hand to our hands. I told her that she was mixed race, that she had brown skin. A leftover from my own childhood, it was important to me that I was the one to tell her that skin has a colour so that she would feel proud and not shame.

I have experienced only one act of racism in Canada in recent years, and it wasn't even addressed to me, it was to my husband. He was at a business meeting and an older man came up to him and said: "I hear you have six kids, that's great we need big families."

"Thank you," he replied.

"It's good that you're keeping the Aryan gene going," the man said.

My husband was taken aback for a moment then said: "My wife is black. I look forward to more mixed families so people don't have the excuse to discriminate based on race or colour." And he walked away. I was so surprised to encounter such outspoken racism again. It has become so rare in my life, that he seemed like a dinosaur out of time, out of place.

I recently went to Vancouver on a school trip to soak up the Olympic experience with daughter number three. There were people of all nationalities walking in the streets, and I noticed a lot of mixed-race children. If they are anything like my own children, hopefully the identity that they feel the most is Canadian and skin colour isn't a part of it.

Do I feel Canadian? I grew up eating white bread, wearing clothes from Sears and watching the same movies and TV shows as the kids I went to school with. My mother still tries to convince me I am as Irish as my red-haired, green-eyed cousins. She taught me to be Irish but I have never felt it. I know nothing about being Mauritian either. I am something new. Canada has given me a place where I can belong, where the definition of "Canadian" includes people like me.

I grew up feeling like I didn't belong anywhere, but when I became an adult I realized an important truth. It isn't that I don't belong anywhere, but perhaps quite the opposite. I belong everywhere. Rather than being scared or intimidated anymore, I feel comfortable sitting with all people no matter their skin colour or culture. Being mixed race, has instead, given me a passport to move comfortably among different kinds of people, and find that I have something in common with many of them.

When I was a child I used to be terrified of South Africa. I saw the signs on the television news, "Blacks," "Whites," and "Coloureds." I worried so much that their ways would spread and the rest of the world would have signs like that too, that I wouldn't be able to be with my mom. So much in the world has changed from my childhood. From Nelson Mandela and the end of apartheid to Barack Obama becoming President of the United States. I am not an American, yet I cried when he was inaugurated. A mixed-race person as President proved to me how much the world is changing. I hear people say that because Barack Obama is mixed race he can represent both white and black perspectives. I don't think so. I think mixed race is an entirely new perspective. It is our actions, what we do, what he can do, that will count.

Being mixed race still shapes me, I will always feel labelled. However, I am comfortable in my own skin and the ghosts of my childhood are just that, ghosts. When people ask my ethnic background I describe myself as mixed race, because I am comfortable with that tag. I don't want to be called half-caste and definitely not half-breed and with all respect to the NAACP, don't call me coloured.

CHRISTINA BROBBY

Of Two Worlds

BEING OF MIXED RACE is like living between two worlds, an alien on both as the inhabitants consider that I belong to the other. I am neither black nor white enough to assimilate into either planet.

* * *

White-skinned faces dominated my early childhood during the 1960s in England, much as they do in my present home in Whitehorse, Yukon. Adopted when I was three by white parents, their 12-year-old daughter, Leeann became my white sister. Though another curly-haired toddler with skin a shade between mine and Leeann's arrived from the orphanage a year later, to become my younger sister, Shannon, I failed to distinguish between the different skin hues within our family.

My blissful ignorance of racial differences continued despite occasional name-calling by children at the primary school I attended in the primarily white city of Canterbury. "Mummy, what does 'wog' mean?" I asked my mother as we walked home one day from school. The boy's tone, matching mine when I called Shannon "stupid," hinted at the likely insult. I was ashamed though I did not know what a wog was. My mother, like bears I've seen in the Yukon defending their cubs, confronted the headmaster the next day, insisting that the offender apologize before the entire school. I still recall the humiliation of being singled out, forced to stand on the stage as the boy mumbled his apology. I learned a valuable lesson from that experience: derogatory slurs are best swallowed and forgotten without being reported.

From an early age, Shannon and I knew our birth parents' cultural backgrounds. Her father was West Indian while mine was Ghanaian. Both of our mothers were British. Still, the significance of having a Ghanaian father never penetrated—my world rarely extended beyond Canterbury's white-peopled borders. I remained unaware that West Indians and Ghanaians might look different from my parents.

"People must think I've been with a black man when they see me with the two of you." Shannon was still using a stroller when my mother first expressed what was to become a constant refrain during our childhood. I walked beside, holding on to the frame as she pushed the carriage down the street. I wore her concern like a veil, wondering whether I should explain to people whom we met that I'd never seen my mother with a black man. The only black characters I had seen were on the television, or on the Robertson's marmalade jar, as the black Golliwog cartoon character who grinned at me while I ate my toast in the mornings. Words like "wog," "black," "Ghana," and "West Indian" scarcely scratched the surface of what I believed myself to be: a white child.

When I was nine, we moved to a suburb of London. Standing at the playground's perimeter on my first day of school, shrieks and laughter issued from children of many nationalities. Looking down at my hand gripped in my mother's, I whispered, "I'm different." As if a pair of protective goggles had been removed, the contrast in our skin colours finally pierced my cloak of naivity. Even while absorbing this new discovery, I assessed the playground scene, determining whether some un-written rule prohibited me from playing with these colourful new school-mates. I continued clinging to my pale-skinned mother until I was convinced that the usual rules applied: girls played with girls, and watched the boys covertly.

* * *

My first serious relationship with a boy when I was sixteen coincided with becoming pregnant. By the birth of Lee, my Caramilk-coloured son, Mum had conceded that I wasn't going to date any "nice white boys." She welcomed her first grandchild and accepted him and his Jamaican father, Mike, into the family.

Embracing Mike's world introduced me to racial politics. At our first party together, Mike strutted over to his male friends to talk man talk. I walked over to the circle of young black women, a smile of greeting etched on my face. A beautiful ebony princess surveyed me from the top of my afro-covered head down to my red platform-shoed feet, then asked, "What you smiling at, girl? Yo think yo better than us or sometin'? Just 'cos yo light-skinned. Well, let me tell ya diss, Miss High Almighty, yo ain't nuttin'." Her words slapped me upside the head. Fleeing to the toilets, I heard them, united in laughter at the light-brown upstart who had assumed that she was entitled to membership in their exclusive black society.

In 1979, when I was 22, Mike and I left our families and England for Canada, and settled with Lee, in Toronto. Early to meet Lee from school one day, I watched him in the playground. Sitting on the grass with boys of various ethnic backgrounds, he blended into the mosaic of children. The scene echoed reminders of my first day in the London primary school and the dawning awareness of not being white. I felt relief: not only was Lee dark enough to be accepted as black, but skin colour mattered less in his multi-racial universe.

In 2005, having survived her husband by years, my adoptive mother died. I had long since split from Mike, and now my relationship of fifteen years with the "nice white chap," as Mum characterized the French-Canadian man with whom I had lived, was also over. Lee had married and settled in the United States. I felt completely alone. Perhaps that was what led me to search for my birth parents. Months later, the adoption agency sent me the package containing my parents' names and other information. The worldwide web and Google's online search engine provided most of the remaining jigsaw puzzle pieces to my identity within minutes.

* * *

A new era of my life opened with the mail waiting in my Inbox in September, 2006: "I have in the last few days been in contact with Barnardos regarding your request for information regarding our father. He had asked me to find you but you found us first… I would be happy to speak to you."

The e-mail was from my Ghanaian half-sister, Glenda.

* * *

Two months after receiving Glenda's e-mail, my old home, London, became the rendezvous point to connect with two sisters—first, Leeann, then the following day, with Glenda. After her initial welcoming e-mail, we talked a number of times by telephone. She sounds like me, her voice soft, deliberate, as if each word is carefully considered before being uttered. There were first telephone conversations, too, with my birth father and another half sister, Karen, both living in Ghana. After London, I would continue my journey and meet them in Accra.

Leeann and I, tired from shopping, sought refuge in a cafeteria. Aware of my discovery mission, she cautioned, "Don't assume that because they're family, they'll accept you, Tina. I know Ghanaians. I see a lot of them in my work at the Immigration Court. They're as black as the ace of spades." She paused, then added, "I don't think they like half-castes."

I had not heard the term, "half-caste" for years. The feeling of being half as good as an unidentified something, lingered. "Why not double-caste?" I mused.

Lowering my gaze from Leean's hazel eyes, I scarcely breathed as she continued: "They parade into court, looking like peacocks in their bright coloured clothes. They bring all these people with them, claiming they're family, but they're not. You can't trust them. Be careful when you're there, won't you?" Concern permeated her advice.

I was furious that I lacked the courage to yell at her, "You're talking about half of me. Is that what you say about your sister to your friends?"

Glaring at the scarlet topping on my strawberry cheesecake, I felt suddenly nauseous. I would not make a scene in the cafe, could not risk losing her. Instead, I convinced myself that Leeann meant to say, "I'm afraid that now you've found your African family you won't want me as your sister anymore." That night in bed though, Leeann's comments replayed, like the needle stuck in the groove of an LP on our old record player: "half-caste;" "peacocks;" "won't be accepted," repeated over and over until sleep finally silenced the record.

Glenda and I arranged to meet the following day after exchanging clues to aid in finding each other. "I'm looking forward to meeting Goddash," Glenda said, bringing to mind a telephone conversation with our father weeks earlier. "I never forgot you, Tina. All my children knew that one day Goddash would come to find her African family. That's what I used to call you. It means God's Gift."

Now, I wondered whether the narrative included Goddash's mother being British and white. Glenda interrupted my reverie with, "I'm five-foot-three and black, like really dark chocolate. My hair's in corn rows. I'll be wearing a red cardigan sweater and jeans."

I responded, "We're the same height. I'll be wearing a brown jacket." I hesitated before blurting, "Look for a middle-aged woman with brown skin like coffee with cream." There. Now she knew I lacked the credentials to become a full member of my African family. I was a fraud, not like her, genuine dark chocolate. I waited for Glenda to say, "Tina, I'm really sorry but I forgot that I have an appointment. I can't meet you." Instead, she answered, "Okay, love, see you at 1:30. I can hardly wait." Warm familiarity lingered like a light perfume after our conversation.

That evening, as we sat at Glenda's kitchen table poring over scenes of the Yukon from the book I brought, I asked if the rest of the family knew my mixed racial background. "I doubt it. I didn't," Glenda answered, then, already attuned to my insecurities, continued, "Don't worry, Tina. It doesn't matter. Our brother, Chris's first wife was white. Their twin girls are fair-skinned, like you. They're family, just as you are." She continued, "You live in such a beautiful part of the world."

* * *

A week later, my half-brother, Tony, hosted a party at his home in Accra to welcome Goddash to the family. Surrounded by forty to fifty relatives, many matching Glenda's dark-chocolate colour, I surveyed the setting: a grand orange-and-white striped tent shaded the garden; white linen-covered tables bore remnants of the meal served earlier by smartly dressed waiters. My half-brother, Chris, his wife and my cousins, Ray, Luke, Marie, and Rose formed a circle around me, attempting to increase my Twi vocubulary, which consisted of little more than *Akwaba* (welcome), and *debe* (no).

"I learned another word yesterday," I announced. "While I was waiting outside the house with Daddy for Sammy to come from school, some of his classmates were staring at me. They giggled and whispered then, after they'd passed, one turned and called, '*Obruni, obruni*.' Daddy explained that they were calling me a white person."

Chris nodded, "Yes, that's right. They wouldn't see many white people where the old man lives."

I laughed, "White people! I'm considered black where I live. I doubt there's more than half a dozen black people in all of the Yukon."

Rose regarded me, as if expecting the punch line of a joke. She waited, the silence lengthening until finally she said, "No, Tina, you're white. I don't think the kids were being mean. But they're right. You'd never be considered black in Ghana. Look at us." Taking my hand in hers, she raised both for inspection by the group. "Now that's black," she stated in a tone that settled the debate. We continued holding hands for long seconds after the conversation shifted to politics, a favourite topic. As I half-listened to the increasing volume of their voices, despite the new classification of being an Obruni, I felt more at peace with that part of my heritage which accounted for my skin being brown than I could ever recall.

* * *

Weeks later, my birth mother and I prepared to share our identities as part of our ongoing e-mail relationship. Fears gathered again, like clouds bringing torrential rains. I fretted that my skin was too dark to be accepted by my own mother. Her photo increased my distress—despite her advancing age, strawberry-blond hair, soft and downy like a baby's framed her face; if she was any more fair she'd be transparent. I searched with increasing desperation for a suitable photo, reluctantly rejecting those taken in Whitehorse, where my face was barely visible beneath layers of winter clothing. The only candidates were from my trip to Ghana, where my skin had deepened to its golden brown shade of summer. As I sent the photo, I hoped that the bold, bubble-gum pink bougainvillea blooms would overshadow me.

"My baby grew into a beautiful woman. I've got tears in my eyes."

Her message dispersed unfounded thoughts of inadequacy, like sun reappearing after the storm. She sent photos of my three half-siblings: their skin, eyes, and hair colour matching mine; their hair and noses divulged their father's heritage, reminding me that my mother married an Indian man shortly after my birth. Months later, fears of being rejected by her proved well-founded, though for different reasons: skin colour mattered less than maintaining family secrets.

* * *

Sometimes I wonder how a city in the far north of Canada, where I have lived for thirteen years, became home. The largest minority population is the First Nations, the original people of the Territory. Their features, like mine, set them apart from the sea of white faces. I am excited whenever a new brown or black person moves to Whitehorse. If I wanted to blend into my human surroundings, I should have chosen to live in Fiji. When I visited years ago, Fijians constantly assumed that I was one of them until I shook my head, indicating I could not understand their language. I enjoyed, briefly, being of the majority, as my partner stood out in the human landscape of brownness.

When I changed my name in 2007, a friend in Whitehorse asked, "Why would you give up a nice name like 'Sutherland' for one that's unpronounceable. You'll be constantly asked, 'how do you spell that?'" She was right. My name suggests that I am foreign. Still, when I write my new name, which incorporates my mother's Irish and my father's Ghanaian ancestries, I recall that despite living in a setting like that of my childhood, where I stand apart from most, I now know people who look and sound like me, whose connections help me straddle the worlds of Black and White.

KAREN HILL

What is my Culture?

What is my culture?
You ask me today
If I say Canadian
Will you look the other way
And murmur that's not
What we meant you to say

What is my culture?
The thumping sound of Basie
"Jumping at the Woodside"
Of a Don Mills house
"da da da da …"

What is my culture?
It's running away to find:
Toni Morrison
Sembene Ousmane
Sonia Sanchez
Marcel Carne
Vittorio de Sica
Luis Bunuel

Naked naturalists
Neo-Nazis
Anarchists
Communists
Dadaists
Fascists and all
Crazy me inside Berlin and its
Concrete wall

What is my culture?
It's soukous, samba, salsa
It's Brecht, Brel, Piaf
Beau Dommage and Paul Piche

It's Bessie's Billie's and Dinah's blues
It's Dionne Brand and Langston Hughes

What is my culture?
African
American
Canadian
French
German
Dutch
Algonquin
And some British slave master
Named Hill

Moʻokūʻauhau (Genealogy)

I picked my last three lovers
for the colour of their skin
deep chocolate brown bodies
radiating the strength of Kāne.

They said they'd be more attracted to me
If I lost weight.
But they picked me anyway
for my green eyes, pass-fo'-haole skin and
ʻehu-coloured hair
"hapa babies are more beautiful"
they whisper faintly in the dark.

While I fantasize about
native children naturally chocolate brown
not bronzed from a bottle
with native names whispered in dreams from the ancients,
          they inquire, "How about Mary? Sarah? Abraham?"

Why do you want to dilute your blood
          your mana
                    your culture
                              your heritage
                                        your ʻiwi
                                                  your moʻokuʻaūhau
I said
Why do you give it away so freely?

I married the last one
with great reluctance

But how do you choose who you love? he said.

Hey, Tina Turner interjected from the FM-tuned speakers,
What's love got to do with it?

She may not have been Polynesian,
but she understood *mana.*

In the days of Civil Rights and Malcolm X
My Hawaiian father
took his white-washed, Punahou-educated self
to the bastion of haole culture — California —
and found himself a haole wife.

In the days when C & K sang with longing
for the "Sunflower with the golden hair"
my native brothers
who came of age during the "Hawaiian Renaissance"
and Billy Kaui
married white women.

They are all divorced now, every single one of them

Leaving green-eyed, ʻehu-hair, children
with skin the colour of sand
blowing in the changing winds
          flotsam and jetsam
                    floating
                              adrift in an unrelenting sea.
          The kalo is uprooted,
          The huli is cut,
          But the mahiʻai has forgotten
          to replant the next generation
          in the fertile soil of Papahānaumoku.

ROBIN M. CHANDLER

Siouxjewgermanscotblack

[cultural software instructions]

Crossing four continents
my ancestors travelled over forty thousand years
to make me.

I am a Siouxjewgermanscotblack(Cherokee)
Of Tribes
And Clans
Among Kin and
Courtiers I will never know.

Surviving holocausts
As stevedores and doctors
Losing at love
Gaining perspective.

Imagine this:
Sioux brotha meets Scottish sista circa 1890 Boston
And 16 galaxies were
born.
Bred.

I descend from
the last galaxy.
She who died in a childbirth of twins.
Leaving my nanny, Emma Fenno,
Who was NOT a black woman, but a SiouxScot.

I am 8.
A voyeur.
She sits by the oversized Victorian

window whistle-whispering prayers
To St. Jude, her face bathed in afternoon sun
And the Great Spirit listened!

Never went to church.
Didn't believe in 'the white Man's' church.
Not this Indian squaw.
Church ain't got no walls, 'cause God ain't got no walls
But her succotash, corn and tomatoes, and blueberry bread
Lingers in all the sacred, sensory places in my soul
Her daily props to the Creator is the air I breathe.

On the other side, few churchmen
Nor did John Schindler, who
Got funky
With
My mulatto grand-*grandmere*
Ever go to temple
Merely begot
Created a Semitic-Nordic-African
Who became
Grandfather.
Who said *sayonara* at 16 to the
chicken coop he was
assigned to
for being
a half-breed.
Was anybody listening?

Part of the great migrating hordes, he railroaded his way Northward
In Chicago, changed his name
To something …
Less tell-tale than Schindler … like Chandler
Lest anti-Semitics and white racists lynch his double consciousness.
Hustling himself east of the Mississippi to Cambridge
Becoming a Massachusetts Yankee landed gentry
Lockheim ! Mazeltov !

married another mixed woman.
And Yahweh/Jehovah listened

I am 8.
This mixed woman, she sits on the porch and holds court
Protecting me from the world.

As eons of women cloistered by windows, on porches, in front yards
Have guided the destinies of generations of children.

From my father's father and
Mother's mother and all that "gettin' busy" from two sides and 15 children
These strands of culture imported all that exotic funk
Into my bloodlines.

I am a 10-year-old girl
Bombarded with
Porkpie and Strauss
The *Dies Irae* and *Take the A Train*
Vaughan and Ellington sandwiched around Tchaikovsky and Doo-wop.

Not music for four hands, but
Music for many brains, many hearts, parallel polyrhythms
The bass AND the treble, not the bass OR the treble.

There are two choices.
Either reconcile the culturesong
Or, on their own, one……
Will kill off the others.
Gang violence with the G-clef.

I am 11 and my dad,
another kin never darkening the door of hallowed ground,
is doing the twist in the living room.
Embarrassed to shades of Chinese red, I pray
For the next dance craze or, perhaps,
His hips will lock or he will cross fade into the stereo?
Is anybody watching?

I don't come with directions.
So I must figure this identity thing out myself.
From hybrid vigor,
to exotic other(ness).

Who cares?

I do.
I very much do.

I am 6 and a saleswomen flees
When the
Little
Brown
Thing which is me
Rushes toward a
White
-skinned
mother, which is mine.
What did I do?
Does this mean something?

I am 13 at summer camp and
Judyfriend teaches me the Jewish alphabet.
We bond because those phrases slipped out
Past my American mask, my disguise
Oy-vey
Oy-vey
With gestures that betray me
An ineffable culturespeak of the bones
I tell her we had Manischewitz wine at the dinner table.
Through her bifocals she grins eloquently.
Running in the summer woods, I am enfolded by greensong.
On the water I am gunwalling in the canoe, humming Indiansong
And the pines and greenwoods and birch voices all sing with me.
Did anybody plan this?

In the '60s, I insinuate this sanguinity into my art.
I am attacked.
'You just don't wanna be black' they say.

Rich memories all and I am a half-century work-in-progress
older now. More vision, better seeing with insight
By legacy I am a Schindler.
I got chutzpa
I got game

and I am mailin' it home, grandpa, mailin' it home.
Yet multiple identities that were born of passion and desire
Have found in me only one love —
for the Creator of this wild and beautiful universe.

I am more things from my past, I have become more things in the now than
    you can possibly dream.
Travelled far and remote to amazons, outbacks and jungles
Across this weary planet
Slipping in and out of whatever
race I share
space
with.
Place to place
where I am
face to face
with family I am not possibly related to
But who stare back with resemblances of
power and
memory and
homefires in the time which has no end and no beginning.
These bloodlines will live forever through my children and grandchildren
Buzzing like bees in and out of the windows of the ribbon-wrapped porches
    of my future.

So here I am.
Did I tell you
I can Irish stepdance
Do the pipe ceremony
Gesture in blatant *Jewspeak* and bargain with God,
Speak ebonically.

You got a box for that, Mr. census!
You got a box for me?
You ain't got a box or a mind big enough for a
Siouxjewgermanscotblack(Cherokee).

The old ones.
They came so far to make us.

The least we can do is be honest.

Laura Kina, "Loving Series: Shoshanna Weinberger," 2006, charcoal on paper, 42.5" x 34".

SAEDHLINN B. STEWART-LAING

A Hairy Question

I AM STANDING IN line in the checkout line at the grocery store when I feel a tug on my hair. I spin around, and see a middle-aged white woman in line behind me, several strands of my long hair still in her hand. She looks puzzled at the anger written on my face.

"I wanted to see if it was real," she says, as though this were a perfectly reasonable explanation for petting a stranger's hair. "It's just so … exotic."

I want to say something sarcastic: No, of course my hair isn't real, I'm an android escaped from a secret government facility. Or I could overwhelm her with a scientific explanation: Well, I have one variant copy of the EDAR gene, which is endemic to indigenous Americas and determines hair strand thickness, a mix of melanin regulating proteins, and a Celtic genotype connected to an increased number of follicles, which express simultaneously to create a blended phenotype.

But I'm in public, so I grit my teeth and reply. "Yes, it's real. Thanks."

***

I explain my heritage, there are two responses I inevitably get. The first is merely dismissive: "But you don't look Indian. No way. You have blue eyes!"

At this point, I sigh, and explain that not all Native Americans are red-skinned, obsidian-eyed clones with straight black hair falling over our shoulders.

But the other, more common response goes something like this: "Wow. Scottish and Carib. What an unusual mix!"

On some level, I understand. But my parents' respective cultures are surprisingly similar, particularly in their additive views of the world. The Carib side of my family, in particular, historically survived by adaptation, first by conquering their island neighbours to the north and absorbing their languages and foods and customs, and then by learning to cope with incursions by the Dutch and the Spanish, the English and the French. Meanwhile, my Celtic ancestors adopted Nordic footwear, and wove Christianity into their own pagan beliefs.

So I think of my hair as a product of adaptation. While my facial features are distinctly Celtic, and my compact, curvy body distinctly Carib, my hair is a blend, the part of me which can be both at all times. Ironically, my hair is also the feature people point to when trying to classify me.

***

When I was a toddler, my hair was pale blond, but curled in ringlets, like my father's hair, and my eyes looked almond instead of wide like my mother's eyes. When my mother would bring me places, people would touch it, and ask what technique my mother used to set the curls. My mother protested that this was entirely natural; the response was usually a scoff: "No white child has hair like that. Come on. You can admit you use a curler."

On the other hand, my blond hair marked me as white, particularly when my father was around. In that case, people were less interested in my curls and more in what they perceived as my irrefutable whiteness, at least compared to my father.

"Excuse me," a white store clerk once said. "Is that man bothering you?"

"That's my dad," I replied, in my snottiest toddler voice.

I remember how his eyes moved: he looked at my father, with his tan skin and long, chocolate-black hair, then back at me.

***

For years, my hair was traditional, a canvas for both of my parent's cultures. I wore it long and single-length, like a Carib woman, but my mother often twisted it into cylindrical Celtic-style braids.

Then middle school came, and like every adolescent, I wanted to fit in. In my grade six class, part of this was having straight, shoulder-length, platinum-blond hair. The other part was designer clothes, preferably pastel, with the logo prominently displayed. Even at twelve, I was acutely aware that the designer clothes were unobtainable; however, I could pester my mother into chopping off two feet of my hair, which I firmly believed would transform me from "weird" and "foreign-looking" to mainstream, whitebread Americana.

My hair had other ideas. I attempted to straighten it; it puffed out like the hackles of an angry cat.

But more importantly, the cropped ends felt uncomfortable. When I looked in the mirror, I didn't look like me.

***

About the same time that I reclaimed my newly grown-out hair, I joined the high school debate team.

High school debate is white. Aggressively white. Nonconformity is frowned upon at the best of times, and a proud statement of culture was seen as an inexcusable affront.

"You need to do something more … professional with your hair," a judge told me, as she glared over her reading oval glasses. "It's too long. It's a distraction. And I'm going to have to mark you down for that."

For the rest of the day, I wondered if I should do something about my hair. Once again, I felt like I was in middle school, longing to look just like everyone else. And fitting in meant success at debate, something for my college résumé.

Then it came to me. Changing how I expressed my cultures by doing "something professional" with my hair for the sake of someone who I would never see again would mean throwing out the incongruity of my identity, my unique and unlikely mixed heritage.

I did not do anything professional with my hair. Embracing my hair is about embracing my identity, claiming my mixed heritage as its own complete identity instead of separate, mismatched puzzle pieces. To me, nothing could be less exotic, or more comfortingly ordinary.

Margo Rivera-Weiss, "Por Vida," 1997, watercolour, 10" x 13".

RAGE HEZEKIAH

Songs Feet Can Sing

Mother fed me on folk music
breastfed me barefoot
Celtic crosses hung between clavicle
my brown neck
their throne

My Feet as the Bodhran
laced in archaic shoe
traced and marked wooden floors of Irish pubs
these dark curls bouncing
with treble reel and jig

Brownness between pale skin and freckle
The features of this face
oblivious to its origins

In the passing of years
My rigid upper body
begs the tales of my ancestory
Pulling island songs from my father's pocket

When I tug his linen shirts
he plays me Harry Belafonte
brings me to my grandfather's backyard

This large man, strong bones
cooks up jerk chicken, rice and beans,
makes sweet drink
"how's every*ting*?
good good good."

I find my hips and let my hair down
hear my father's hands upon tightened skins
drum circles pulsing of djembe and conga
my core heated with dance

Movement has always been my medium
This body of the Moors of Ireland
This body of the West Indies
This body, dancing.
Dancing.

LISA MARIE ROLLINS

Opposite of Fence

my mother gazes at me silent
as we turn this dying pasture into itself,
we prepare the earth for the cold winter to come
she averts her eyes from my skin
and I from hers
both denying how when side by side
we ignore our differences

I watch her lithe, sure fingers
nails engrained with black earth

I set down the shovel, turn to her
am earnest as I reach to hold them
a moment of recognition for us both

I drop her hands
and we return to hack down the corn stalks
my biceps singing as side by side we unroot them from the fields

she is gentle in her reminder to pick the last of the cobs
even if they are light green
there are animals to feed and more earth to fertilize
for our next harvest season together

I am terrified I will forget
that she has taught me how to love
well and strong
more freely than any one I know

LISA MARIE ROLLINS

Appliqué

we shop for textiles, fabric and thread
as if it is the only thing we have to discuss

we pore over colours, cut shapes of disjointed edges
I ignore how our bodies aren't the same

you teach me patterns, flowers, log cabins, strips connecting
pretend not to read what I write about the world

we align the squares, sew them with articulate stitches
deny how much work it will take to make them fit

blue veins of your hands come through your skin clear now
I am afraid when I look at my brown fingers, of what will tear us apart.

but we stitch and iron and hum with this strong thread
cover the floor we sit on with laughter as I pull out a crooked stitch
and re-do it, tighter.

*"Appliqué is a great technique to cover stains, rips or other problem areas."

ADEBE DERANGO-ADEM

Blanqueamiento

The land that's yours is mine,
is shadows, which I see
both dreaming and in the night
when drums make our old selves dance,
bring us to embrace those old ghosts
weaving through. No one owns them
or us,
   nor the fearful asymmetries
of our lineage, of our Caribe we left
for new callings,
   a new response
from Yoruba to Cuba we work hard
to reflect. This land that's yours
is a patria of poes'a mulata;
   we shan't forget
these shanty towns, this Afroantillana
beyond the pale, beyond even Matos
and Guillén there is a spirit
unlearning its colour and shade, becoming
the Veil we pull out
from the eyes,
challenging the dark.

What else to say in this assortment of
motion, stars,
this strange green sky,
waiting for the train

in the certainty of night:
these may be the last grey days

where light bends

through glass and the spring
and is reborn again,
wandering

among names of the dead, remembering
the peace of communion,
the landscapes which fade

at the edges but hold our bodies in place,
the letters written in a furtive ink
stitching promises
   of pilgrimage,

towards the sea that calls
me to embark
into a dialectic of light and dark,

and then hopefully light again,
back to the theories and poems we wept for

a true pledge for morning,
for the momentum to run,
to sing as a way of traveling

to await only
the moment where all that is static
shatters into hope.

FARIDEH DE BOSSET

The Land

The land is brand new to me,
unknown to my ancestors.
It is not my birthplace.

But it has made me its own
as much as herons, muskrats
and frogs in the lake.
We are all pilgrims
hearing each other's prayers
and gratitude.

The land claimed me
as one of its pine and maple
trees.
 It found me
hearing my yearning to belong,
less audible
than the chorus
of the Canadian Geese,
always on the go,
agitated,
looking for another settlement,
 farther and less visible
than the patches
of the blue sky reappearing
among the cumulus

The geese will fly high to catch
their dreams
leaving me

in the great stretch of the moment
sheltered for now
from the protests of difference
and belonging.

ANDREA THOMPSON

Legend

In this time
of post-racial fairy tales
we still have a story to tell

the election of a mixed-race president
didn't cure the disease
of injustice and discrimination
merely provided a band-aid
to cover what is still
in the process of being healed

in our journey
towards social maturity
this current growth spurt
is a landmark way-station

this freedom train has yet
to reach its final destination

in this changing landscape
we —
are the confounders
of strict definition
are life beyond the boarders
of racial expectation

we are incarnate questions
of loyalty and identity

we do not fit in

the Dewey decimal system
of restrictive human categories

we, the often fetishized
exotic objects of fascination
of idolatry and suspicion
of assumption and rejection

are our own north
star — to freedom

beyond the bondage
of an other-centric
dichotomous dialectic

we are the human race taking a step
from murky sea to dry land

we can breathe both
water and air

we do not live in the margins, but
at the centre
of this ongoing evolution

we are racial redefinition
in flesh and blood
in celebration

we —
are re-imagining ourselves
and what it means to be human

beyond the borders of either / or

image by image
word by word

Native Speaker

Daring to Name Ourselves

"N *as in Nancy, F as in Frank, O, N, O, Y, I, M as in Mary.* (Insert heavy sigh.) *Yes, N as in Nancy, F as in Frank."* I remember the countless times throughout my life that I heard my father, head nestling the phone, or bent over a customer service counter, reciting this refrain in his Cameroonian cadence with its rhythmic smoothness sung low. This sentence was so embedded in my mind, a part of my earliest memories, that I myself have used it for as long as I've had to spell out my last name.

The names "Nancy, Frank, and Mary" just as dated as the vinyl records my parents jammed to and not nearly as classic. Yet the names, over thirty years later, are still so perfectly (almost eerily so) "American" conjuring up idyllic (read: white) cookie-cutter images of U.S. life. It's a simple translation for a last name that has no coherence in this hemisphere, has no history in this land before my father arrived in 1979 suitcase full of dreams and phantoms.

The translation my father and I continuously offer is always followed by a perfunctory explanation: "The 'N' is silent." Before the confused pause or a prompt to spell it out even comes, I parrot out the same apologetic line, stringing it in seamlessly as if it, too, were an inextricable part of the name itself—an apology for the difficulty of a name so brazenly foreign, spoken in my clear, practiced, unaccented English. The silent 'N' in my name carrying with it the silences and secrets, the erasures of my history and marking, perhaps, the completeness of my assimilation growing up mixed/black/African/Latina and American in this self-proclaimed multicultural mecca.

The first intelligible words I ever spoke were in Spanish, my small ball of a body nestled in the soft lap of the brown-sugared Dominican women who took care of me in my first year of life. They, the warm hands and strong arms that jet in and out of my hazy rememory and whose faces and names I strain to but can no longer recall. My early imagination full of Spanish names for things, places and people. I entered elementary school in 1990s Jamaica, Queens then the land of names from Diaz to Rampersaud and I, barely bilingual, already knowing somewhat vaguely that I was a bit *differente*. I would pronounce my name clumsily, struggling under it's three weighty syllables.

I see her, my five-year-old self, navy-blue uniform jumper on, rocking an '80s-style side ponytail carefully tamed by her Abuela and a slip of cardstock hung around her neck with the name "Nicole Nfonoyim." I hear her introduce herself as "Nickul Fooonojeem", elongating the "O" and extending the "I."

I used to say that the day I stopped speaking Spanish—the day I could no longer remember how to say the simplest words, the day my dreams switched to the English channel, was the day I became half ghost. Somehow, all the food my mother made connecting me to homes I had never known, washed down with Malta Goya and canned coconut water, could not fill the void where my tongue used to be, where my voice could have been.

Is culture and identity really just the sum of the languages we speak and the foods we eat? Must we as mixed people or immigrant children always frame our stories around lack and loss instead of the intensity of our creative, productive and perhaps even transgressive possibilities?

In many ways, my "mixedness," my "blackness,"my "latinidad" and, the strongest contender of all, my "Americaness" were always in a constant battle to the death. The world and even my own heart told me there was no way all *that* could exist harmoniously and unchallenged within me. Standing firmly and unapologetically amidst all the contradictions I embody was a long process of finding my voice, creating a language and ultimately (re)naming who I am. Finding a voice was perhaps the hardest part because it was so inextricably tied to the loss of my first language and the yearning to transform my newly acquired yet still tongue-tied bi-culturalism into a wholly new form of speech and fluency, legitimate in it's own right.

Growing up I didn't know how to tell my story. My story juggling too many different worlds and my body the bridge I at once struggled to build and then burn to the ground. I was in a world content to name me and never caring to ask what I wanted to call myself. The grand narrative of race and immigration in America played to the tune of School House Rock's *The Great American Melting Pot,* which managed in three minutes of animation set to a catchy jingle to effectively erase the histories of people of colour in the formation of the United States. No one had to tell me that my story was "Other," I already felt it branded across my brown skin.

I see her sitting in a classroom, silent tears inexplicably rolling down her face as her classmates present family trees and say where their names came from, what they mean and who named them. All the "Katie Russos," "Danielle Espositos," "Chris Murphys," and "Michael O'Connors" take turns, while she struggles to bridge two worlds and connect the branches of her family tree. She mutters the meaning of her middle and last names as if ashamed—as if saying her name were more about baring her soul than a simple class exercise on Ellis Island.

Why had I been so ashamed of being the only one with my picture tacked on the west coast of Africa on the giant paper map of the world in the front of the class? I didn't have the words to proclaim confidently, "My name is Nicole Asong Nfonoyim. I was born between pride and two continents. I was lulled to sleep with the dreams of my ambitious father and raised in the heat of my mother's kitchen. My name is a mouthful of edges, bitter earth and foreign spice. It tastes of tropic sea water and falls with the weight of Ejagham women wielding giant wooden pestles to pound cassava into *fu-fu*. It carries a touch of sweetness depending on who's saying it, a nanosecond of a melody as the tongue moves around the "Ono" only to be met once again with the pointed, exaggeration of a "Y." My name carries with it the songs of fierce ancestors—the legacy of family and of a people who's masked faces whisper of who I once was and who I could someday be. And yet this name is only a part of my story."

There she is, a few years later in the school yard, hip to the fact that speaking Spanish and "looking black" somehow makes no sense in the United States. I hear her bold-face lying, saying "Well it's 'cause I have two last names: "Lopez" and "Nfonoyim" already myth-making to make sense of her interraciality and bi-culturalism, an aching to make visible all she is.

Like a wonky pendulum I'd swing unevenly between being ashamed of my difference and suddenly wanting to tell everyone just how "unique" I was. I'd accept the names and labels placed on me all the while writhing rebellious under their weight. I was named by school teachers, by classmates and friends. But was first named by my mother who understood all too well the way race works in America. She'd say bluntly, "You are black and you are a woman, my Colé you'll always have to work twice as hard."

My mother, bi-racial herself, never speaks of her mixed identity. She's black. Period. Growing up Afro-Costa Rican and living through the '70s as an immigrant and a woman of colour in New York City didn't grant her the luxury to call herself anything else. I, the privileged American daughter, came of age in the "multiculti" 1990s when the world had deceived itself into thinking it looked like a glossy print United Colours of Benneton ad. Yet in my little corner of the world, being black and being mixed still seemed like two disparate halves of me that refused to seamlessly come together and no one was telling me it was okay to pull a Tiger Woods and break free entirely. Ultimately, I *became* who I was told to be.

Number 2 pencil at the ready, she stares blankly at the discreet bubbles of the standardized test form and raises her hand. The young white teacher complete in an ankle-length flowered skirt and twin set moves toward her. The teacher listens to the question, smiles with a look of feigned understanding, and says simply "You're 'African American'." The pencil shades in the bubble and moves on.

It's funny the way impersonal, sterile forms for tests or applications can have the power to cause a momentary existential crisis for the mixed and bi-cultural.

These forms becoming symbols of a history of being defined and named according to the colour of one's skin and one's perceived place of origin, of being reduced to statistics and multi-coloured pie charts, of allowing oneself to become subsumed into a discreet box or run the risk of being a perpetual outlier—eternally "Other."

After my teacher told me I was African American as if it were the definitive correct answer to a math problem, I became vaguely aware that I was *becoming* a black American. At 14, I didn't know anything about "passing" or about "colourism" and "racialization"—all that would come years later in the hallowed halls of higher learning. But being seen and named as "black" in America, inevitably made me African American by default. My biculturalism, marked first by being an immigrant child learning the language of white America, began to demand I speak fluent *black* American as a matter of survival and resistance in the wake of the volatile racial inheritance of the United States that rendered bodies like mine marginal and unassimilable.

Despite being made marginal, I can speak proudly and fluently with the tongues which I have had to master, those which I have had to create and those which I have been given.

First week into college. Ignorant to that fact that she's sitting in a room where student activists and revolutions were born. Surrounded by multilingual people with names, and complex histories rivaling her own. That night she's given other names—new names, a new tongue, and a new voice to speak her truth.

I began to find my voice in college. It was there that I learned what it meant for our identities to always be in both the process of *being* and *becoming*. My higher learning was about finding empowerment in self-naming and demanding to exist in spaces on my own terms. I came to understand that my identities did not exist separately within me and that I could be "Camstarican," "Black-American," "Multi," "Afro-Latina," and any other name I chose to give myself at any time. That seemingly simple space to name myself meant that I could, for the first time, see myself clearly. It meant that I could also think critically about racial and social justice and just how significant speaking for ourselves from the multiple places we stand, truly is. For too long marginalized communities have been named and spoken for. Perhaps as we embark on this the second decade of the millennium, we mixed edge-walkers can finally proclaim the all too difficult names of who we are.

I look at myself reflected in my bathroom mirror. My eyes tracing the contours of my face. I think of all I've grown with, of the insidious and pervasive nature of marginalization and the layers of self-silencing and doubt that once threatened to break me and all it has meant to be mixed, to be a woman of colour, an immigrant daughter and a black American.

I have no single, complete "mother-tongue" and my identity has ever-proverbial "roots." But while my branches stretch far they have grown sporadically—breaking off, changing course and bearing altogether new and multifarious fruit. Against all odds, I have learned to love the entirety of that woman I see reflected before me. I have learned to call her by all the beautiful names she has dared to carry.

III. REVELATIONS

Colour Lesson I

Family Studies, age ten:

when asked what colour
I thought described who I was
I wrote down "everything"
a chameleon, cool and smooth
but the class laughed
and my teacher asked
why would I want to be that
so that I can be anything,
I replied
years later
my blond highlights
do all the talking, and are
definitely more fun
less work and less laughter,
the rest of the animal kingdom
now quiet and aroused
by my silence
and less chaos

ADEBE DERANGO-ADEM

Concealed Things

colour in the mechanism
of concealment,
lineage a dangerous dream

of children marked forever
into the gaze,
pushed into alleyways

roads, orchards, skylines;
but look closely,
in these whole anthropological worlds

you may find my people —
they look like yours
merged in the pure gaze of the sun

with Exodus in their eyes,
spectrums for skin,
my sisters.

PRISCILA UPPAL

Serendipity

Were I invited to name a planet
(& why not?), such a globe in the universe
would be called Serendipity. We would live there.

We'd wake to the smell of Columbian coffee
engage in Chinese calisthenics before
a rodizio lunch
siesta then squaredance
read old Russian novels while
sipping champagne &
throat-sing into the night.

Our flag would be a bird without borders.
Our anthem composed by shooting our names out
of a canon & catching the rain.

We would speak only when absolutely necessary
& in oxymorons.

Work days & holidays indistinguishable.
My mother = my sister = my grandfather =
my long lost neighbour = my hairdresser.

Every object in our homes native & artifact.

We would dream all possible permutations
of planet, animals, & species. & each
would be a paragon of you.

Margo Rivera-Weiss, "Ultramarine," ca.1990, watercolour, 10" x 13".

KATHERENA VERMETTE

before i was this

before i was this
i was more

before i was this i was
the dream of a hundred martyrs
the sort of wish that lingers
under young girl whispers
into young girl ears

before i was this i was
what all the old ladies knew
would happen when
all the old man ideas died out

before i was this
i was the high plateau
on the mountain of revolution, the one
the women would look up to and say,
"one day"

i was that light in a fear filled eye
that gift floating in the wind
i was as light as those white seeds
sprinkled about the wide red earth
and i was as certain as the future

and my birth has taken centuries
a labour that nearly killed us all
but now i have
emerged, infantile

though fully grown
and i may not look like much
but i have so many gifts, i have so many
stories that have waited
lifetimes to be told

Firebelly

I was once
a nappy headed
Barbie wielding
cartwheel turning
little girl

deliriously playful
obliviously brown

adolescence brought
scalp burned
straightened hair
            initiation
skin grown fairer
with hormone change
and less playing in the sun

brought passing
            accidentally
getting dates, being in
on nigger jokes told
by a soon to be embarrassed
smarty pants kid at the party
who doesn't know my ancestry

Brian Brinkman waited for me
every day after school
behind the same snowy hedge
three years in a row
him, a big gangly teenager

me, between training wheel
and training bra
still just a kid

but I never did
take the long way home, no
just stood my ground
fought tooth and nail
reclaiming my right
to walk down the street
with my head held high

and the boys who do
date me eventually
are heroes
for not listening
to the teasing
are brave in heart, and
soft in skin

(also
 often
 later)

                      disappointing
                 as they mistakenly
                   stake flag on me
                     brave explorer
                        first to see
                       this exotic
                      and erotic
                         foreign
                         colony

                        now
                       the dic
                       tionary
                       states

something that is

exotic, is such that is
from elsewhere, over there
overseas, once upon
a time in a kingdom
far, far away
not native
not from here

and here, my dear
beats the heart of pre-
judice, assume first
and think later

Mr. Man-on-the-street
this girl will not
give you the answer
you may so want to hear
when you ask:
Where are you from?

I will not
banter in Swahili
or the long drawl of Patois
will not enthrall you

with captivating tales
of the Ivory Coast

lazy days spen'
wit muddah and sistah
singin' folk tune
weavin' from dah loom
undah de broad shade
of de coconut palm

cause that's not where I'm from
I come from a land where
the people all share
a firebelly ferocity
about their belonging

a land
of strip malls
snow tires
driveways
microwaves
cottages, camping
K-Tel, Kool-Aid
mashed potatoes
skateboard
bacon bits
convenience stores
skating rinks, barbecues
backyards and swimming pools

of coming home
when streetlights go on
of hide-and-seek after dark

 if any further questions
do not insinuate exile, I will
offer clarification
a biographic explanation
will expand upon the blood
newly brewed in this nation

it's from the land
of Buckingham, marmalade
BBC, Royal Brigade
and a little nosh with tea

and the blood that is
from the rest of me
tells a tale
of North Star, railroad
underground
near escapes
and bondages broken
of hundreds of years
working this land
headstones marking ancestors
born on and buried in this soil

I am slave
and slave master

but
I am not
a hot chocolate
sweet ginger
butterscotch
brown sugar
toffee, coffee
caramel, coco
maple fudge
cappuccino
honey dipped
mocha, oreo
lightly toasted
cinnamon girl

I am not dinner
at the afro-congo
brown girl café

where am I from?
really from?
my parents?
parents' parents?
before that
or-ige-jan-al-ee?

I come from the land
of snow job
and firebelly
where the neighbours
are Brinkmen
and the natives
are brown

JASMINE MOY

From Chopsticks to Meatloaf and Back Again

"I DON'T KNOW HOW to eat with chopsticks," I once said to a friend within earshot of my mother.

"You wanna bet?" she challenged.

I'd tried to use them in the past and failed miserably so I doubled down. "Yeah. I'll bet."

I should have known better. My mother isn't the gambling type. She scurried off to her room and came back waving a photo in the air, and tossed it on the kitchen table triumphantly. I was barely one and a half, still a baby, when it was taken. I had chubby cheeks and a thick layer of glossy bangs and was sitting in a highchair; a bowl of food in front of me … chopsticks perched perfectly between my tiny fingers.

"I'm leaving. If you ever come after me for child support I'll kidnap your children and you'll never see them again." My father had been cheating. Those were his parting words and she didn't call his bluff. Penniless and with two children under the age of three, she moved our family to Chicago and in with her parents. As a result, the most direct contact I've had with my father is limited to a phone call I overheard him having with my mother when I was eleven. Her name was on the house that he wanted to sell and he needed her signature to do it. I could hear the tension in her voice, could see her back stiffen. I felt afraid. I heard a question and answer I'll never forget.

"Don't you want to know how your children are?" my mother asked. Before my mind had time to start properly racing it was followed with, "Well I'm going to tell you anyway," succeeded by a list of our virtues, how well we were doing in school and what sports we excelled at.

Yeerik Moy, the only other Asian kid at my high school, asked me to every dance because his parents only wanted him to be with other Asian people.

"But I'm only half, I don't really count," I'd tell him. But he and I shared a last name, which meant I was Chinese enough. I wonder whether it would have been good enough for my father's family who greatly disapproved of my curvaceous German mother.

"She is not Chinese!" they hollered when they met her and almost never spoke another word to her again. I couldn't understand any situation in which I was only allowed to date people who looked like me. Nobody looked like me.

"We can make fried rice," she said. Fried rice? I'd never, in my life, seen my mother make fried rice. Meatloaf and the occasional spaghetti were the main dishes in my mother's repertoire. We were mostly a McDonald's family, but my third grade class was having an "ethnic foods" potluck at school and I needed to bring something. (In retrospect, the effort at culture introduction is quaint. I was the only "non-white" child in my class in a town where all the money was old money and nothing was "ethnic." I imagine there were several seven-layer dips and dishes of meatballs.) She dumped the rice in cold water.

"But it's not boiling yet!" I protested. Already she was messing it up.

"We're rinsing the starch off," she said, frustrated by her know-it-all daughter. Her short, pale fingers sinking into the water, swishing and shuffling the grains as one would tousle late-forties pin curls or rake lines in the sand of a Zen garden. The water gradually turning milky with each pass, we rinsed and rinsed again. "Until the water runs clear." My mother, secretly, had a whole cookbook's worth of Chinese recipes up her sleeve. My father insisted nothing but Chinese be cooked under his roof so it was her first project as a young wife: mastering the art of Chinese cooking. I pictured her as a concubine, following orders, bowing to the will of a man who married a white woman but wanted a traditional Chinese wife. "When we got divorced I never wanted to cook Chinese food ever again." It was her way of putting her foot down, escaping the oppression after the fact. I wished she'd have been able to take that stand while they were married. I felt guilt at being the reason she was revisiting painful memories and, the straight A student that I was, anger that it was for a stupid class project that I wouldn't even get graded on.

Even though she's the white one, I look a lot like my mother. The resemblance is so strong that friends of mine have stopped her on the street saying, "We've never met, but you must be Jasmine's mother." I have high cheekbones and almond eyes, just like her. We both have the same long straight thin nose. At least I thought we did, until I found out that she'd had a nose job in high school to remove a bulbous knot along her ridge (a gift passed on from my grandmother). I'm left to wonder whose nose I have after all. I didn't know what my father looked like and never much cared, but when my brother, Ken, needed to do a family tree for school in fourth grade and needed pictures to go along with it, my mother dug out one of the only photos that she refrained from cutting my father's head out of: their wedding portrait. Ken, it turns out, looks just like our father. It's strange to think about in hindsight, but when you're young, you don't question things that aren't there or things that used to be. It was shocking to find that he was a dead-ringer. I wondered how often my mother was reminded of my father when looking into my brother's eyes.

There is a vast disconnect between what I've received from my father and the reception of his genes. Of feeling white without looking white, if feeling white means being raised in a suburb and going to good public schools with all white people and having no discernable connection to anything outside the suburban bubble, all while having a pretty harsh Chicago accent. Confusion runs rampant.

"What are you?"

"Excuse me?"

"I mean, where are you from?"

"I'm from Chicago."

"No, where are your parents from?"

"They're from Chicago, too."

"I mean what ethnicity are you?"

Finally, the words match up to the question that we both know they're asking. This happens at least once a week. Almost always from people working behind cash registers. In response, I often hear something along the lines of, "Ah, it's a beautiful combination." Though nosy, most questioners are kind.

"Ooohh!" the owner exclaimed in a sound that resembled "Eureka!" the first time I ever went with my mother to pick up Chinese for dinner. "You no look like Moy" he said, pointing my mother's way. "You! You look like Moy!" he said, pointing at me and sounding quite satisfied. White women, apparently, weren't supposed to have Chinese last names.

At the nail salon they'll occasionally start speaking Mandarin or Cantonese to me. "I'm sorry," I say, and I mean it. Asian cultures are rich with things so exotic, so foreign, that they might as well be from another universe. My only time in Asia was on a visit to the southern coast of Turkey, the decidedly least Asian part of the continent. While I'm not white enough to pay for paper towels at the drug store without being interrogated, I'm also not culturally aware enough to feel like I deserve the Asian side of me either.

"You don't remember that time you were beat up?!" My mother was incredulous. Had she believed me I'm sure she'd have used more tact in bringing the subject up to begin with, but I had no idea what she was talking about. "Miss Kime called me. She was leaving school and saw you on the ground, two boys kicking you."

In small waves, memories begin to come into focus. Like the tide, inching further and further up the sand at dusk. The vision of Miss Kime, frantically running over and picking me up off the ground, fills my head. I don't remember pain, just confusion.

"Chink," I hear one of them spit at me. I don't know what it means, but I can tell they're cursing me and they know they're in big trouble. I'd been close with Miss Kime, the principal, all through grade school and junior high, feeling quite like the teacher's pet. For years I'd blocked out the reason why.

My growing acceptance of who I was and where I'd come from was somewhere in my subconscious, imperceptible. If forced to trace it back, I'd start with college, where I'd matured enough to think I might be pretty and that being unique was something to luxuriate in, not hide from. I made some friends who were Jewish and Latino and African American and started seeing the world as a place where mixing and being mixed was the future.

My brother never had these issues. As my father's duplicate, nobody has ever stopped him to ask where he's from. He's long had the nickname "Moy Sauce," he has the bar code for soy sauce tattooed on his inner wrist and he is covered with Chinese letters and symbols from dragons to koi fish. He's been my bridge, guiding me across the expense between my halves. With him, I tried sushi for the first time. It was love at first sight. From katsu to sashimi, from kimchi to kalbi, bun to salted plum soda and back around to pad see eu, I've developed an obsession for Asian cuisine. I take authority with a menu that my non-Asian friends watch with awe.

This transformation showed itself one night over dinner. I was in a wealthy Connecticut town at an expensive restaurant with the first serious boyfriend I'd had since college. Looking around, the fact of looking different being part of my daily routine, I said, "I'm the only non-white person in this place."

Surely coming from a desire to make me feel included, he responded, "You are white, honey." As quickly as the words registered, my disbelief came even faster.

"What the fuck are you talking about?!"

"Oh, come on Jasmine. You're one of the whitest people I know. Your English is perfect, you don't speak with an accent. You were raised by a bunch of white people in a white town…"

My heart was pounding, my blood rising to flush my cheeks. Hearing him say the things I used to tell to myself, I was being confronted by a reflection of my own childhood ignorance. I was looking at the denial I'd possessed for most of my young adult life and my desire to fit in, and it wasn't pretty. Yet here we were, adults, and somewhere in his head, denying my ethnicity was not only supposed to be socially acceptable but also comforting?

I was awash in thoughts of grade school textbooks teaching the one-drop rule, of voices asking me what I am, the image of Ms. Kime reaching down for me, the smiling child in her highchair.

"I am not white" It was both a true statement and a defence of what I'd come to embrace about myself. Much debate can be had about whiteness and how it has evolved over the decades and generations that preceded my own, but the difference between "white" and "non-white" has always been crystal clear. I was not white. An asinine statement by an ex may not have been the cause for this acceptance, but it was the first time I had ever had to defend my heritage and in doing so, I felt a sense of pride in what I was, who I was, and what I looked like.

"Half-Asian babies are the cutest. Am I right?" is something I've uttered on occasion, and then to not seem too vain I'll mention that mixed anything is gorgeous. Someone who is Asian or mixed themselves usually asks in one word: "Half?" They want the specific type of Asian cloth from which I'm cut. It feels like membership in a club with the cool kids.

"You're a hapa!" someone once proclaimed. I had just finished reading Obama's *Dreams from My Father,* where I had heard the term for the first time. His memoir affected me profoundly. It documents his struggles to come to terms with his own issues with being of mixed race. It was revelatory to read someone writing so eloquently about the problems that I grappled with so clumsily all my life. We were both born in Hawaii, where the term "hapa" originates. We were both nearly fatherless, and raised by some pretty hardworking and generous white mothers and grandparents. Though having spent some time in New York, we both call Chicago our home and became lawyers. Our life paths diverge pretty dramatically after that, but I still consider him a bit of a kindred spirit.

My Power

is the perceptual place

where Ɨ feel the light through my skin
and through my skin the force
of gravity,
that stretch of energies
at work, at once.

Ɨ as heliotropic grounded reaching.
Ɨ as small satellite
launched at dawn
and each night rebecoming earth.

Ɨ, G‑dness:

that awakeness,
that perfect acuity

that holds at the snap
of the other's
approach,

that listens
for the space
between options.

I, no‑not‑just‑I,
then yes, the thisness
refusing its own negation.
The Ɨye

that knows
the differentiated plurality
of its own knowing
cells
as what touches

        ular conscience.
the glob
        al consciousness.

Whitewashed

IT STRUCK ME AS funny when George told me. But it was one of those situations where the words don't quite mean anything at first until you have had a chance to let them resonate inside you, and then they sink into your gut like stones thrown into a lake, taking their time to reach the bottom where they stay and build up like sediment. What did he mean by whitewashed?

That people were even discussing me struck me as odd because I never considered myself to represent anything out of the ordinary. But perhaps to the black boys at my school, I, a mixed-race girl, was white-washed. Washed in white. I dissected the vocabulary. Am I a black girl washed with whiteness? Am I a white girl hiding her blackness? What am I? It was the first time that I had to think about that consciously, and I resented that it took some insignificant boy in high school to throw me into my personal race consciousness.

"What did he say exactly?" I asked for clarification.

"I don't mean to offend you. I just thought you should know" George replied with a smirk. "When I asked Carl if he would date you, he said 'No' because you are whitewashed." Carl was born in Trinidad but raised in Canada. George was from Trinidad too, and he was practically my family. His grandmother lived down the street from my grandmother in Trinidad, and his aunt happened to be my babysitter in Canada, which is how we realized that our families were old friends. Mere coincidence.

"Well what does he mean by that?"

"It's a term we use to refer to a black girl who is trying to be white." He said it so frankly that I was dumbstruck by his ease in discussing my racial subjectivity.

"So am I whitewashed?" I was completely ignorant to what I represented to my peers. I wondered about how many other students had the same thoughts. Danielle? No, she was my friend. She never made me feel like I was different from her. I understood her West Indian culture, for it was my own, and we discussed many interesting things for high school students: music, clothes, school. What about Donna? She was nice, but I understood that she was one of the few black students who did talk to me. Were most of my friends white? I went through the list … yes. Being the deconstructionist that I have always been, I began to analyse why I had mainly white friends. And it occurred to me, I had the same friends from elementary school. It was not my fault that I grew up in a predominantly white school. There was one other black kid in my grade then.

So from that moment on I really made a concerted effort to appear blacker. My daily concerns involved embodying the cultural representations of what blackness meant to me. I became a product of small town Canadiana trying to represent a subculture I learned about from media misrepresentations. My understanding of blackness was baggier pants and men's shirts. I started to pay more attention to the black students in my high school. However, rather than relating to them like a person, like I was doing before, I began to study them like specimens, like people different from me. I viewed them like a singular group of whom I peripherally belonged, but as a group that would never accept me by virtue of the fact of my upbringing and perhaps my skin colour: I was *whitewashed*.

Later on, in my adult years, I read much of mixed-race theory, and I suppose I had, in that conversation with George in my adolescence, what can be called an "epiphanic moment." An "epiphanic moment" is described as when a mixed-race subject realizes her blackness. However, for me, I realized my whiteness in that moment because with brown skin in Canada, you are always aware of your blackness or, in my case, my black daddy who no one else had while I was young growing up in my hometown. However, I was never made aware of my whiteness until that moment. I never saw my mother as different because it was my father who stood out. And through the race consciousness I received at home, I understood how I was and always would be linked to a certain ontology, an ancestry, a root, that was deeper and more connected to my core than the other side of my family, my mother's side. It is not that I don't love and admire my mother's family; I do. I was raised with them. I saw them frequently since they lived in Canada. But my father's family represented an imaginary and originary place that I thought of only in stories from my father and grandmother.

That epiphanic moment led to a passion to research and critique mixed-race subjectivity in Canada as a personal journey to discover who I was. That journey guided me to write a Master's thesis on mixed-race subjectivity in Canadian literature. Through that work, I came to realize that my experience of being mixed race in Canada is troubled by the fact that racial categories are too distinct. Growing up in the predominantly white suburbs of Toronto, I have experienced the ambivalence and alienation of not fitting in my hometown. The consequences of the racializing gaze, the feelings of in-betweenness and fragmentation, as well as being able to cross borders, have affected the way I have developed a sense of my mixed-race subjectivity. For these personal reasons, my thesis became a mixed-race response to what it means to be mixed-race in Canada. As a result, that work put things into perspective for me.

But before this self-realization, I had my upbringing, my past, and it was haunted by an accusation that I was whitewashed. And that moment marks a significant shift in my perspective of myself and where I fit into Canadian society (and the world). From that juncture, I had two choices. One was either to go with the way I always was, whatever that was, and the second was to enter into a strange territory that began to actively reject a part of my cultural heritage, in this case, my Trinidadian (black) heritage. That was what I found myself doing. This happened because, as an "authentically" Trinidadian student in my high school dictated it, I did not have claim to that ancestry because of the so-called white strand in my DNA. I also began to perform a commodified blackness that would be conveyed to all the Carls in my school that I was somehow authentically black even though my skin or behaviour seemed to say otherwise.

I was thrown into a sort of catch-22. I could perform a kind of blackness informed through perhaps cultural stereotypes and adolescent media-influenced subcultures, or I could be white. As far as I'm concerned, I didn't seem to have a choice since, in this dilemma, pretending blackness was contrived, whereas whiteness was posited as natural. I suppose I could have a third choice—to not care—but as an impressionable, overly sensitive adolescent, who already experienced feelings of ambivalence and in-betweenness as a consequence of being mixed race, it was impossible not to be affected by this seeming powerful, culturally secure young man who rejected the idea that I could ever belong to anything he represented.

So, at that juncture, I somehow started to reject the blackness that I was told I could never represent and, in my search for certainty, I had better odds at being white than black, I believed. Of course, I didn't know at that time, as is common in the lives of mixed-race people, that I could be both simultaneously. This self-awareness took years and many difficult experiences to recognize.

Now at 31 years old, a mother and married to another mixed-race person, I feel comfortable in who I am. It took discovering myself through graduate school, moving to an African country to simply remove myself from the Canadian racial framework for a while and develop my subjectivity as I saw fit … for me. Now, I embrace by mixedness, my multiple heritages, my experiences, and what I have to offer. I like that I am fluid, indefinable, and diverse, for that is what truly reflects the Canadian reality today. But the Canadian system has yet to catch up to that reality. When I see the large amount of mixed kids around today, I just smile to myself, secretly happy that we are "taking over the world" and hope that they grow up with less confusion than I did. And when I listen to CBC radio reports that mixed-race coupling is on the rise, and it is an important issue to talk about, I laugh to myself. For they are only now getting it.

Actually, I am Black

G RESHAM, OREGON 1992. MY brown mother, my pink father, and their two olive, kinky-haired children pull up in our dented blue Oldsmobile to the only breakfast place in town. John Deer sits across the street renting tractors to the tree nurseries that threaten to take over more old growth forest. I'm six and only familiar with dirty loud city buses, the big street cleaning machine that I named Happy and Giuseppe's bakery that sold our daily Italian bread. My father, the inherently flamboyant Italian man, steps out of the car in hot pink short shorts and hair longer than my mother's. My mother follows with my little brother in her arms. I trail behind, managing my way up the creaky steps. The diner by day, tavern by night is packed with overalls and flannel, confederate flags and beehive hairstyles. A few people have BB guns sitting up next to their chairs. Noticing my mom's uncertain face, my dad assures us it's going to be okay. The waitress seats us in the back and I can feel stares from all directions. The man with the BB gun sitting behind us is talking loudly about how he's "Damn sick and tired of these dirty Mexicans and coloureds coming to his country."

We decide it's time to leave.

At twelve my only friend at school tells me I have Black people's hair. "What's Black people hair?" I ask. "You know, like horse hair." So I sit under my mom's flat iron, burning the Africa out until it's dry and brittle but still never like Kate Moss or the white girls at school. This is when I learned that beautiful was white. I was too light to be black, too dark to be white, but something didn't fit. Something made me just not right. I still look too … something. Not light enough to be white. Not Black enough to be Black. Not anything enough to be seen.

It took a long time for me to realize I was Black. My mother was Black but I wasn't. My grandmother was always my mom's mom, not grandma; my mother's family, but not mine. In 1967, my mother peered out the window to see tanks with white men in them shooting out the grocery store. At eight she could tell you the sound a tank made as it searched Newark's streets for Black people, who were tired of living in 14-storey buildings with no heat. Crimson droplets stained the streets. Tear gas saturated the air. The National Guard came in, shot at young children, bombed their stores, forced people to leave their homes and the media called Black people savages.

Inside her home, her father, my grandfather, was an abusive alcoholic. After returning from World War II, he brought the war home only finding comfort in Jim Beam.   One evening she hit him over the head with a wine glass when he was about to beat her sister for walking in the house with snow on her boots.

She decided to leave.

When I was five, my family gathered everything and moved to Oregon. My mother left by marrying a white man, and took her blond children somewhere that had to be better than where she came from. I don't blame her for leaving. I would have too. But she also left the Gumbo that only my grandmother knew how to make. She left the wisdom that is whispered amongst the elders at kitchen tables. The laughter that's loud and unapologetic, bellowing over candied yams, collard greens and black-eyed peas as hips swayed to the rhythms of Smokey Robinson and the Temptations. I never grew up playing hopscotch. Couldn't tell you how to jump rope. Didn't know that Black girls come in all shades and all kinds of hair just like me. I didn't know that I came from somewhere.

And yet, she raised me on Anansi's Web and Mufaro's Beautiful Daughters. At seven years old I knew the real name of Egypt was Kemet translated into Black Land.   Somehow I don't believe culture can live in only one person. What is "Blackness" without black people? Africa was an abstract concept, one that was not reflected in my skin colour.

I remember sitting in the back seat as we drove home and telling her black people looked like monkeys. I was eight. At 14 I dyed my hair blond and went tanning. Bought all my clothes from Gap and Old Navy and said "dude" too often. White was beautiful and normal. I was drawn to anything that would make me pass as normal even if it was painful. His name was Jason. He was tall, white and handsome. His pants sagged; he always had a naked lady on his shirt, smashed beer bottles over his head and would pick me up in his father's vintage blue sports car. He was a dreamboat. Jason, myself and his three friends, would sit around his apartment drinking Coors Light with the football game blaring in the background. A half empty pack of Marlboro cigarettes sat lying on the burned wood table and Dr. Dre was on the radio rapping about dirty bitches. I can't say I felt comfortable. A part of me knew I was better than this situation but I was so desperate for validation and acceptance that I stayed. On one of these nights, as I curled up to Jason's apathetic arms I heard him say he didn't like those nigger's on TV. "But I'm black" I said. "Come on, you know I'm not talking about you!" He staggered as he picked up another Coors, "You're different, you're probably whiter than me."

I decided it was time to leave.

Around 19 years old I decided Black was beautiful. I finally met my Black family in the mist of my punk hippy years, with my leather jacket, hairy armpits and vegan diet. There was nothing at that Thanksgiving feast that I could eat, yet I sat happily munching on my tofu dog wrapped in whole wheat bread. My uncle Will sat on an old La-Z-Boy watching the football game with the other men in my family. I told him about school and the film I was making about the Newark riots.

"How's your dad?" He asked, "Your mom and him, they still together?"

"No, they split up four years ago." I said, sad that he missed so much of my life.

"What about that farm? Does your mom still live there? Hmm ... It's a good thing she took y'all out there instead of staying here."

"Yeah, but I didn't get to know you or any of my family."

"It's a good thing though, cuz you livin' out there made you able to go to college. And make movies about this stuff."

"This stuff" meant his reality, like his house that had its windows blown out by the fire across the street. He said the insurance money that the owners would collect was worth more than the building. Or that he only had one chair in his entire house, a lawn chair. Or his daughter, my cousin, who had two kids at 16 and that Administration for Children Services is threatening to take away. I could make movies about the violence instead of live it.

Although I was welcomed I could feel their hesitancy in relating to me. I didn't get the "Hey girl! How you doin'?" I got the "Hi, How are you? What do you do? Where are you from?" It was like a part of me, blood that I came from, a shared absent grandmother, wanted to know who I was. They were really asking what are you? You don't look like us, talk like us, act like us. But I didn't care. I had read about this in books and had seen it in Spike Lee movies. Family. Community. Africa had names and faces that looked like my own. Maybe here I could re-root myself and uncover my ancestry.

I shed the leather jacket, thick Carhartts and saturated myself in African print fabric, red, black and greed buttons and carried around the *Autobiography of Assata Shakur*, certain only she knew my struggle. I laughed at the white girl with dreads and hung my head when my people gave me the same dirty looks when I wore my African print dress. In search of community I sought women of colour spaces. Spaces that were about healing, and transformation with sage burning and India Arie playing in the background about how she is a queen. I entered knowing my hair hung like long twisted vines and not the curly kinks I wish I had. I had tried locking my hair and it refused only knotting in the back where my mother's hair grew. But maybe they would see the hues of my grandmother's skin in my own. Or maybe they could tell by the way I walked that my hips knew the beats of the drum. Maybe I would be seen as I am.

A beautiful woman with long locks, draped in white and yellow fabric, greeted my darker friend, Shalea, and me at the door. She gave Shalea a hug and said,

"Welcome sister. The other sisters are inside. Take off your shoes and make yourself comfortable." To me she said "Hello. You know this is a *woman of colour* healing space. I'm sorry where are you from?"

Actually, I come from the same place you came from. My grandfather came on that same ship yours did five generations before me. And no, my family was not house slaves. We worked in the fields, our hands bled; our backs were sore and our skin cracked. We resisted. Escaped North. Bore children. 11 children and left our husbands when they beat us. I am an African and I've earned it.

"I know." I said, "I'm African-American and Italian." Confused she said, "Oh, okay." Her raised eyebrows revealed the questions burning inside her. "But you don't look like what black is supposed to look like, talk like black is supposed to talk like, or act like black is supposed to act like. How do you exist? What are you?"

I still don't know. I just know I exist somewhere between the margins where my mother and my father mixed. Where they blurred and confused the lines of race. Maybe almost like an experiment. Will a light-skinned mixed girl know she is black living on a farm in a white community separated from her people? Something still drew me out, made me reshape my community, learn my herstory, and re-affirm, "No actually, I am Black."

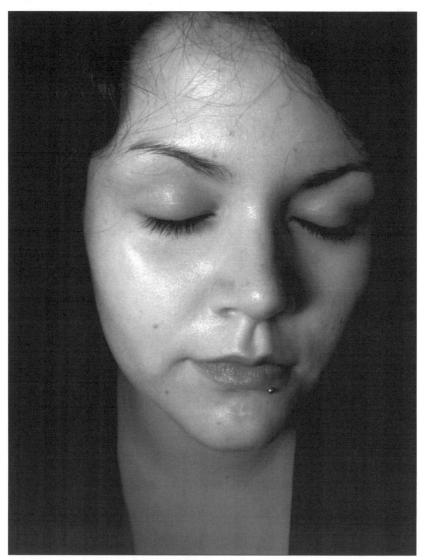

"Self." Photo: Lisa Walker.

SONYA LITTLEJOHN

Grey (A Bi-Racial Poem)

"If you try to walk a path in the middle of the road, there is a greater chance of being hit by traffic from both directions."
(Advice from my father)

I am the confluence
Of their two rivers

I am the creation of disparate characters
Entwined

I have bred the same,
reproducing infinity

in the grey line.

I am loved by many,
Understood by few,
Overstood
Though I am without engagement,
Without marriage
to any single philosophy.

I am the place no one wants to be.
Maybe I am everywhere we wish
they were?
The unspoken and often misplaced
border of human intellect and emotion.

A raging river of mud
and the settling of sediment.

I am the dark that
light sees
the light that
dark sees.
Perspective.

I am my own truth

MICA VALDEZ

Nubia's Dream

First, cross the tumultuous river
near the damn
Careful of the pull
of the rough waters

Seek refuge
            from the cold reptilian world

Open   lush forest
sanctuary

        Look there,   you will find me
half Indian   half snake

JONINA KIRTON

both sides

the drumbeat of my heart knows the truth
when you speak of those white folks — it is one
when they speak of you "indians" — it is one

the drumbeat of my heart opens and closes
with each blow, that look; you know
"you" don't belong here; you know

the drumbeat of my heart knows its place
despite its time in the white mother
never forgets its red father

the drumbeat of my heart knows this land
ancestors on both sides
of the ocean it belongs

white picket fences
school houses, churches inside
buffalo plains, sweet grass
smell of smoke, leather
medicine wheels inside

the drumbeat of my hear knows this land
ancestors on both sides
of the ocean it belongs …

Mulatto Nation

W HITE GRAMMA AND BLACK Gramma share the space. This is the spirit world; things happen slowly. White Gramma represents earth and downward direction. Black Gramma represents air and upward direction.

Black Gramma slowly pans her line of sight across the audience.
White Gramma makes quick looks from side-to-side, arms crossed and feet apart.
Black Gramma steps in a half moon shape, posing with a bevel and hand on hip.
White Gramma does a two-step shift, three times.
Black Gramma closes her eyes to inhale, and moves her hand away to blow smoke.
White Gramma holds her hand close to her face to drag deeply, and coughs.
Black Gramma rests her hands on her chest and thigh and throws her head up to laugh.
White Gramma puts her hand to her head as she laughs.
Black Gramma sits on a chair and strokes her granddaughter's hair.
Black Gramma becomes Maizey, resting her head on her grandmother's lap.
Maizey becomes Black Gramma, and continues stroking hair.

White Gramma: Have you seen her daughter?
Black Gramma: Beautiful.
White Gramma: Must get it from you.

0.

Narrator: The near future has arrived. We are living in a truly blended society, where mocha-lattes outnumber regular coffees, and grandparents eagerly welcome their little bundles of interracial love, wondering if they'll look more like Paula Abdul or Nicole Richie. Hair troubles are a thing of the past—white, black, and brown mamas alike buy "Mixed Chicks Leave-In Conditioner" for their curly-locked offspring, whose wild curls blow freely in the winds of change. Life seems to be easier for those carrying the genes of both the slave and the colonizer. But as in photography, some of us wish for the days when everything was black and white…

1.

A young woman (Maizey) is waking up and going through a morning ritual. Maizey stretches, prays aloud (improvised), and checks text messages.

A crowd is heard chanting outside the window: "Make mulattoes, not war!" Maizey goes to her window and looks out. Maizey decides to go.

Maizey puts on an indie rock outfit like skinny jeans, a beater, and a rock-n-roll belt. She considers her outfit, and adds a hip-hop/bling accessory, like a Rocawear pendant or slouchy cap. Takes the accessory off. Puts it back on.

Maizey *(to audience):* What do you wear to a Miscegenation Pride Parade?

(after a pause) Off-white.

2.

Maizey is on the sidewalk, observing a large, spirited march. She is transformed into a young woman in a t-shirt that says "Mulattos Unite! Take Back the White" (Cassie). Cassie wears a two-way radio with an ear bud.

Cassie: Good morning! Welcome to Mullatopia! Join the march!

Maizey hesitates before stepping onto the street to walk with Cassie.

I'm Cassie. What's your name?
Maizey. That's a pretty name. Where's it from?
Oh.
Nice day for it; we really lucked out… And I'm not just talking genetically! Kidding aside, I'm really happy with the turnout. And no five-O anywhere. I know it's not a black people thing, but, you know, we thought they'd send *half* the force.
So, what's your mix?
You just came to support?
Mmm… Not mulatto: just "light skinned." Hey, sis, there's no such thing as light-skinned blacks, only self-hating mulattos. Just because the original mixture happened a long time ago, and probably through rape, doesn't mean it didn't

happen. You're clinging to your so-called racial purity, mamacita. Let it go. Here. Read this.

Cassie pulls out a pamphlet and extends it towards Maizey.. But really, Maizey...

Awkward pause.

    What's your mix? Come on. What are the ingredients in your cocktail? Hm? What kind of tropical fruit got blended up in your smoothie with that vanilla ice cream? "Black." Are you? Be proud, Maizey. It's okay to be what you really are. Mixed is the new white. You should think about joining the Mulatto   N a -tion. No pressure. Take my card.

    Not mulatto? You're telling me there's no white in you?

    Zero percent.

    No eighths.

    You say you're black, but I think you're not. And I know how to spot a muli. For starters, you have all the characteristics of a standard mulatto: loose afro; Germanic features, with a touch of the continent; beautiful caramel skin; extreme defensiveness... Whoa. Settle. Down, It's okay; enormous chip on the shoulder is also part of our phenotype.

Cassie snaps her head to observe another group of marchers.

    Whoa! Did you hear that??

Cassie turns to watch the scene unfold on the street and immediately begins using her radio; Maizey also turns to watch.

    "Ho-latto"? Who says that?!

    (into her radio) Yeah, we've got a bit of a situation at the rear of the march; one of the Jewlattos starting is making slurs towards a group of what appear to be Gelattos... I need *all* the marshals at the back ASAP. Okay. Roger that. Over.

Cassie disengages her ear bud and turns back to Maizey.

    Yes, unfortunately, there are factions. It's not encouraged, but it happens. Usually to do with money, or what part of the city people live in; some superficial, divisive crap.

    Sorry?

    No, you're absolutely right, class divisions aren't ... superficial... I certainly didn't mean to imply that. What I said ... what I meant ... did I say that? Hey,

I'd love to talk more, but I've really got to take care of the situation here. We can't have any violence going down at our first public event. There's already enough rumours flying. Like the whole body odour thing.

It was great to meet you; please be in touch. There's a Velvet Revolver cover band playing tonight at the after party, if you're into that sort of thing.

Yeah. Slash is mixed. Bye.

Cassie walks purposefully towards the scene of the altercation, speaking into her radio.

Maizey: Cassie Washington, Senior Vice President of Recruitment. Mulatto Nation. "Mulatto Nation"! Who *are* these people?

Maizey studies her pamphlet. A young man, D, approaches Maizey without her noticing, and gently takes hold of her wrist.

D: Maizey?

Maizey: Yes?

D: I'm with the MNA: Mulatto Nation Authority, the organization's oversight and foresight body. We've recently received a report of several mixed-race indiscretions on your part. There's no need to be afraid, but this is a serious matter. I'm going to have to ask you to come back to our headquarters with me so we can talk.

Maizey: What did I do?

D: What did you do? I have the evidence right here.

D pulls put a mini recorder and presses play. We hear a garbled recording of Maizey from minutes earlier: "I'm actually not mulatto, I'm just light skinned…"

Maizey: I'm not going.

D: Maizey, I hope you'll cooperate. But I am prepared to use force if I need to. By any means necessary. Little known fact: Malcolm X was a mulatto. I have the scooter parked around the corner. Follow me, and you'll be home by suppertime. Resist, and I'll bring in backup.

Maizey: So, not only do I have to get interrogated by a miscegenation enforcement goon, I also have to risk being seen, on a motor scooter, riding behind your yellow ass?

D: So much self-hate. That doesn't hurt me, Maizey, but it hurts you. Don't think of this as an interrogation. Think of it as a therapeutic lesson in self-knowledge. Okay? Are you here alone?

Maizey: Yeah … left to the wolves!

D: A more apt analogy would be "Left to the coyotes.". A coyote is half dog, half wolf.

D tries to place his hand on Maizey's arm as he leads her away through the crowd.

Maizey: Whatever. Don't touch me.

3.

D leads Maizey into a holding room. It is lit with fluorescent lighting. There is a long table with plastic chairs, and a kitchenette on one wall. Along another wall is a couch with a pillow and comforter. A long-handled mirror, a clipboard, and a pencil sit on the table. D pulls a chair for Maizey and takes a seat. D makes notes as he talks to Maizey.

D: Okay, Maizey, complete the following sentence—I call myself black because:
Maizey: Because … I look exactly like my mother, and no one ever questioned her race.
D: Got it. Next: I started feeling the need to stand out when:
Maizey: What do you mean, "stand out"?
D: Okay, how about this—I want to be different because:
Maizey: Different than what? That doesn't make any sense.
D: Well, for example, do you think that being "black" will get you a better job?

Maizey gives D an icy, mean stare.

D: Fine, we'll move on. These are hard questions. Date of birth?
Maizey: Why?
D: So we can look up your astrological chart, if necessary. Sometimes it's relevant.
Maizey: Aries.
D: I see. Can you tap dance?
Maizey: No!
D: Who was Sammy Davis Jr.?
Maizey: Uh, well, he played … he was in…
D: Next. Preferred musical genre…
Maizey: You care why?! Stop asking me questions! What's in this for you??
D: Shh, shh. It's just an intake survey, it's designed…
Maizey: Intake?
D: Calm down, Maizey. What's in it for us is a more in-depth understanding of the tastes and values of young mulattoes in this geographical region. We need to know

how to reach you. But if you don't want to finish the survey now, that's fine.

As he speaks, D pokes his pencil into Maizey's hair and lets go of it. He then picks it up and scribbles on his clipboard.

Maizey: What are you doing?
D: Pencil test. We have to do it to everyone.

Horrible silence.

D: I'm sorry.

Maizey shrugs.

D: Now, our research department in conducting a study in economics, to determine some … things. These next questions are part of the investigation. One. How much do you tip?

Maizey looks quizzical.

D: Tip. Waiters, bartenders, estheticians, cabbies… Let me re-phrase. If the bill for dinner is twenty dollars, would you tip a) ninety cents, b) a dollar fifty, or c) a dollar ninety-five?
Maizey: Those are all bad tips.
D: Yes, but, well, it's widely acknowledged that black people are… lousy tippers. So, if the average black person tips three fifths of what the average white person tips … does the average mulatto then tip half of the black tip; half of the white tip; or, split the difference between the black tip and the white tip? Can you see…
   Fine. Let's just … talk.

Horrible silence. Finally, D blurts out what he has been dying to say.

D: Why do you insist on calling yourself black?!
Maizey: I am black. I was raised in a black family. Till high school, all of my friends, were black. I don't usually have to defend who I am. Can I go?
D: Maizey, you've mentioned a lot of other people—black people—who are part of your life. But you haven't actually spoken about yourself yet. Why can't a mulatto woman like you—a mulatta, if you'll allow me the liberty—be surrounded by black friends and family, the way you are? Hm?
Maizey: "Mulatto" sounds so cheap! It's a cop-out—black people trying to get away from being black. Why do I have to hide? I'm proud.

D: And aren't you proud of your white heritage—your father?

Maizey: No! Capitalism … slavery … genocide … sitcoms … that's your fucking white history.

D: Hm…

D furiously takes notes.

Maizey: Are you going to use that in your next pamphlet?

D: No. It sounds like something an angry white person would say. The way you identify yourself doesn't help black people, Maizey. You need to take a long look in the mirror. You need to stare that poor, self-hating white girl inside of you dead in the eye—and tell her that you love her.

D lifts the handled mirror off of the table and holds it up to Maizey's face. She pushes the mirror away.

Maizey: I see a black girl.

D: I see a mixed girl.

Maizey: This is insane. And, racist. Every black person who isn't the appropriate shade has to call themselves "mixed"? There'd be no "black" people left.

D: Interesting, isn't it? Maizey, who benefits if self-identified "black" people make up a larger percentage of the census population?

Maizey: Black people. Obviously.

D: Really?

Maizey: Yes, white people don't know how to deal with us. We're their worst nightmare.

D: And you think they know how to deal with *us*? If you ask me, white people seem to have figured out exactly how to deal with black people. That didn't take them long. It's when things get more complicated that they get confused. It's not black and white, Maizey. And as hard as you try to see things that way, you can't make it so. You can't polarize … zebrify your world.

Maizey: *Zebras* are the problem! You know kids used to call me that after they saw my parents together? Fuck! Can I go now?

D: *(looks at Maizey seriously, a look of appraisal)* Are you still black?

Maizey *(looks at her hand):* Yeah.

D: You're going to need to convince me of your identity before I can release you. I'm going to leave you alone for a while to think. Make yourself comfortable—this isn't supposed to be torture. And here's the mirror. In case you need it.

D places the mirror on the table and moves to the door.

Maizey: When are you coming back?

D: That depends. I've got a lot to do. We picked up a few today based on remarks that were overheard at the march. I'll be making my rounds.

D exits.

4.

Several hours have passed. Maizey is exhausted. She is humming a tune trying to keep her spirits up. Maizey sings the song now, loudly.

Maizey's singing brings ancestor and descendent spirits out, as if they are coming out to hear her sing. Maizey stops as she notices the spirits of her grandmothers entering the space.

Black Gramma slowly pans her line of sight across the audience.
White Gramma makes quick looks from side-to-side, arms crossed and feet apart.
Black Gramma steps in a half moon shape, posing with a bevel and hand on hip.
White Gramma does a two-step shift, three times.
Black Gramma closes her eyes to inhale, and moves her hand away to blow smoke.
White Gramma holds her hand close to her face to drag deeply, and coughs.
Black Gramma rests her hands on her chest and thigh and throws her head up to laugh.
White Gramma puts her hand to her head as she laughs.
Black Gramma sits on a chair and strokes her granddaughter's hair.
Black Gramma becomes Maizey, resting her head on her grandmother's lap.
Maizey becomes Black Gramma, and continues stroking hair.

Black Gramma: *(tersely)* Well. We're all here. Yes, I'm happy to see you. Of course. It's just that … it's not often that we're in the same room with all of them.

Black Gramma indicates the space where a crowd of spirits has gathered behind White Gramma.

Black Gramma: Can't you tell who they are?

Shhh! You've always been awfully flighty, haven't you? Use your head, dear. They're your father's people. Your white family.

Oh yes, I'm sure. His parents. His grandparents. His grandparent's parents…

Well. We're equal in numbers. But that's where the similarities end.

It's no use, they won't speak so don't bother. We had a bit of a falling out, and, well, now the cat seems to have gotten everyone's tongue. Except mine. Well. That was never an option.

We'd go somewhere else if we could.
Can't. Don't be silly.

Black Gramma gestures to the downstage area, where many smaller spirits are crowded.

They need us to stay.
Ohhhh … she's cute. But this hair is a mess!

Black Gramma begins to comb the little girl spirit's hair.

You're allowed to touch. They're not dead; these babies haven't lived yet. They're yours, or rather they will be.
Yes, your children. And their children, and theirs, and … I've been minding them, for the time being. You know—"high class gal, stay home and mind the baby…" Remember?
Pardon me, dear? They're beautiful children.
Oh, You were a lovely child, too, Maizey. These ones have started to grow on me … and what's this Mulatto Nation?
Well, I don't have anywhere to be. You?
Oh? Trying to tell you you're not black?

Gramma pauses to consider.

Good. They're right. You're sort of beige.

Black Gramma sits on a chair and strokes her granddaughter's hair.
Black Gramma becomes Maizey, resting her head on her grandmother's lap.
Maizey becomes Black Gramma, and continues stroking hair.

Black Gramma: *(after a pause)* Have you seen her daughter?
White Gramma: Beautiful.
Black Gramma: Must get it from you.

5.

D enters. Maizey is sitting on the couch. Has she been crying?.

D: Maizey? Is everything okay? What's wrong?
Maizey: Um…
D: Did you look in the mirror?

Maizey: No…no…

D begins to leave again.

Maizey: Look, I'm sorry. You know … I wasn't always like this.
D: Like what?
Maizey: Like, so angry. Uh, do you ever think about…having kids?
D: Yeah, for sure. You?
Maizey: Yeah. Um, a lot. Can I tell you something?
D: Okay.
Maizey: Okay. I want to have kids, some day, but … do I deserve one? I don't know. I almost had one, sort of. I think I didn't care about her enough to bring her to life.

After my first ultrasound, I started thinking about what the baby was going to be. As in, maybe white. When they asked me if I wanted to know if it was a boy or a girl, I practically screamed "NO!" Like I was fighting off a rapist. Yeah. I was very assertive. I did want to know the sex, but I couldn't get the image out of my head of this smug little white baby—girl, boy, whatever—floating in *my* uterus, just chilling, wearing like plaid and listening to Broken Social Scene—capital W-h-i-t-e, right? And I ask it, "Where did you get that ipod, baby?" but it doesn't hear me—it's rockin' out.

I really didn't want to know anything more about that baby; it would have made it real. I would have started picturing her as a white five-year-old, and then as a white high school kid, imagining how she would have worn her hair. I was thinking bangs.

They didn't ask: "Do you want to know what race your baby is going to be?". They don't. I guess they figure you've got that figured out. And, I had to face it: chances were, the baby was going to be pretty much … white. That really fucking freaked me out. I mean, that's gotta mess with you to see that come out of you. This is not something I want to think about. It made me feel obscenely white. How could it be? Me. A black girl, a Black Woman, was gonna give birth to a baby with no trace of my race? A person of non-colour? … No!

I lost the baby about two weeks later. Two weeks ago, now. It felt like murder.
D: I'm sorry…
Maizey: It's okay. I was sad, but I haven't dwelled on it. So, after that, I decided that I would never, never let that happen again. No. Now, the buck stops here. I don't want to dilute myself. No offense, but I'm not here to mullatify the next generation. It's predictable. Besides I can't imagine how we would be close. I'd just look at her, like some weird thing from nature, wondering if she was computer-engineered. Like how I'd look at a transparent frog, or flowers that look like they can't be real.

I look nothing like my father, but I know his genes must be hiding out in me, just poised for a comeback. The "damage" that my mother did to their family line—I would have practically restored it.

But not. Because my kid wouldn't have been a run-of-the mill curly-hair white child. No. Her eyes would have glowed with the hazel of my Carib great grandparents; every single black freckle would have held the strength and pride of my ancestry. And Poland in her hair. Generations of nations, legacies lurking inside of this little off-white person. And if I'd have loved her—loved her properly—she could have loved herself, and maybe… Oh, I wish she'd been born.

D: Maizey?

Maizey: Hey.

D: Are you still black?

Maizey: I don't know.

D: You're free to go.

Colour Lesson II

the academic in me is waiting
for the time when contours dissolve
and bodies really don't matter
The artist in me
when flesh becomes abstraction
becomes song
not something that falls
between the cracks
or stalls, tries to pass
but when flesh becomes dance
a body that can turn to itself and say
what will it be? what will we be
and then everything
crumbling
into legitimate freedom

KIMBERLY DREE HUDSON

racially queer femme

IT MIGHT BE TRUE that I have never written about myself before. That it's always been a fictionalized version of who I've thought myself to be, written for purposes of both acceptance and opposition. To declare and undeclare, create space and remove myself from space and certainty. It is both white supremacist culture and the heteropatriarchy—representations of language that have become useful to me lately—that have taught me that I am here to be consumed; that I cannot claim full ownership of my mind and body, that others dictate the rules by which I live and exist, and that to be healthy I ought to allow for the unregulated and free access to and abuse and misuse of my most intimate parts. This is my attempt to undo, to heal, and recreate.

Today, I turn to the mapping of my own "intellectual" politics, positioning, and pathways. When tending toward radical separatist ideals—that healing and repair can only happen in the absence of the oppressor, in a place safe from domination—I insert myself into my own paradigm of resistance and resilience I realize that I land, by result of my own hand and mind, in a place of impossibility. I've had to conclude, for many intents and purposes, I existed somewhere I didn't want to and couldn't be. How did I end up imagining in a way that doesn't allow me to exist? This has made me reflect on where my accountability lay and to whom and to what exactly I am related and responsible. Where the existence of ME and US could be possible. Where the imaginings made sense. I am only beginning to better understand the racially queer self: cultural and contextual meanings attached to history and politics that seep through every facet of the lived experience, and the structural and social environment: what it means to interpret and be interpreted, to read and to be read, to express and be an expression.

As I walk through the world, I am both a queer femme of colour and a straight white woman. In my history I am both the colonizer and the colonized … more exactly, both the object and subject of colonization. This contradiction carries me. Digging deeper into our contradictions brings us closer to, and more intertwined with, our humanity. Being "queer" today is racialized, gendered, sexualized, classed, ableized, aged, nativized, and languaged. It is always already intersected.

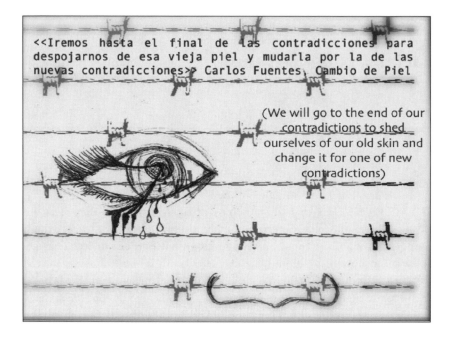

<<Iremos hasta el final de las contradicciones para despojarnos de esa vieja piel y mudarla por la de las nuevas contradicciones>> Carlos Fuentes, Cambio de Piel

(We will go to the end of our contradictions to shed ourselves of our old skin and change it for one of new contradictions)

For me, intersectionality is not only about which identity category becomes how important when/where/why or under which conditions. It is about designing a geometry of wholeness. I pass, intersectionally. I pass as a White woman and a woman of Colour. I pass as a straight woman and as a queer woman. My femme-ness intersects with womanhood and both with the institution of gender. So by way of distribution and permutation, I essentially find myself exploded. I experience intersectional passing as a type of action that manifests, or takes form, as a place, as passages. At the margins of a marginalized identity, I've learned how to negotiate the material and spiritual resources that exist between these identities and spaces. It's a praxis between how we understand our identities and how identity places us in a certain place. It's being aware of who I am, aware of how other people see me, and also aware of how I can manipulate those spaces in between: how other people see me and even how I see myself.

I am keenly aware that in queer spaces I am more often "of Colour" and in White spaces I'm more often straight. How do I know? I get spoken In, I get spoken Out, through microinvalidations and microinsults. But then again, there's not such a big difference between White spaces and straight spaces: they're both bullies. All of my relationships have been interracial and all of them have been queer—especially the ones with men. Apparently, I do what they call "passive" passing. I rarely correct people in their assumptions and perceptions about me. Sometimes I lie. Sometimes not correcting is the lying. Sometimes it's not. Just as the idea of borderlands can be interrogated at the physical border, in the idea of community, in the home, and in the body, mind, consciousness, and spirit, so can intersectional passages. Intersectional passages are where we look both our parents in the face and see ourselves in both and in neither at the same time. Intersectional passages are where our histories of colonization grow up in Seattle, and the wars that tore our country apart made for the opportunities for our grandparents to meet, and our parents to meet. And to create us. Intersectional passages are where we are waiting for an invitation while anticipating a request to leave. Intersectional passages are where in the choice of two groups, we demand a third: the neither/nor, both/and spaces that don't exist. Where it's not about being bisexual, biracial, or straddling classes, identifying our generation or our history of immigration. It's where all those things happen at the same time, and we constantly negotiate our privilege, our power, our oppression and our differences through the eyes of others that look at us in a different way than we look to them. When I consider what it means to be me, a racially queer femme, I realize that I not only need to understand what my existence means in the world, but also and maybe more importantly, what the world means to my existence.

I have too often been challenged with the question: What are you? Throughout my entire life, the only constant to that answer has been the changing ways I have been able to respond to it. I have realized the importance of place, politics, and history in not only understanding who we are, but in how and who other people understand us to be. We are not only individuals with personal experience, contradictions and strife, we are also symbols of contradiction, struggle, place and time: where and when we are necessarily impacts the meaning of who we are. The conditions that have made the possibility of my existence unlikely are not happy ones—centuries of global slave trade, neoliberal globalization, colonization, anti-miscegenation laws, and racism, to name a few. In my family's history, it was unlikely that my grandparents would immigrate to the United States during anti-imperial struggle in their country, and while being hotel cooks in Las Vegas they would raise a child, my mother. It was unlikely that my mother would be afforded a college education by the parents of the American children who she nannied, during which time she would meet my father, and in turn raise her own family.

The products of colonization and globalization have come to bear different faces, meanings, and continue to live through different forms of resistance, preservation, and celebration, a contradiction that permeates ancestry, culture and location, social and structural divides. It carries a unique yet universal story of cultural imperialism, occupation, and migration, embodied through the artifacts of multiracial and queer resilience and vibrancy. My story is just one of an infinite number of unlikelihoods and contradictions. Intersectional passings and passages happen in a place, and happen in a real place—not a completely subjective, fluid, "neither here nor there in the middle of nowhere" space. It happens in places and at borders that are patrolled, that are monitored, that take a count as you enter and leave, reporting back to the very structures that push us through these borders. Intersectional passages are where our queer identity meets our heterosexual partners, and our multiraciality meets our whiteness. Where growing up poor meets getting a graduate degree and having a stable income. Intersectional places hide what could never and should never be hidden. It's hiding what has never been hidden from us. It's learning to love and to be healthy in ways that aren't allowed to us. This healing takes place often at the exclusion of some others, rarely at the exclusion of all, never at the exclusion of the whole Self.

Intersectional passages are knowing that as people of Colour we enact our whiteness through our intimate relationships with men, while we yearn for the love of women. Intersectional passages are where we look for approval from our white parents while they'll never understand what it means to be a little brown girl. Intersectional passages come from a torn family where histories don't allow us to know ourselves, that make us fear who we love and who we're intimate with, whether it be our families, our partners, our friends, our communities, or our struggle. These places emerge from a place of yearning for love. Intersectional passages are just that: places of love and liberation.

RUHA BENJAMIN

mypeople

mypeople
(re)cover
they cover with chadors
silken spun with intricate design
and original flow
subtly
let you know
their originality.

mypeople
(re)cover

they cover with
kente headwraps
smuggled 'neath ships
to southern shores
that couldn't washaway
how they dye-n-tie
their originality.

mypeople
prostrate
and they
innovate
which means
when i fall to myknees
and pray
i become a creator
metaphysical entrepreneur
sewing mystrength

weaving mydestiny.

mypeople
are Most Wanted
pulled over by the PD
frisked by airport security
damn!
they can't go anywhere
without being
Wanted.

mypeople
just don't know
they're related
long nosed villagers
in yazd, iran
stocky brown folk
in a west african town
mypeople
don't know they're related
in me.

from different regions
of mypsyche
they commune
one day soon
i'll introduce them
salaam | amen | allah'u'abha | ashe

we'll crack (open-)up
watching ced the entertainer
and maz jobrani on split screen
we'll freestyle to a beshkan beat
or chant southern spirituals in farsi.

one day soon
i'll invite all mypeople
to a huge reunion
and serve
bbq tofu and tadik
gorbe sabzi with collard greens

wash things down
with some sugar cubes
and sweet tea.

mypeople...
have a lot
of catching up
to do.

JENNIFER ADESE

My Life in Pieces

I STRUGGLED TO FIND a format that would do justice to both my voice and to the anthology at hand. I wasn't sure—should I write a poem? Should I write a fictitious story? Or should I write a personal narrative of my experiences growing up as a "mixed-race" woman? I find it quite fitting that as a mixed person I should struggle "to choose." Choosing, I think, has defined my and many other "mixed" persons lives. From the day which we become cognizant (or for some of us are made painfully aware) of our difference from the majority of those around us we are thrust into a world characterized by the act of choosing. In my experience this choosing always had a companion riding side-saddle called "defending"—the act of defending the choices that we are forced to make. It's somewhat contradictory, that as we are forced to choose, so too are we expected to defend the choices that we do make. Here's a bit of my story.

I born in British Columbia and raised in Ontario, raised by my mother in her hometown, who although adopted and with unknown origins was for all intents and purposes classed as, and considers herself to be a Caucasian (white) woman. She has two children from a previous marriage, a daughter and a son, who like her bear sandy-blond hair, flawless fair skin, heights of NBA-like proportions, and lanky builds. Like three ivory pillars they towered over me with my ever-changing light-to-dark brown hair, light-to-golden skin, and stocky build. I was proud of my brown legs and as my mom would say my "brown berry nose." I've been told that I take after my father more times than I can recall. I never knew my father, have never been able to eye him up and down, and have never been able to search his face like I have my mother's for the nuances of my own.

My father has always been a mystery to me. Committing suicide just a couple of years after my birth, I can rattle off a list of things I know about him. In photographs his hair appears to change from light-to-dark brown, straight to curly, his skin from light-to-golden brown, and his physique somewhat stocky in the ways I've been told of my own. He was born in Alberta and met my mom in North Vancouver at a party in the building they both lived in. He left home at 18 to join the navy and upon his return worked on the railway. An entrepreneur of sorts, he was always trying to find ways through woodworking and other crafts to lift himself out of the poverty he'd been born into. Anyone who met him adored him—he was quick-witted and enjoyed pulling pranks on his close friends. He would lovingly hoist me high on his shoulders for walks to the local corner store to buy penny candies.

He also had a penchant for "Native things," like the beautifully-stitched hide and beaded wallet that reads "Inuvik, NWT 1977" (in which he carried a school picture of his Other daughter, my raven-haired half-sister), and a flower-patterned, beaded fringe jacket. As early as I can recall my mom told me that by way of my dad's family I was "part-Cree." I didn't know what this meant and she had little information beyond the simple point of fact that she'd overheard during family gatherings when we still lived out West. Somewhere inside of me though, I knew that these beaded things, things I'd never seen on any of my white friends' fathers, signalled part of my father's "difference."

Without anyone explicitly telling me so I came to associate the "darkness," the dark hair, eyes, and occasional brown skins that I saw in the faded photographs of my father, sister, grandmother and great-grandparents—with "being Native" and with being "different." I knew as much, that something was "not quite right," or as I've mused over the years "not quite white," about the family members I came only to know through black and white and Polaroid photographs. Before I had the language of "race" I came to understand that the "light people" dominated the world around me, in my school, my community, and on television, and that the "dark people" like those in our photo albums, were fewer and further between. I searched the faces of classmates and teachers for traits like those I saw in the photos and present in my grandma's face during her all too infrequent visits from "out West." The light people usually lived in nice houses, drove nice cars, and took vacations with their families. As we drove by detached houses that unlike mine weren't attached to anyone else's, I wondered what it would be like to be them, to live in those fancy houses with their perfectly trimmed hedges and twinkling Christmas lights. I wondered what it would be like to be a member of a light family. Since the people in the nice houses were only light people, I internalized from a very young age that having both light and dark meant that I would never end up living in a Christmas house. Further, from what I'd seen light families lived together while my own mixed family, light and dark, seemed (to my six-year-old brain) to fall apart.

I desperately searched my own face, looking back and forth between the light people in front of me and the darker people in our family photographs in an attempt to understand why I didn't look like one, or the Other. The only wave of comfort I felt pass over a deep and growing sea of uncertainty came in the form of a photo of my two sisters standing together, one six-foot-three and blond, the other five-foot-three and black-haired, a photo taken shortly before my dad passed away and calling out to me my two, seemingly oppositional sides. I imagined myself standing in between them, not the tallest yet not the shortest, not the darkest yet not the lightest. It is here, in between these two poles, that I have spent my life.

As I reached high school confusion over my identity increased. Throughout my childhood I had been told that when my father died he simply "fell asleep," never to awaken. I spent many terrified nights sneaking into my mother's room long after she slept, placing my tiny hands beneath her nose, hoping to catch her breath and reassure myself that she had not and would not leave me that night. Then, one night shortly before my high school career began my mom sat me down to tell me that while my dad did fall asleep and had not awoken, it was not by some fluke or random occurrence that he did not. My dad had, methodologically, planned and executed his own death. When I started high school a few weeks later under extreme duress I met with the school nurse who referred me to the school's counselor for help in coping with the pain and the knowledge of my father's horrific death. Within a few minutes of speaking with her, the counselor asked if I was "Native," to which I replied "Yeah, part-Cree." In what seems now like such a distant memory, I recall she made immediate arrangements for me to join what was called "Native Circle" which would allow Indigenous students to leave our regular classes to participate once a week in sessions aimed at fostering a sense of connection and pride in our various Indigenous heritages.

"Being mixed," I realized, would continue to be a very isolating lived reality despite the presence of fellow students of varied European-Indigenous and African-Indigenous mixtures. While the group and the various people I connected with through the group helped me understand more about what it meant to be "part-Native" I still struggled to reconcile all the "parts" of myself. The hairs on my arms stood up when I was faced with the cautionary acceptance of FBIs (full-blood Indians), whose skepticism towards my increasingly pale skin was fuelled by an understandable fear that my mixed-ness might also mean that I was being "mixed in the mind" and behave predominantly in Eurocentric, disrespectful or appropriative ways of thinking and ways of being. Yet there were many Native people who embraced me as I was, and attempted to instill within me a sense of pride and respect for the remarkable pasts, presents, and futures of Native peoples.

It was, and continues to be the "white" people, the non-Indigenous, that pose the greatest challenge to my attempts at feeling at home in my own skin. By my late teenage years and early twenties my skin no longer browned under the sun, retaining instead an unearthly white glow, and so there was no questioning for white peoples that I was "one of theirs." When I opened my mouth and proudly declared my "mixed-ness" I was told by more than one "well-meaning white person" that they "couldn't tell I was Native" and that I could "pass for white." Funny, I thought, hadn't I already been doing so? By virtue of my physical inability to meet their criteria for Native appearance and their assumptions of my white-ness, hadn't I already passed for white? I came to understand then, that I had been given tacit acceptance based on my appearance, however in order to pass *fully*, I needed to stop opening my mouth and *telling* about my Native-ness. Not looking it and not speaking it would apparently allow for my total transgression into whiteness and signal the death of my Indian-ness. By that time I had seen enough of both worlds and of the far too frequent presumptions of superiority and arrogance of white ways of being, and the outright racist hatred by many whites toward Indigenous peoples, to know that as confusing as it was, I'd *rather* stay as the title of a Renisa Mawani essay suggests, somewhere "in between and out of place."

Eventually though, I did grow weary from living in "parts." I grew tired of living in a world that told me to choose one, or the Other. I felt like I was being ripped into pieces by Census forms, scholarship applications, surveys, and by white people whose world commanded my allegiance to a particular side. Sometimes I felt my skin burn as I glared down upon these forms or spoke to people demanding that my allegiance be identified. My head and my heart pounded, engorged with red blood and threatening to break about my white skin as I struggled to reconcile the fragmented and conflicting pieces of my self. I never talked about the aching in my heart or the desperate longing for peace that I sought. There were many times when I looked at the photo of my two sisters, wanting to be fully absorbed into one of their worlds.

I refused in those moments, and continue to refuse, to give in to centuries old attempts at assimilation by white peoples that say by virtue of a portion their blood running through my veins I *must* renounce any claims to my Indigeneity, that I must "pick a side" or that I must reduce the significance of my Indigeneity only to the superficial—I can wear beaded earrings, hairpieces, and moccasins, but I cannot and should not align myself with "their" politics. I reject the implication that I must make the "logical choice" and *choose* to immerse myself totally in whiteness. When people ask how I can ignore my whiteness I unwaveringly point out that I don't need to ignore it, that I *live* in whiteness—I live in a white world structured in and around the ethos and ethics of whiteness—economically, politically, and in many cases socially. When I apply for a job or apply to live in a particular apartment or neighbourhood and my whiteness goes "unchecked," when I am invisible to the white power structure as it absorbs me seamlessly into its framework—willingly or not—that's me living my whiteness. I do not need any more exposure to the world of my non-Native family and ancestors—nearly every one of my day-to-day activities centers around them and the world that they built for themselves. As an urban "mixed-blood" I am at no loss for a connection to the markers of whiteness. It is the "Other" side, my Indigeneity, that daily I fight tooth and nail to hold on to.

In recent years I have begun to tap into the historical linkage which some of my family has had to a Métis identity, Métis being the term for peoples of French and (predominantly) Cree ancestry. As I meet more and more Métis peoples who have been raised within a Métis sense of identity and share with me that they are not "part this" or "part that," that they come from Métis families and are 100 percent Métis, I wonder what my life may have been like had I not grown up thinking of myself in "parts." What would it have been like, instead of thinking of myself in fragments, if I saw myself as whole? After years of learning about and considering myself in relation to, I've come to embrace Métis identity for myself but I am haunted by the memories of my life, of my soul, in pieces. As I look toward having children with my partner, a man of the Isoko tribe of Nigeria, I wonder if I can save them this pain. If I explain to them as I understand my relationship with my partner, that we are in an "intertribal" relationship and will be an intertribal family, I wonder what will become of my children? When I ask my partner he bristles as I remind him of his "difference" and he says I've put him, as the one with the darker skin, at the centre of the "problem of mixedness." I don't know how to tell him that while it *is* about him, it's *not*—that white-skinned as the day is long, I'm still confused about how *I'm* still neither *here* nor *there*. I don't know how to tell him that so much of it is about *me* and my skin, my blood, my in-betweenness, that after all these years still has me so damned confused.

WORKS CITED

Mawani, Renisa. "In Between and Out of Place: Mixed-Race Identity, Liquor, and the Law in British Columbia, 1850-1913." *Race, Space, and the Law: Unmapping a White Settler Society.* Ed. Sherene H. Razack. Toronto: Between the Lines, 2002. 47-69.

ANGELA DOSALMAS

Burden of Proof

From Colón-eyes to Kaleidoscope

In the womb
the first shot rang out
Gunned down
by a mythical norm intended to impede
Amniotic tears I did not cry
As a shotgun shower fractured my identities
Severing the ties that kept me whole
One

Biological warfare saturating my soul,
Pathogens embedded in my brain,
Weaponized messages of mass destruction
Coursing through fetal veins
Summarized in every heartbeat:
Worth–less   Use–less   Un–wanted
Waste

My heart
a child's first teacher
struck down
Before … it … had … a … chance … to … breathe.
Bioterror.
Black baby: white host
Miscegenation.
Literally composed of the sin of my father —
involuntary absorption of light
Race
Choose one.
One.
Just one.

Only one.
Mom or dad?
Girls or boys?
Colonizer or colonized?
Choose.
One.
Now!

Oppositional birth
ammunition scraps wedged cerebrally
vital organs with gaping holes
Fragmented
Because divided
I fall.
born a sin.
born illegal.
Forever viewed with Colón-eyes.
Colliding.
Scoping.

Much of my youth was spent colliding against barbed-wire borders that created wounds akin to Gloria Anzaldúa's "una herida abierta where the Third World grates against the first and bleeds" (25). And, I have bled. Too much blood. My mixed-race experience began with profound pain. So much so that I rarely revisit it. When people have asked me if I could go back in time, what would I change, my answer is always the same. I would not go back. Period.

My experience is coloured not only by the social and political context of the time, but also by intra-familial racism. A remnant of the late '60s, post-Civil Rights era, I was conceived in the wake of the U.S. Supreme Court decision declaring anti-miscegenation laws unconstitutional, in the wake of my mom's parents' white flight, and in the wake of my mother's ejection from her parents' house for loving my black father. I was the result of such turmoil and my physical presence a constant reminder of it.

The first few years of my life were marked by extreme sadness. My mom cried nearly everyday. Most often after phone calls. Most likely from my dad who was in high school for the first year of my life and stuck dealing with his own mother's undiagnosed mental illness or from her sisters who hounded her about "how much she hurt mom and dad" for falling in love with my father. I was not something my mom chose; I just sort of landed in her lap at the worst of all possible times. One day in particular, when I was two and a half, I remember just sitting quietly and watching her, helplessly. And, I sat there, watching. And, I began to absorb her pain. I could feel it in my bones. I could feel her shame. I could feel her fear and I could feel her eyes, pleading. And, in that moment, I remember only that I never wanted anyone, least of all my mother, to feel that way again. And, I made a vow. That I would be good. I would be so good that people would see that Black is good. And, my mom's parents would love her. And, they would love me.

In that moment, unknowingly, I had accepted the torch of the "burden of proof." Generally aligned with the Latin dictum *semper necessitas probandi incumbit ei qui agit* (the necessity of proof always lies with the person who lays charges) in law, in life the burden of proof is placed upon those arguing against popular beliefs. Some how, my mom came to believe that if she could prove that black folks (with me as conduit) were just like everyone else then she would be atoned for her supposed transgressions. (Nevermind that these thoughts themselves are racist.) And, in that moment, I surrendered to it. With one split second decision, I ceased to be me and became whatever everyone else wanted me to be. I came to see myself and the rest of the world through Colón-eyes.[1]

By the time I was three, my Colón-eyes made it impossible for me to look in a mirror. The ways people treated me and looked at me, illustrated to me that I was not yet good enough. Though I could read, cook, clean, and take care of myself, it was not enough. My mother would remark to me years later that by the time I was three she felt as though I was "all grown up." And, so I was, in a strange dysfunctional sort of way. I sometimes wonder if it was not just a matter of "being good," but was also a way to not need anyone. If I could do everything myself and not need anyone, then I couldn't hurt like my mom did when she needed her parents and they were not there.

One weekend, I remember that my grandmother, in her infinite, bipolar wisdom, decided to stand me in front of the mirror and force me to repeat, "I'm Black and I'm proud," over and over again until I could say it without crying (James Brown's song had just played moments before). I stood in front of the mirror for hours that day, crying and crying for as long as I had tears. I couldn't do it. I could not say the words. I am ashamed to even write this now. There was such inner turmoil. In my young mind, Blackness kept me from being loved by my mom's parents and siblings, it kept my mom from being loved by her parents, Blackness got me spit on, Blackness made people look at me disapprovingly and Blackness made people exclude me from friendships and games. In those moments, from where I stood, Blackness was the sole source of all the pain I saw in the world and I was the one who brought it into my mom's family and I was far from proud of that. At this time in my life Blackness was a rootless, concrete entity that simply existed in the world and that could be crumpled up and thrown away or reversed with goodness. I did not understand that it was an intangible idea created by the imagination of White people and linked to certain physical characteristics. And, if I felt all this about Blackness, what did that say about what I feel for my dad?

For his family? I cried myself to sleep many nights throughout my childhood after this. I cried for my dad. I cried, "I'm sorry." And, I clung to him because I did not want him to feel the pain of Blackness either.

Sesame Street generation
"One of these things
 is not like the others.
One of these things
doesn't belong"

"What are you?"
Not "who," but "what."
An object that requires a label.
Initial collegial achievements
A quest for mere humanization
At times a dire plea.
A search for dignity and belonging
And sometimes pure defiance.
A middle finger to the keepers of "can't," "shouldn't," "don't," and "impossible,"
And those who collude with silence.
Toeing a very fine line.
Mathematics a masculine realm
Defended by rape
No merits for brown or breasts,
Certainly not breasts with children attached.
Tug of war to hold my own.
Kaleiding.
Scoping.

While I loved Sesame Street as a kid, its song about things that aren't the same, not belonging, really got to me. It was the soundtrack in the movie that was my life. I lived in all White neighbourhoods and went to all White schools. I was always the only person of colour. One of these things don't belong … and, its you. After a while, I continued to be wounded and I still bled, but I no longer felt pain, I just saw red. Somehow, wounds began leading directly to anger. There were no more tears. This anger was responsible for most of my accomplishments, but I often wonder at what cost? Anger was the source of a dogged determination. Whatever someone said could not be done, I did, whether it was something I enjoyed or not. When they said boys are stronger than girls, I beat every boy in my school at arm wresting. When they said girls can't play football, I played. When they said white boys don't go out with black girls, I got myself a white boyfriend. When they said people like you don't do well in math, I got an advanced degree in statistics. I guess it was my way of saying "Fuck you," while still being good, but I spent so much of my young life proving other people wrong that I never truly lived. I began other silent rebellions as well. I would scratch out "Choose One" and write in "Choose all" when asked for my race. If Other was an option, I'd check it and fill in bi-racial: Black/White (though it was obvious to my young mind that Other was not a real category, but a limit to someone's imagination). Sometimes I'd scratch out the question altogether. I started coming up with names for myself to beat everyone else to the punch. When asked, "What are you?" I answered anything from mixed, to oreo, to zebra, to a human, to mutt. I called myself brown and I called myself grey (equal parts of black and white mixed together). One word that would send me over the edge though was mulatto. I despised that word (still do). I remember hearing my mom talking about someone using that horrible word, so I looked it up in my dictionary. It said something to the effect of: *the sterile offspring of a female horse and a male donkey; jackass.* Hell, no.

"You don't meet our qualifications."
Credit check not required,
Brown need not apply.
Homeless.
Baths in the rest stop sink by night,
Preschool teacher, grad student, TA by day.
Choices constantly questioned.
Inequity not even reckoned
Poverty deemed a one way street
Initiating at poor choice avenue.
But look over here on my other hand.
There is another middle finger.
Degree granted.
Kaleiding.
Scoping.

Back to grad school
TA evaluation:
"Needs to learn that appearance matters."
Now, as another student from the same class remarked,
"I would have thought she was talking about your clothes, but I was in the class and know that you dressed professionally everyday,"
So this woman is not referring to my clothes.
Does she honestly think that I, a queer woman of colour,

Do not know that appearance matters?
When I walk into a medical office and before I get to speak am told,
"We don't take medi-cal."
Do I really have the privilege of not knowing that appearance matters?
Would I waste time waxing my eye brows,
shaving my mustache and beard,
if people could appreciate me as I am?
I am well versed in the code.
"One of these things,
is not like the other.
One of these things
doesn't belong…"

And what of the presumption of ignorance?
That there is something I am lacking,
Something that I "need to learn."
It did not cross her mind for one second,
That I could possess the knowledge
And be actively resisting conformity,
Or better yet, that I actually know who I am
And take pride in this wisdom…in my difference.
It does not cross her mind that someone might actually value their difference.
Of course I know that appearance matters.
It matters most to racists, sexists, homophobes, ablists, classists…the border patrol.
Those who use my transgressions to define who they are
Which means *I* define *you*
So, be careful what you wish for because if I lose sight of me,
You lose you.

Kaleiding.
Scoping.

Race continued to affect my life in profound ways and once I went back to graduate school (in a field not dominated by dead white men like those I previously persued) I was able to recover from old wounds and think about identity in whole new ways. "Identity is about situatedness in motion: embodiment and spatiality. It is about a self that is constituted through and against other selves in contexts that serve to establish the relationship between the self and the other" (Rodriguez 5).

My mom's parents never did come to love me, at least not in the way I had hoped. Not in the same way they relished their other grandchildren. I suppose their life was too short (they were barely in their sixties). I remember the last time I cried as a child. It was when my grandmother, my mom's mother died. I was around ten and while the grownups were working out the details of the funeral I was banished to the outdoors. I immediately went into the garage and started looking through my grandmothers' things. In her dresser drawer, I found her wallet. I silently pulled out her driver's license and tucked it into my back pocket. I flipped through her pictures and was happy to come across one of my brother and I. But, my happiness was short-lived. The remaining 24 pictures in her billfold were of my three white cousins. I cannot express how much that reality hurt me that day. One out of twenty-five oddly, sums up really how much value I had in that family. But, somehow at some point, I was able to realize that they don't set my exchange rate. I came to terms with how other people saw me. I came to terms with being ambiguously ethnic and being constantly misidentified. People know I am not white, but place me anywhere from South Asia to South Africa to Mexico to Latin America to Egypt to the Caribbean to various islands. What I know is my truth. And, in my truth, my identity requires ambiguity and fluidity. It cannot be contained. It changes from one instance to the next. I can now look in the mirror and say, "I'm Black and I'm proud." I am also Multi-racial: Native/Black/White. I am also a same-gender loving sistah. I also have become adept at recognizing my Whiteness and associated privileges. I am a woman of colour raising beautiful, strong women of colour who teach me more about identity everyday. I like to think of myself as a kaleidoscope. The literal translation of which is "observer of beautiful forms," but which itself is also beautiful and fluid and constantly changing.

My spirit continues to grow
And I continue my flow,
A continual pattern of changing shapes.
Kaleidoscoping
Connecting the dots that stitch
My fractured identity whole.
4000 cookies.[2]
14 days.
Pay or leave.
No rest for the weary.
Community.
Brown, white,
Queer, non-queer,
Faculty, staff,
Grads, undergrads,

Entire departments.
Coming together.
To invest in me.
Power ... collectively.
Supporting one individual.
Me.
And I am still here,
With my kaleidoscope heart,
An "observer of beautiful forms"
Kaleiding and scoping.

Notes

[1] A reference to the in/famous colonizer of the West, Cristóbal Colón AKA Christopher Columbus.

[2] Refers to 4000 Cookies—Will Bake for a coupla letters separated by a period (Ph.D.)—a Facebook group I started in 2006 in attempt to raise $4000 to pay my school fees and keep from being dropped out of school.

WORKS CITED

Anzaldúa, G. *Borderlands/La Frontera: The New Mestizia.* 3rd ed. San Francisco, CA: Aunt Lute Books, 2007.

Rodriguez, J. M. *Queer Latinidad: Identity Practices, Discursive Spaces.* New York: New York University Press, 2003.

TOMIE HAHN

Recipe For Mixing

for Kimiko

EVERY FALL TENDRILS CREEP out of my mulch pile, out of my half-eaten debris, carted out religiously after the kitchen scrap bucket holds no more. What climbing plants could these be, wandering from the muck, reaching to warm sunlight?

To my delight, the first year these mystery plants bore fruit—pumpkins and carnival squash.

The second year, similar leaves and vines crawled along the rich soil, grasping at any stable staff to hoist skyward. The trailing green vines—now bearing pumpkins with speckles, squash, and ornamental gourds—seemed to intertwine sensuously. Caressing gently here. Climbing and interweaving almost competitively there. Prickly broad leaves forming shade, camouflaging fruit below.
What's to hide?

Year three, delicate tendrils return.
I watch eagerly as each vine sprawls out with whimsical, yet slow dance steps.
Later, after the performance, they recline longingly.
What secret appears under shaded leaves?
Radiant orange hybrids of gourds, squash, pumpkin—striped and speckled pumpkins, carnival squash with gourd knobs, and long gourds wearing stems befitting jack-o-lanterns. Three years of fertile cross-pollination, as one anther's pollen mingled with the other. None can simply pass for pumpkin, nor squash, nor gourd any longer. The labour from mulch bore no Latin-named offspring. Each vine offers unique offspring with no sense of belonging, except with those travelling along the vine.

GENA CHANG-CAMPBELL

Metamorphosis

There was nowhere to turn.
Running had long been impossible
And sanctuary existed only inside the self.

Faced with dichotomous understandings
Of my body, my presence
I sought refuge in the only place
That welcomed the mulata, the mestiza
The exotic product of uneven histories
And crashing worlds
That always unsettled, always disrupted
And therefore was silenced on glass shelves
On curio cabinets
In dusty tourist-shop windows
That proclaim an impossible dream as reality.

"Yours is the future," social scientists say
Insisting that the margins are coming to Centre.
But that's not enough
For the little girl searching for her place
In the *present*, the here and now.
She is told she possesses a unique beauty
A gift that marks her as "Special"
But the sneers from black girls stun her shy heart
And the endless questions from white girls
Make her feel like an unclassified species
One that does not include the aspirations
And desires, and anxieties
Of naïve youth.

As a woman she faced the world bravely
Accustomed by now to her teetering pedestal
She learned how to turn it all to her advantage.
The hyphen became her springboard
Her leverage for success
The eyes that followed her confident gait
No longer pierced fragile armour
Instead, she fed ravenously on their curiosity
Defied them to put her wordliness in a plastic box.
Men and women wanted her
Black and white
For very different reasons.
To one, she embodied the ideal partner

Café con leche
"Respectable" and "beautiful"
To another, a trendy trophy to impress the crowd
A hot-blooded commodity inciting unconscious lust
To sleep with her was to sleep with Self and Other
Subject and Object
Virgin and whore.
She is the B-girl, B-side
B-movie star
Claiming every contradiction contained
In each label
(None sticky enough to hold her together, or even in one place).
In no case could she ever truly be certain
That it was SHE, and not the token of her mixture
That was valued or loved
That found its way into poems songs and neo-ancient rituals.

Now when asked, "What are you?"
Her response is not static
It no longer involves endless punctuation
To qualify and quantify her existence to others.

For this is a *homecoming*
No more delays or denials
Ochun opens wide her arms
And Erzulie Freda's mirror reflects

Truth reconfigured
From the shards of non-being.
In one metamorphosis
La *Chingada* becomes
La *Virgen* becomes
Me.

SHANDRA SPEARS BOMBAY

The Land Knows

Can't see mixed-race when I look at it directly
It sneaks away when I turn to see it
It is in the eyes and mouths of others
When they tell me how it is for me

Most often these words come from
Those who sit in one racial place
Foolish enough to explain mixed-race
To a mixed-race person

Light-skinned Indians, they say
Native community problems
Blamed on Indians like me who are half-white
White Indians get all the jobs and ruin everything

Not Indian enough, they say
Arriving with expectations about me
Mixed-race Native people are white to them
Dismissed as fakers by newcomers to our land

Sheltered middle-class suburban girl, they say
You do not know how we really live
Violence and shame not my rez experience,
True, but not exactly safe and easy

Light-skin privilege, they say
Folks talking about racism
To Native folks who've seen their share
Silenced in struggle and invisible in our skins

It's just a phase, they say
Like your punk thing, or your music and acting
But I still like that music and that's my career
It's my life; Native identity is, too

You're beautiful, they say
But being raised to be white
I looked in the mirror and knew that I
Just wasn't getting it right

You're worthy of love, they say
Ugly, or awkward, or just not white,
Untouchable in a desperation that's
Almost impossible to voice

Don't limit yourself, they say
When I talk of a Native partner and children
You might be narrowing your choices
What they mean is choose a white guy

Ugly, unlovable, misunderstood
Ignored, erased and dismissed,
Sounds like not too much fun
But this is normal life for me

***

You don't look Native, they say, they all say
But the land knows me, the Elders see me
And when I stand with my family
We are who we are, who we have been in this
Place for thousands of years

I find words that will help me stay strong:

> gaawiin nizhaagwenimosii
> gaawiin gaye niwiiaanizhiitanzii

I am not discouraged and I will not give up

I hold on to teachings that give me strength

That give me a way to place myself
A single drawing in the sand
From an Elder who showed me how to choose

Identity is not a measure of blood quantum
It is nationhood, it is language, it is family
It is in my blood, my blood memory,
My DNA that responds to these shield rocks

But I am not Anishinaabe because some
Percentage of me matches up to some
Percentage on someone else's chart
I am Anishinaabe because that's who I am,
Who I was born to be

He said you have to choose
Stand in one place or the other
People say the mixing of races
Will make all the races one
He said the Creator gave us
These colours and directions
And we can choose which place to live

People of one racial identity tell me
I am both, and they're right
But I do not have to run back &
Forth with my little suitcase
I can choose one that is my home

***

Be white be white be white, they say
But I'm not good at being white
Being pushed to be white only made me a ruin
When they say I look white, I say
"you're half-right!"

And when one annoying white woman
Asked if I was part-white,
I felt satisfaction in the moment when replying,
"Yes, but I'm not ashamed of it"

***

I write from my homeland
Surrounded by the rocks and waters
The land knows
The land knows me

I walk around the rez sunburned
My face a red burned flag, announcing in case it's not clear
That I am half-white
Acting like a tourist, I am okay with this
I am not discouraged and I will not give up
The land knows

JOANNE ARNOTT

Land in Place

Mapping the Grandmother

It is not just white people who have
Métis grandmothers

It is not just black people who have
Métis grandmothers

It is not just yellow people who have
Métis grandmothers

It is not just red people who have
Métis grandmothers

From all the directions
the grandmothers come

intermingling languages, stories, blood
braiding a river of human

inter-relations
interlocutions

bawdy songs and body songs and
storied landscapes

Think of the old communities, and our ties
to the lands of our old stories

our minds returning our selves to mother tongues, to native tongues
re-wrapping our bodies around these new-old sounds

new-old syllables
new-old rhythms

new-old sensibilities & loves
redrawing the maps, and pulling

fresh wisdom from the old music
we formed around

inside the dancing vessels of
our mothers, vital daughters of

our
grandmothers

Still, so often it comes, the time returns
when we have to pack our things and move again

every single time we move, some thing
is left behind

a ladle
a small cup

an obstinate person
a story, cherished much

We have our desperate moments, too
when memory of all that is lost rises full

casting long shadows across the moon-tinted & starlit
landscape

and so the sorrow of the long good-bye
becomes a part of our heritage

the sorrow of the unspoken, unwilling partings
the sudden deaths, the midnight moves, the lost children

sighing in our dreams
the silent elder

look around you
look around you, now, and know this

There are Métis Grandmothers standing
all around you

some rising to cusp the horizon
some falling to blanket the earth

some growing between blades of grass
some winging across a concrete-shackled homeland, still

very much alive
still singing

"I am the leaf, you are the wind." Photos: Lisa Walker.

DEBRA THOMPSON

Language and the Ethics of Mixed-Race

BEYOND THE STEREOTYPE OF the tragic mulatto, the recent Obamafication of racial politics, and rhetoric of an inevitable multiracial future, the very concept of mixed-race simultaneously hides and enshrines both promising and problematic elements of our understandings of that four-letter word, RACE. How can we ethically (and ethnically) respond, when the question "*who do you think you are?*" is literal?

This is clearly a personal question. But there are important political elements at play here. In Canada in particular, we are fundamentally uncomfortable with the notion of race. Our democratic conceptions of equality, social justice and citizenship demand that the superficial morphological and physiological characteristics used to distinguish supposedly distinct races matter not; the self-evident truth of the liberal ideal is that all are created equal. Yet, both the historical legacy and contemporary politics of western societies—including Canada—are plagued by massive racial inequalities. We now face an unavoidable paradox: on the one hand, using the language of race runs contrary to dominant norms of liberal democracies; on the other, in order to challenge racism, we need to come to terms with the fact that race matters to all those whose skin colour or eye shape betray a status of privilege or subjugation.

At the same time, we are witnessing challenges to the very notion of racial classification by the mixed-race people who defy its logic. We, the straddlers, transgressors, fence-sitters, disruptors, undefined and perhaps indefinable, who challenge classificatory schemes while at the same time providing more of an imperative for racial categorization because of our contraventions. It is precisely because the concept of mixed-race operates at the points where categories collapse, classification schema crumble, and race is revealed as a social construct *that nonetheless carries ontological meaning* that it poses ethical challenges to our understandings of race itself.

Take the terminology of mixed-race as an example. The main epistemological issue with using the term "mixed-race" is that it implicitly and unavoidably reifies the concept of race itself. Mixed-race can refer to categories, ideas, individuals and groups that identify or are identified as the product of two or more distinct races. But there is a dangerous potential here: even self-identifying oneself as "mixed-race" does, to a certain extent, reify the notion of race as a biological truth.

Indeed, there is a history to be told of how the classification of mixed-race has at times challenged and at other times reified the hierarchical reliance on discrete racial categories. From nineteenth-century debates over the nature of racial difference through Social Darwinism and eugenics, for nearly three hundred years race was interpreted as and believed to be wholly biological in nature. Importantly, biology was considered to be determinative, though it was unclear how, exactly, somatic differences such as skin colour, body and eye shape, hair texture and skull size determined the nature of those so marked (Miles and Torres 27). F. James Davis argues that the idea of biological racialism consists of five key beliefs, all of which scientists now generally agree to be false: (1) some races are physically superior to others and can be ranked from strongest to weakest based on differences in longevity and rates of selected diseases; (2) some races are mentally superior to others and can be ranked from most to least intelligent; (3) race causes culture, to the extent that each race's distinct culture is genetically transmitted along with physical traits; (4) race determines temperamental dispositions and behaviours of individuals within racial groups; and (5) racial mixing lowers the biological quality of all (Davis 23-25).

Mixed-race is simultaneously fundamental to but problematic within this paradigm. In the age of scientific racism, the fertility and longevity of mixed-race progeny were critical for assessing the validity of doctrines of racial superiority and inferiority (Young). For example, the theory of polygenesis—the contention that different races were, in fact, different species—hinged on the question of whether or not mixed-race people were fertile (and hence, "Negroes" and whites could be traced to a common ancestry) or infertile (inconclusive proof that the two races were actually separate species and differential treatment could be justified on this basis). Robert Young points out that the dominant view of racial hybridity from 1850 to 1930 was the argument that races were either "proximate" or "distant" species—unions between proximate races, such as the Irish and English "races" would be fertile, while those between "distant" races, such as between blacks and whites, would be infertile and degenerate (18).

However, the many forms of racial transgressions—of which mixed-race is an important, but not the only, example—were also disruptive to the varied gendered and racial configurations that relied on the coherence of racial and colonial regimes: for example, concubinage, prostitution, rape, love and/or marriage across colour lines, "going native," non-white property and inheritance rights, notions of legitimacy and illegitimacy, and so on (Winant 115; see also McClintock; Stoler 1995, 2002; Hodes; Levine; Pascoe). Multiraciality itself was also highly problematic for unfettered beliefs in racial hierarchies, as the most important thing about races was the boundaries between them—those on top of the hierarchy had to work actively to maintain the boundaries that defined their superiority and keep others from surreptitiously advancing (Spickhard 15).

Most now acknowledge that race is a social construction—though it has clearly been constructed with incredible longevity and permeating power. Regardless of its constructed nature, race is commonly perceived as "lived experience"—while the concept itself may refer to an illusion, racial identities carry symbolic value and determine material advantage and limitations. To this end, mixed-race is also socially constructed and much like the social construction of race the label "mixed-race" has a tendency to essentialize the experiences of a particular group. Racial essentialism is the belief that there is a monolithic "Black Experience" or "Chicano Experience," what Angela Harris calls a "second voice" that "claims to speak for all." She argues that essentialism is both intellectually convenient and cognitively ingrained to a certain extent. Racial essentialism naturalizes race and racial differences, arguing that the "essences" inherent in the members of a given group are immobile, unchanging and fixed in both time and space. Essentialism ultimately reinscribes the precarious nature of biological racism; as cultural studies theorist Stuart Hall writes,

> the essentializing moment is weak because it naturalizes and dehistoricizes difference, mistaking what is historical and cultural for what is natural, biological and genetic...as always happens when we naturalize historical categories ... we fix that signifier outside of history, outside of change, outside of political intervention. (472)

This naturalization of race invents multiraciality as a mixed-ness to be measured against the standard of being either one race or another, suggesting that as a "mix" of two different racial groups, these racial group differences *exist* and are *real*.

Academic work on mixed-race has acknowledged the dangerous potential of the terminology of mixed-race. Ann Laura Stoler (2002), for example, calls the mixed-race offspring of Dutch colonialists and Indonesian natives the *métissage* and Jayne Ifekwunigwe uses *métis(se)* to describe multiracials, both of which are attempts to demonstrate the fluidity of hybridized racial identities and to resist essentialist frameworks. The vernacular designation of mixed-race is also contingent on location: in the United States and Canada, "mixed-race," "biracial," or "multiracial" are often used while "hybrid," "dual heritage," or "mixed parentage" are more likely to appear in the British context. The application of the label "mixed-race" is rarely applied to indigenous populations. In Canada, for example, mixed-race Aboriginal people are identified as "non-status" Indians in accordance with the *Indian Act*'s regulatory regime, originally designed to manage and control the indigenous population. There are also terms that refer to specific groups that identify as "mixed"; for example, the Coloureds in South Africa and the Métis of Canada are both groups that find their origins in white/non-white intermixture, but have since become recognized (racial) groups in their own rights.

However, in my work and my life, I use the term *mixed-race*. I'm going to give you three valid reasons why.

First, in Canada, we avoid all language of race, preferring instead to use the kitten-hugging terminology of "visible minorities" and "multiculturalism". On the one hand, this is a promising development. It means that Canada has recognized that there is no such thing as race and has attempted to move beyond the idea that humanity can be divided along such arbitrary colour lines. On the other hand, however, the dominance of multicultural rhetoric in Canada has functioned not only to avoid the language of race, but also to avoid issues of racism, racial discrimination, and racial inequalities, allowing Canadians to, as Constance Backhouse writes, maintain a stupefying innocence about the history and enormity of racial oppression in this country. The elusive search for a Canadian identity, resolved to a certain extent by the utopian myth of multiculturalism, is continually defined against American nationalism. The classic American melting pot versus Canadian mosaic metaphor, inaccurate though it may be, has instilled a logic that denies by comparison.

Canada is constructed as the original "promised land" sought by fugitive slaves along the Underground Railroad; contrasted always, of course, with the oppressive and discriminatory realities of American politics and society. However, a fact check is in order: slavery was not officially abolished in Upper and Lower Canada until it was abolished throughout the entire British Empire in 1833. The Underground Railroad, the subject of many a "heritage minute" commercial, was originally created to smuggle slaves *out* of Canada and into the free northern United States (Cooper 103). Further, upon arriving in Canada many ex-slaves found that discrimination and segregation were just as prevalent in Canada as in the U.S. and returned to America after the end of the Civil War. In contemporary times, racism is clearly a facet of Canadian society, whether it be indicated by under-representation of racial minorities in the House of Commons, the "entrance status" of highly educated and skilled new immigrants into the Canadian labour market, or the informal racial boundaries that permeate social life in Canada. For example, Reitz and Banerjee's recent research indicates that 35.9 percent of racial minorities in Canada report experiences of discrimination, and while most Canadians deny they are racist, they still maintain a "social distance" from minorities, preferring not to interact with members of other racial groups in social situations (Reitz and Banerjee 12). Yet, to admit that racism exists in Canada, as most refuse to do, would be to admit that the moral superiority Canada holds over the United States in terms of race relations is unfounded and misleading.

Multiculturalism deprives us of the ability to combat racial discrimination and drains the notion of race of its emancipatory power for collective memory and mobilization. So any chance I get, I talk about mixed-*race*.

The second reason for using the term mixed-race is because of recent debates about this very issue. In the 1990s, post-modernists, post-structuralists and critical race theorists reclaimed racial discourse. Race, they argued, is a social construction. And so it is. But then the neo-conservatives took their assertions and threw it back in their faces, arguing that race is a social construction, and therefore, it doesn't exist. And what doesn't exist, doesn't matter. Those on the right of the ideological spectrum believe that the civil rights movement was successful and racism no longer exists (in the U.S.), had only existed in the U.S. (in Canada) or is of little consequence (in Britain). If racial inequalities persist, the moral and cultural failings of individuals and groups are to blame, not structural, systemic circumstances of inequality. Based on liberal values of individualism, state non-intervention and market-based opportunity, state policies that engage in "race-thinking"—such as affirmative action—simply continue an unwarranted emphasis on the saliency of race. And thus the neo-conservatives used Dr. King's dream of colour-blindness to blind us all.

So I use the term *mixed-race* because *race matters* and it is time to reclaim the language once more.

The final reason is because of the variety of interests that can be mobilized in the name of mixed-race. My academic research is on racial categories in national censuses. When I first started reading about the push to get a "mixed-race" category on the U.S. census in the 1990s, I was absolutely on the side of the multiracial movement. I thought the census should recognize our identities, no matter how complicated they may be. Then I kept reading and realized that the multiracial activists were only concerned with recognition and didn't care that it potentially came at the expense of civil rights agendas. Being counted is crucial in the U.S.—and elsewhere. It is linked to money, political power, grassroots mobilization and even community cohesion. Having a separate mixed-race category threatened all that—and the hard-fought victories of the civil rights movement. The multiracial organizations that testified before Congress in the 1990s were mostly white mothers of multiracial children who did not want their children to have to choose one race over another. But they failed to recognize what else was at stake - though the census was once an instrument used to manage and control racial populations, it now has a political power that racial minorities can access and use to advance their claims. The entire U.S. civil rights regime rests on the idea of discrete racial categories. One group's recognition could lead to another's oppression. But the mixed-race activists didn't care—they went on to argue (unsuccessfully) for their cause and even struck alliances with Republicans, including Newt Gingrich, whose ten steps for better race relations in the U.S. included adding a multiracial category to the census and doing away with affirmative action.

So I use the term *mixed-race,* but do so cautiously, so no causes other than my own will be advanced with my words.

Identities are most often assigned. We have preconceived notions of what racial identities are, what they look like, who belongs in what box. But sometimes, we can choose our own identities. But with the promise of choice come the potential for consequence and the need for ethical consideration of our options and obligations.

Works Cited (and Further Reading)

Backhouse, Constance. *Colour-Coded: A Legal History of Racism in Canada: 1900-1950.* Toronto: University of Toronto Press, 1999.

Cooper, Afua. *The Hanging of Angelique: the Untold Story of Canadian Slavery and the Burning of Old Montreal.* Toronto: HarperCollins Publishers Ltd., 2006.

Davis, F. James. *Who is Black? One Nation's Definition.* University Park: Pennsylvania State University Press, 1991.

Hall, Stuart. "What is this 'Black' in Black Popular Culture?" *Stuart Hall: Critical Dialogues in Cultural Studies.* Eds. David Morley and Juan-Hsing Chen. London: Routledge, 1996. 465-475.

Harris, Angela. "Race and Essentialism in Feminist Legal Theory." *Critical Race Theory: The Cutting Edge.* Ed. R. Delgado. Philadelphia: Temple University Press, 2000. 261-274.

Hodes, Martha. *White Women, Black Men: Illicit Sex in the Nineteenth Century South.* New Haven: Yale University Press, 1997.

Ifekwunigwe, Jayne. "Diaspora's Daughters, Africa's Orphans? On Lineage, Authenticity and 'Mixed Race' Identity." *Black British Feminism: A Reader.* Ed. Heidi Safia Mirza. London: Routledge, 1997. 127-152.

Levine, Philippa. *Prostitution, Race and Politics: Policing Venereal Disease in the British Empire.* New York: Routledge, 2003.

McClintock, Anne. 1995. *Imperial Leather: Race, Gender, and Sexuality in the Colonial Contest.* New York: Routledge, 1995.

Miles, Robert and Rudy Torres. "Does 'Race' Matter? Transatlantic Perspectives on Racism after 'Race Relations'." *Re-Situating Identities: The Politics of Race, Ethnicity and Culture.* Eds. Vered Amit-Talia and Caroline Knowles. Peterborough: Broadview Press, 1996. 24-46.

Pascoe, Peggy. *What Comes Naturally: Miscegenation Law and the Making of Race in America.* Oxford: Oxford University Press, 2009.

Reitz, Jeffrey G. and Rupa Banerjee. "Racial Inequality, Social Cohesion and Policy Issues in Canada." *Belonging?: Diversity, Recognition, and Shared Citizenship in Canada.* Eds. K. Banting, T. Courchene, and F. L. Seidle. Montreal: Institute for Research on Public Policy, 2007. 489-546.

Spickhard, Paul R. "The Illogic of American Racial Categories." *Racially Mixed People in America*. Ed. Maria P. P. Root. Newbury Park, CA: Sage Publications, 1992. 12-23.

Stoler, Ann Laura. *Race and the Education of Desire: Foucault's History of Sexuality and the Colonial Order of Things*. Durham: Duke University Press, 1995.

Stoler, Ann Laura. *Carnal Knowledge and Imperial Power: Race and the Intimate in Colonial Rule*. Berkeley: University of California Press, 2002.

Winant, Howard. *The World is a Ghetto: Race and Democracy Since World War Two*. New York: Basic Books, 2001.

Young, Robert. *Colonial Desire: Hybridity in Theory, Culture and Race*. London and New York: Routledge, 1995.

JACKIE WANG

Hybrid Identity and a Writing of Presence

*Each of us is here now because in one way or another we share a commit-
ment to language and to the power of language, and to the reclaiming of
that language which has been made to work against us.*

—Audre Lorde

I WRITE. AND I write for the present. I *write myself* without writing to *know
myself*. I write myself in order to undo myself and to create myself in an
instant. I am always remaking myself in this way—through writing, through
a continuous creative process of identity-construction. Many of us are in this
anthology because we are invested in different writing projects in some way.
We may find ourselves here because we believe in the power of words, the
richness of our stories—yours and mine, shared. We move between worlds; we
move between tongues; we unsettle gender and racial narratives and fashion
our own. I write because I believe that it means something, because I have *a*
story, although it is not *the* story. The final pages are missing. As long as I am
alive, there is no conclusion.

It is the life of writing that interests me. The temporality of my writing revolves
around the now-moment, the formation and birth of particular *presences*. If to
write is to engage in a process of becoming, the goal does not have to center
around becoming *something*, but can remain a continual process of becoming.
For me, writing is a twofold process: on one hand, it allows me to critically
contextualize my racialized and gendered experience. On the other hand, it is a
way to make myself, to tease apart how I have been made and to make myself
anew. It is a way to *work through*, while eliminating the goal of arriving at some
finishing point.

THE POLITICS OF WRITING

*We are wedded in language, have our being in words. Language is also
a place of struggle. Dare I speak to oppressed and oppressor in the same*

voice? Dare I speak to you in a language that will move beyond the boundaries of domination—a language that will not bind you, fence you in, or hold you? Language is also a place of struggle. The oppressed struggle in language to recover ourselves, to reconcile, to to reunite, to renew. Our words are not without meaning, they are an action, a resistance.

—bell hooks

The *I* that I write from is grounded in life. It does not know the past as an objective thing. It partakes in the making of stories, is always partial, is always running ahead of itself. The question is: how do I speak the personal without lapsing into writing myself in a way that is closed-off, that engages only its *self* and concerns itself solely with reconstructing an accurate account of the past? There is always the danger of creating a fixed representation, a notion of "authenticity" whereby the weight of what I have to say is measured by the truthfulness of my account. Paradoxically, the pressure to be "authentic" can produce the opposite effect: only certain narratives that adhere to a pre-established representation may be considered to be "authentic," flattening the range of possible representations into a narrow set of familiar tropes and representations.

Where was my story? I saw it nowhere. The either/or mentality of the American cultural landscape of my upbringing left little room for my hybridized background. As a child I was confused. I didn't know what it meant to be mixed. I didn't know where I belonged. I looked into the mirror, alien to myself. Who was this person? I don't look like the people around me. My family doesn't fit. We must be from somewhere else. We have no place here.

In my adolescence I grew into my queer sexual identity. When a complex and unclear sexual identity was integrated into an already muddled racial identity, I was even more confounding to curious onlookers. What was I? Could I ever be a "positive" entity within the narrow discourses of insiders and outsiders if I was incapable of fitting neatly into any category? Could I learn to embrace my fractured identity and see it as a source of strength, not a watered-down weakness?

A LETTER FROM CHINA

In china i feel so strongly that i am a product of language and history and culture and all of these things outside me. in a cafe a guy mistakes me for straight up shanghaiese. i tell him i'm not shanghaiese, but my dad's jia xiang (native or home land) is hangzhou, only a couple hours from shanghai. then while talking to some old british guy who refers to me as an "ABC" (american-born chinese), he interrupts and says i'm not a REAL abc. yesterday, while driving through the yunnan countryside, i saw all these tombs tucked away in mountains and in fields. generations and generations of

families that have lived and farmed on these lands. they must feel so connected…to the people in their village, their family, to this place … but maybe that's stifling? the villages look like the village i visited when i was seventeen and didn't know how to speak hardly any chinese or know much at all about my family or this place but that's when i became ready to learn, maybe. i remembered a photograph next to the tomb with all the names of my dad's family members inscribed on it. in the picture, on one side of the tomb was my dad's extended family, farmers that still live on the same lands, and on the other side was my dad, me, and my dad's cousin, who left the village and became head surgeon at a big hospital in hangzhou. the placement in the photograph seemed significant, like it represented some fundamental divide between the uprooted and the rooted, those who left and got educated and learned a new way of living and those who stayed and remained rooted. we are blood but what does that mean? it was hard to feel a connection to the place or the people because i have no memory of ever belonging to it. My friend from hungary believes in the history of places, in the memory of language and families and he feels such a strong connection to it all. can it be erased, this memory that runs so deep? can it be forgotten or does it leave something on you somewhere? my dad has never known his jia xiang, home lands. he was born during the civil war to a military father and they moved to guilin and that's where he was born. after the KMT lost the war my dad's family retreated to taiwan with the other nationalist supporters. what if the communists had lost? what if my dad had never gotten a scholarship to go to grad school in the united states? at home my mom showed me a picture of her grandfather at a fruit stand in new york city, after immigrating from italy. the sign next to him read "5 cents" and she tells me they made enough money to support family members back in sicily. it's strange to think about, all this history and displacement. i don't know what it means but I know that people are malleable. and i don't feel bad or confused about "what i am supposed to be" or whatever identity issues anymore but when my hungarian friend asks me if i feel a connection to the english language, i can't help but think "no," and that every time i sit down to write i feel as if i am using someone else's language.

WRITING AND IDENTITY

> *To write is to become.*
> —Trinh T. Minh-ha

I am writing from the position of a queer biracial woman of colour, but what does that mean? It is through this unique positionality that I have come to understand the insufficiency of categories and prefabricated identities. So I write against the narratives of narrow identities. In regards to my personal experience as a gendered and racialized subject, one way this experience has informed by my perspective on writing is my interest in hybridization as an identity configuration *and* as a strategic approach to writing. Writing can be a way to engage in a practice of identity-making when dominant categories are too limited to speak to our complex experiences.

Not surprisingly, many people who feel like cultural, linguistic, racial, and gender exiles (in that they don't have any comfortable home because they don't fit neatly into categories), find a home in writing. Writing can be a way to make oneself. Hélène Cixous, in a poignant discussion on her relationship to Algeria (her country of origin), her relationship to France (her country of immigration), and her ethnically mixed family, describes how living between cultural and linguistic worlds prevented her from feeling completely comfortable in any single place. However, Cixous saw her status as an exile and perpetual outsider as a potential source of strength. In "The Writing, Always the Writing," she notes: "I did not have the need for a country, I had already entered the borderless country of texts." For Cixous, "The impossibility of an identification and any settling down" is her "historical luck." In another work, Cixous writes that, "I adopted an imaginary nationality which is literary nationality."

SELF-REPRESENTATIONS AND THE REMAKING OF RACIAL NARRATIVES IN ZINES

The dominant discourse on race and sexuality tends to either portray mixed-race and queer people negatively and stereotypically, or ignore them altogether. Many activists and scholars of multiracial issues have noted the remarkable absence of mixed-race people in historical discussions, which is a peculiar oversight given the large population of mixed people and their existence throughout America history. However, if racialist ideologies function to serve certain political agendas, than a discussion of multiraciality may undermine the very foundation of racialist ideologies, which assumes that racial categories are pure, discreet, and separable. It could be said that the invisibility of mixed-race people is a political issue in itself. Recently, visibility of queers and multiracial, and multiracial queers, has increased. Most of this increase in visibility has come about by queer multiracial people demanding visibility themselves, by writing personal narratives, demanding visibility at conferences, networking on the internet, and creating message boards and groups.

In 2007 I started publishing my zine, *Memoirs of a Queer Hapa*. One location where the articulation of a queer hapa identity ("hapa" meaning a mixed-race people of Asian decent) has emerged is in the zine community. Zines are self-made publications produced and distributed outside of mainstream culture. This style of publication allows direct-access to self-representations by mixed-race queers, who may be distorted, unrepresented, or misrepresented in other outlets. Pamphlets such as *Angry Black-White Girl, Quantify, Borderlands: Tales from Disputed Territories between Races and Cultures,* and *MXD: True Stories by Mixed Race Writers*, all contain narratives that articulate experiences that are multi-racial, queer, and multi-cultural. It is interesting to note that many mixed-race and queer writers are beginning to forge a community with each other regardless of their diverse mixed backgrounds (an essay by a half-black butch-identified person may appear next to an essay by a Chinese-Jewish queer feminist). Transracially adopted people are also often included in these compilations given the tremendous overlap in their experiences (which may include pressure to assimilate, challenges to ethnic authenticity, loss of language, and so forth). These zines provide a place where self-representations can be produced. It is possible that exclusion from both *dominant* and *minority* groups has led outsiders of varying backgrounds to construct a "home" on the hotly contested middle ground of racial and sexual identities.

In an excerpt from "The Mixed-Race Queer Girl Manifesto," Lauren Jade Martin, a writer and artist of Chinese-Jewish decent, reflects on how being biracial affects her sexual identity, and how being queer affects her racial identity. She writes:

> As a mixed-race queer girl, I am an example of one who can slide in and out of identities and communities, either by choice or through others. For me, queerness seems like a natural progression from bi/multiculturalism: growing up biracial, I am already familiar with shuttling back and forth between being an outsider and an insider, not fitting into others' convenient little categories, and intimidating people with

ambiguity. As a mixed-race individual, I am the physical result of an already-broken taboo. (13)

She notes that being both mixed-race and queer "decreases tunnel vision," which leads to a more heightened awareness of the interplay of multiple systems of oppression. She emphasizes how a single racial or sexual category does not sufficiently capture who she is, for they are too rigid and narrowly-defined. Martin also explores the frontiers of exclusion and inclusion based on slippery racial and sexual identifiers.

When I self-published my zine, it opened me up to a world of queer, mixed-race writers who were similarly frustrated with the narrow-narratives available, and the little xeroxed pamphlets we were exchanging seemed suddenly significant—a collective re-writing of history through the sharing of our complex and bewildering experiences.

THERE IS AN-OTHER STORY

You think of your friend, the humanity in the way she treats people, the way she was so open, didn't judge, and engaged you and your ideas without making you feel stupid. Something about people who look other people in the eyes and can see past the immediate things that others perceive. Clothing, skin, exteriors. And other signifiers that indicate something, setting us apart. Looking people in the eyes. Eyes tied together by invisible string moving between all these millions of people who are connected maybe only for seconds through their eyes. This acknowledgment of another, so powerful, and we close our eyes and look away because that's frightening and we feel weak, maybe aren't even ready to be seen like this; not as an object but as another person, another subject. Maybe we turn ourselves into objects, start to see ourselves that way because that's what we're trained to do. And we become a picture they handed us as they said, this is you. My vision wavers. I escape their grip, shed my sunglasses and am overwhelmed by the clarity; the suspicion and fear turning to love, I open my mouth. I'm usually so afraid, live in this silence but some days I overcome silence. I say it to myself everyday: I don't want anyone to ever be driven to silence because they're afraid. This silence is political. I do not trust their monopoly on voice, the way they demarcated who is worthy of speech, of words. And I can no longer internalize this feeling of unworthiness, of self-dehumanization. So much has been lost and they should feel like shit. Colonization, patriarchy, slavery and all other systems of dehumanization. So much has been lost, never even given a chance to live or grow.

Our lives are not flat. They are round like unopened buds, as alive as an ecstatic forest—sonorous and unending. They are songs not meant to be looked at, but listened to with a quiet and open mind. I hear something different every time.

Works Cited

Cixous, Hélène. "The Writing, Always the Writing." *Hatred of Capitalism: A Reader.* Eds. Chris Kraus and Sylvère Lotringer. Cambridge, MA: Semiotext(e), MIT Press, 2001.

hooks, bell. *Yearning: Race, Gender, and Cultural Politics.* Boston MA: South End Press, 1990.

Lorde, Audre. *Sister Outsider: Essays and Speeches.* Trumansburg, NY: Crossing Press, 1984.

Martin, Lauren Jade. "The Mixed-Race Queer Girl Manifesto." *Borderlands: Tales from Disputed Territories Between Races and Cultures.* Ed. Nia King. Denver, CO: Author, 2008.

Trinh, T. Minh-ha. *Woman, Native, Other : Writing Postcoloniality and Feminism.* Bloomington: Indiana University Press, 1989.

Wang, Jacqueline. *Memoirs of a Queer Hapa.* Sarasota, FL.: Author, 2007.

Contributor Notes

Sheila Addiscott lives on Vancouver Island, British Columbia. She is mixed race; her mother is Irish and her father is Mauritian. She is married and has six children aged five to fifteen. She is currently writing a children's novel.

Jennifer Adese is a proud Métis woman descended from the historic St. Albert Métis and a Ph.D. Candidate in the Department of English and Cultural Studies at McMaster University in Hamilton, Ontario.

Mica Lee Anders is an artist and arts educator based in the Twin Cities. She has shown her work in various venues in the Midwest, at Work Gallery in Ann Arbor, MI, and in Anji, China. She participated in an artist panel discussion at the Loving Decision Conference in Chicago.

Naomi Angel was born in Kochi, Japan and grew up in Vancouver, Canada. She is currently a doctoral candidate in the department of Media, Culture, and Communication at New York University.

Joanne Arnott is a Métis/mixed-blood writer and mother of six young people, all born at home. A frequent presenter and performer, Joanne is author of six books including *Steepy Mountain love poetry* (Kegedonce Press) and *Mother Time: Poems New and Selected* (Ronsdale Press). She is one of many Indigenous artist-activists working toward a greater wholesome for us all.

Tasha Beeds is of Cree and Caribbean ancestry. Culturally, she was raised within her mother's Cree and Cree-Métis family in Saskatchewan. Currently, she is in her first year of the Indigenous Studies Ph.D. Program at Trent University. She is also co-editing a book on *Indigenous Poetics* for Wilfrid Laurier Press. Poetry, for her, is a way of expressing her love of words and her respect for their power.

Ruha Benjamin is professor (of Sociology and African diaspora studies at Boston

University) by day and poet by night. She is a Baha'i, a child of the half-light, working to animate unity and justice in the minutiae of every day life and craft r/evolutionary discourses that intervene in planetary strife.

Christina Brobby was born and raised in England but has for a number of years called the city of Whitehorse in Yukon her home. She is presently working on a memoir of her experience finding her birth family, including her journey to Ghana to meet her African family.

Marijane Castillo graduated in Spring 2010 and received a B.A. in Chinese and a minor in Spanish from the University of California, Berkeley. In 2008 she published *Las hojas que caen sin fin*, Spanish poetry that explores the end of the Porfiriato in Mexico.

Robin M. Chandler has been a practicing artist-sociologist for more than 30 years and has exhibited in the U.S. and abroad. Chandler has been a guest artist-in-residence in France, South Africa, and the U.S. and her work is included in corporate and private collections in the U.S. and abroad. A widely published author, international lecturer, and development specialist in gender issues, her latest book, *Women, War, and Violence: Personal Perspectives and Global Activism* (2010), includes her book cover art entitled "Capoeira." Her work as a poet is available on the CD collection *Blackout: The Poetry Collection*. Her work can be viewed at <www.DiscoveredArtists.com>, on their vimeo <http://vimeo.com/10185971>, and on her website at <www.robin-chandler.com>.

Gena Chang-Campbell is an intensely hyphenated individual who thoroughly enjoys confounding expectations and dodging labels, racial and otherwise.

Jordan Clarke was born in 1984 in Toronto where she currently maintains a studio. In 2007, she received a BFA in Painting and Drawing from the Ontario College of Art and Design. Her studies included a year in Florence, Italy. <www.jordanclarke.ca>.

Farideh de Bosset was born in Tehran, Iran where poetry is part of everyday life and conversation. She has been writing poetry in Farsi, French and more recently in English. Her poetry has been published in *Canadian Woman Studies/les cahiers de la femme* and *Carousel*.

Adebe DeRango-Adem is a writer whose words travel between Toronto and New York. She recently completed her MA at York University, where she also served as Assistant Editor for the arts and literary journal, *Existere*. She is a former research fellow at the Applied Research Center, home of *ColourLines* magazine, and current Cultural Editor of Race-Talk.org, a blog dedicated to writing on race politics and pop culture. She won the Toronto Poetry Competition in 2005 to become Toronto's first Junior Poet Laureate, and is the author of *Ex Nihilo* (2010), her debut poetry collection that considers how art can respond to the annihilation of particular identities struggling to exist in an impossibly post-racial world. *Ex Nihilo* was longlisted for the Dylan Thomas Prize, the world's largest prize for writers under thirty.

Angela Dosalmas is a spoken-word artist, scholar, mother, warrior and an editor for *Spaces for Difference: An Interdisciplinary Journal*. She resides in the U.S. with her supportive wife and youngest warrior-daughter hopeful of a post-doc and/or academic position in the near future.

Anjali Enjeti-Sydow lives in Atlanta with her husband and three children. Her essays have appeared in print and online publications including *Mothering, Catholic Parent, Hip Mama*, and *VerbSap*. Her essay, "Fade to Brown," is included in the anthology *Call Me Okaasan: Adventures in Mothering Across Cultures* (2009).

Marcelitte Failla was born in Newark, New Jersey, and grew up in rural Gresham, Oregon. She is an artist, filmmaker, seamstress, and community organizer, and has worked with numerous community organizations in New York City. She is a Hunter College graduate and currently resides in Brooklyn, New York.

Kali Fajardo-Anstine is a fiction writer from Denver, Colorado. Her stories have appeared in the *Bellevue Literary Review* among other publications. She is currently at work on a novel and collection of short stories.

Kay'la "Kiki" Fraser is a poet and youth facilitator who first entered the world of poetry slams in July 2008 and found a way to combine her passion for theatre, music, and writing through spoken word—establishing herself as a serious competitor and artist in the community. She has competed in slams across the Greater Toronto Area and beyond, and has shared the stage with artists including C. R. Avery, Truth Is… and Dwayne Morgan. It is a well known fact that she is a cheesecake fiend, a wearer of many hats, and a purveyor of random acts that has been known to drop a poem or two on occasion. For more information contact <fraser.kayla@gmail.com>.

Tomie Hahn is a performer of *shakuhachi* (Japanese bamboo flute), *nihon buyo* (Japanese traditional dance) holding the professional stage name, Samie Tachibana, and experimental performance. She is Associate Professor of performance ethnology at Rensselaer Polytechnic Institute. Tomie's research spans a wide range of topics including: Japanese traditional performing arts, Monster Truck rallies, and issues of identity and creative expression of multiracial individuals. Her book, *Sensational Knowledge: Embodying Culture through Japanese Dance* (Wesleyan University Press) was awarded the Alan P. Merriam Prize from the Society for Ethnomusicology. <http://www.arts.rpi.edu/tomie>.

Rage Hezekiah is a queer, BlackIrish, sister, who followed her dreams of farming, dancing, baking, and assisting birth, to Oakland, California. Originally from mostly white suburbs in the Northshore of Massachusetts, Rage has found the queer community of colour she has longed for, as well as love, inspiration, and strength.

Karen Hill is a Toronto-based poet and writer who is working on her first novel. She lived and worked for many years in Berlin and is the mother of 21-year-old Malaika.

Kimberly Dree Hudson is a racially queer femme and pseudo-artist-activist-scholar. Born in Seattle, raised in San Francisco and nurtured in Los Angeles, she is currently a doctoral student in social welfare, personally studying healing and resilience, professionally studying ambiguous social positions and community/organizing.

ku'ualoha ho'omanawanui is a hapa (Hawaiian, Chinese, haole) poet, artist, educator, and mālama 'āina advocate born in Kailua, O'ahu, and raised in Wailua Homesteads, Kaua'i. An east-side "Ko'olau" girl her whole life, she currently divides her time between Anahola, Kaua'i and Ha'ikü, O'ahu.

Liberty Hultberg is a freelance writer and editor. She holds an MFA in creative nonfiction from the University of Pittsburgh, where she now teaches composition. She's writing a memoir about her experiences with hair, race, and transracial adoption in America.

Michelle Jean-Paul currently works as the vice-principal of a Manitoban high school. She is passionate about issues of identity and equity in educational settings. Her work as founder of the Educators of Colour Network and as a graduate student are examples of that passion put into action.

Sandra Kasturi was born in Estonia to a Sri Lankan father and an Estonian mother. She is the poetry editor of *ChiZine* and the co-publisher of ChiZine Publications. Sandra's poetry and fiction has appeared in various magazines and anthologies, including *Taddle Creek, Prairie Fire, Contemporary Verse 2, TransVersions, On Spec,* and *Shadows & Tall Trees*. She managed to snag an introduction from Neil Gaiman for her first full-length poetry collection, *The Animal Bridegroom* (Tightrope Books). Sandra recently won the 2010 Whittaker Prize for poetry.

Alexis Kienlen published her first collection of poetry, *She dreams in Red,* in 2007. She holds an International Studies degree from the University of Saskatchewan, and a graduate Diploma in Journalism from Concordia University and currently works as an agricultural journalist. Originally from Saskatoon, Alexis has lived in numerous cities in Canada, and currently makes her home in Edmonton.

Laura Kina is an artist who focuses on Asian American and mixed-race identities. She is an Associate Professor of Art, Media, and Design and Global Asian Studies and a distinguished Vincent de Paul Professor at DePaul University. Kina is one of the founders of the Critical Mixed-Race Studies conference and a board member of MAVIN. Born in California to an Okinawan father from Hawai'i and a Spanish-Basque/Anglo mother, Kina was raised in the Pacific Northwest and currently lives in Chicago.

Jonina Kirton is a Métis/Icelandic poet/author. Her writing, often contemplating the practicalities of embracing a spiritual life, has been featured in *Pagan Edge, First Nations Drum, Toronto Quarterly, Quills Canadian Poetry Magazine, New Breed Magazine,* and *emerge: Simon Fraser University's Writers Studio Anthology 2007*. Please visit her at <www.sacredcirclesbook.com>.

Erin Kobayashi is a writer, journalist and editor in Toronto. She is currently studying English Literature and Aboriginal Studies at the University of Toronto.

Sonnet L'Abbé is the author of two collections of poetry, *A Strange Relief* and *Killarnoe,* both published by McClelland and Stewart. She is working on a new collection that explores the language of plant sentience, neurology, and spiritual development. Her recent work has appeared in *Best Canadian Poetry 2009* and *Best Canadian Poetry 2010*. She lives in Vancouver.

Tru Leverette is an Assistant Professor of English at the University of North Florida where she teaches African-American literature. Her research interests broadly include race and gender in literature and culture, and she focuses specifically on discourses of mixed-race identity and interracial romance.

Sonya Littlejohn was born in Williams Lake, British Columbia. She is of English and Bermudian ancestry. She attended The University of British Columbia for an undergraduate degree in Canadian Studies, graduating in 2002. She teaches English as a Second language and volunteers as Volunteer Coordinator for the Vancouver Poetry House. She is also a member of the Black Dot Roots and Culture Collective.

Michelle Lopez-Mullins is a psychology major at the University of Maryland, College Park and serves as President to the Multiracial Biracial Student Association. She is an artist of many mediums, owns her own clothing line, Hydrolicious Apparel, and hopes to publish her first book before she turns 22.

Miranda Martini is a musician, playwright, and journalist. Raised in Calgary, Alberta, Miranda writes to unpack the experience of growing up half-Black in the prairies. Miranda's work has appeared in various Canadian publications, including *Reader's Digest* and *Discorder Magazine*. She currently resides in Vancouver, British Columbia.

Kathryn McMillan is a writing specialist in a student learning centre at a greater Toronto area university. Her Master's thesis looks at mixed-race subjectivity in Canadian literature. She is married with a daughter.

Rea McNamara is a writer and editor living in Toronto.

Natasha Morris is a born storyteller and emerging playwright in the Toronto arts community. Her creative roots stem from poetry, acting, and sketch-comedy. Presently Natasha is enrolled in b current's rCurrentz artist development program. Her recent and past theatre training background includes graduating from d'bi young's anitafrika! dub theatre residency program, the Paprika Festival's Old Spice and Creators Unit, and Etobicoke School of the Arts' drama program.

Jasmine Moy is a lawyer and freelance food and travel writer living in New York City. Her work can be found at *Esquire.com, Eater.com, The Awl, The Huffington Post, Mediaite* and *Capital New York*.

Cassie Mulheron is a photographer currently based in Richmond, Virginia. She will be graduating from Virginia Commonwealth University in May 2011 with a Bachelor of Fine Arts in Photography, a Bachelor of Arts in Gender, Sexuality and Women's Studies and a minor in Psychology. Her personal work focuses on aspects of racial, gender, and sexual identity through performative photography.

Amber Jamilla Musser teaches gender studies in New York. She is working on a book about the history of masochism.

Nicole Asong Nfonoyim, born in the Dominican Republic and raised in New York City, is a warrior scholar and "artivist" in training. She currently serves as the Assistant Director and Africana Community Coordinator in the Multicultural Resource Center at Oberlin College.

D. Cole Ossandon is a Canadian writer (as well as a musician, actor, and artist), with a Scottish/English/Irish-Chilean background, based in Toronto and Guelph, Ontario. Her work has appeared in *Matrix Magazine, Shameless Magazine, Books@ Torontoist*, and *Canada Arts Connect.*

M. Ann Phillips, Ph.D. is a mixed-race Jamaican/Canadian renaissance woman of African, Indigenous and European ancestry. Her eclectic talents include: researcher, educator, health and wellness consultant, poet, writer, photographer, natural health practitioner, martial artist and traditional "medicine woman"/shamanic healer.

Amy Pimentel currently resides in Oakland, California and earned her MFA in Creative Writing from Antioch University. She was a Student Teacher Poet in 2008-2009 in the program, Poetry for The People, started by June Jordan. She hopes to win the Lotto so she can visit the Azores islands that her paternal grandparents left decades ago. However, she doesn't ever buy Lotto tickets.

Gail Prasad is an elementary and secondary school teacher of East Indian and Japanese Canadian heritage. She is completing a Ph.D. in Second Language Education at the Ontario Institute for Studies in Education and she lives in Toronto with her husband, Michael Sullivan.

Rachel Afi Quinn was born and raised in Durham, North Carolina, and is currently a Ph.D. candidate in the Program in American Culture at the University of Michigan. Her current research is on mixed race and blackness, queer sexuality, and transnational identity in Dominican popular culture.

mónica rosas is an educator/agitator/artist whose work aims to challenge and provoke community discussion on gender, race and the environment in compassionate ways. mónica is the curator of Cha Cha, a yearly women's literary event in Toronto and she is working on a novel, *Salt Water & Cinammon Skin.* <www.monicarosas.com>.

Phoenix Rising (Debra M. Guerrero) was born and raised in Denver, Colorado. and is a known poet in the GLBT community and varying poetry venues in Denver. Currently, she is a guest instructor of her poetry for a pilot program "Intro to Urban Education" at Montbello High School, Denver.

Margo Rivera-Weiss is of Mestizo Peruvian and Ashkenazi Jewish descent. Margo was one of the co-founders of "Mongrels" a group for women of mixed heritage begun in the San Francisco Bay Area in the early 1980s. More art can be seen at <margoriveraweiss.com>.

Lisa Marie Rollins is a Black/Filipina writer, multidisciplinary performance artist, adoption activist, and educator. She is currently developing her one woman show, "Ungrateful Daughter: One Black Girl's Story of Being Adopted into a White Family … that aren't Celebrities." Lisa Marie is the Founder and Director of Adopted and Fostered Adults of the African Diaspora (AFAAD) and author of "A Birth Project," a blog focusing on transracial adoption and black diasporic identity and politics. She is a dramaturg, and teaches poetry and writing in both academic and community spaces.

Nicole Salter was born in Brooklyn, New York in 1978 to an Italian mother and African-American father, but grew up in Old Toronto. She currently resides on the Danforth in a fragile ecosystem consisting of one husband, one turtle, two cats, and a multitude of tropical fish.

Marika Schwandt is, among other things: an actor, dancer, and creator from Winnipeg, based in Toronto; Co-Artistic Director of a young multi-arts company called The Movement Project; 2010 OAC Playwright in Residence at Mammalian Diving Reflex; one-half of PPMV? Apparel, a streetwear line celebrating mixed-race identity. "Mulatto Nation" is a work in progress. <www.emarika.com>.

M. C. Shumaker earned her Bachelor of Arts in Creative Writing from Florida State University in 2002. She resides in Tallahassee, Florida with her mad scientist husband. When she isn't deflecting the question of what she is, she continues to work on the Great American graphic novel.

Shandra Spears Bombay (Ojibway) is an actor, singer, writer, and educator. Her work has been published in several anthologies, including *Strong Women Stories: Native Vision and Community Survival*, (Sumach) and *Outsiders Within: Writing on Transracial Adoption* (South End). Shandra has an Honours BA in Drama and Communication Studies, and is a part-time professor at George Brown College. She is a member of Rainy River/Manitou Rapids First Nations and a member of the wolf clan. Raised in Chatham, Ontario, she now makes her home in Toronto.

Saedhlinn B. Stewart-Laing has lived and worked in the United States, Scotland, Canada, Dominica, and on a research vessel in international waters. She is currently at the University of Glasgow, where she is writing a dissertation on fisheries management and global warming.

Aja Sy was born in Bawating (Sault Ste. Marie, Ontario) region of the Robinson Superio Treat area. She is blended ancestry with Anishinaabe roots from Obishkikaang (Bay of Pines/Lac Seul First Nation), Walof and Pulaar roots from Mauritania and European roots. She attends Edmison Heights Public School and performed her first public reading of "pick one" at Sounding Out Indigenous Poetics, Trent University, Peterborough, Ontario.

Christine Sy was born and raised in the Bawating (Sault Ste. Marie, Ontario) region of the Robinson Superior Treaty area. She is Anishinaabe of mixed ancestry whose roots emerge from Obishkikaang (Bay of Pines/Lac Seul First Nation) through her mother and from Belle Island, Newfoundland through her father. Christine began writing poetry and participating in public readings in 2003. She has read publicly at various student events and magazine launches in Sault Ste. Marie, Peterborough, and Montreal. Christine has published in *Algoma Ink, Rampike* and *Matrix Magazine.*

Andrea Thompson is a writer and spoken word artist who has performed her poetry, at venues and festivals in Canada, the U.S., and Europe. Dynamic and innovative, Thompson is a pioneer of the Canadian Slam Poetry scene, whose work has been featured on film, radio, and television; and included in magazines, literary journals and anthologies across Canada for over 15 years. Her spoken-word CD, *One,* was nominated for a Canadian Urban Music Award in 2005, and her poetry collection, *Eating the Seed,* has been featured on the reading lists at the Ontario College of Art and Design and the University of Toronto. Thompson is the host of season two of the 13-part television series, *Heart of a Poet* (Bravo TV, 2007), and the writer and performer of the one-woman spoken word/play "Mating Rituals of the Urban Cougar." She is currently attending the University of Guelph where she is completing a Masters of Fine Arts in Creative Writing.

Debra Thompson completed her Ph.D. in political science at the University of Toronto in 2010. She is currently a SSHRC Post-Doctoral Fellow at the Center for American Political Studies and Department of Government at Harvard University, and will be an Assistant Professor in the Department of Political Science at Ohio University beginning in fall 2011.

Kirya Traber is a nationally awarded spoken-word artist, and has been featured across the country for her work as a writer and performer. She is a former Brave

New Voices International Teen Poetry Slam Champion, and has been featured at the United States Mayor's Summit, San Francisco's National Queer Arts Festival, the Stern Grove Festival, and San Francisco's Lit Quake, among other notable stages. Her work has appeared in *Tiny Little Maps to Each Other*, a First Word Press collection, and in her self-published book of poetry, *Black Chick*.

Natasha Trethewey is the author of three poetry collections, *Domestic Work, Bellocq's Ophelia*, and *Native Guard* (2007 Pulitzer Prize in Poetry). Her latest book, *Beyond Katrina*, is a personal account in both poetry and prose of the Mississippi Gulf Coast and of the people there, including her family, whose lives were forever changed by Hurricane Katrina. She teaches creative writing at Emory University in Atlanta, where she is the Phillis Wheatley Distinguished Chair in Poetry and Professor of English.

Priscila Uppal is a poet, novelist and York University professor. Her international publications include *Ontological Necessities* (shortlisted for the Griffin Poetry Prize), *Traumatology, Successful Tragedies* (Bloodaxe Books), *Winter Sport: Poems* (written as Canadian Athletes Now poet-in-residence for the 2010 Olympic and Paralympic Games), and *To Whom It May Concern*. *Time Out London* (UK) recently dubbed her "Canada's coolest poet." For more information visit <priscilauppal.ca>.

Katherena Vermette is a Métis writer of poetry and fiction. Her work has appeared in several literary magazines and compilations, most recently, *Home Place 3, Prairie Fire Magazine*, and *Heute Sin Wir Hier / We Are Here Today*, a collection of Canadian Aboriginal writers, compiled and translated into German by Hartmut Lutz and students of Greifswald University. A member of the Aboriginal Writers Collective, and 2010-2011 Blogger in Residence of <thewriterscollective.org>. Katherena lives, works and plays in Winnipeg, Manitoba.

Lisa Walker is a photo-based artist born in the small town of Kitimat in Northern British Columbia, Canada; she is currently living in Vancouver. As a half Haisla First Nations half British female, Lisa attempts to comment on binaries, barriers, and explore duality in identity. Through photography, Lisa encourages others to relate, to remember, and to create dialogue.

Jackie Wang is a writer and artist who is interested in postcolonial feminism, theories of writing, and hard femme identity. Her writings on literature, art, film, music, theory, politics, and culture can be read at <serbianballerinasdance-withmachineguns.com>. Her work often uses a hybridized style that combines criticism and memoir.

Adebe DeRango-Adem won the Toronto Poetry Competition in 2005
to become Toronto's first Junior Poet
Laureate, and is the author of *Ex Nihilo*
(2010), her debut poetry collection
that considers how art can respond to
the annihilation of particular identities
struggling to exist in an impossibly post-
racial world. *Ex Nihilo* was longlisted
for the Dylan Thomas Prize, the world's
largest prize for writers under thirty.

Andrea Thompson received the
2009 Canadian Festival of Spoken
Word's Award for Outstanding
Achievement for her contribution
to the form over the last seventeen
years. Her CD, *One,* was nominated
for a Canadian Urban Music Award
in 2005, and her poetry collection
Eating the Seed has been taught at
Ontario College of Art and Design
and the University of Toronto.